WHEN WAVES
Break

WHEN WAVES
Break

Allison Wells

Ambassador International
GREENVILLE, SOUTH CAROLINA & BELFAST, NORTHERN IRELAND

www.ambassador-international.com

When Waves Break

ISBN: 978-1-62020-721-5
eISBN: 978-1-62020-740-6
Library of Congress Control Number: 2019957884

This is a work of fiction. Names, characters, and incidents are all products of the author's imagination or are used for fictional purposes. Any resemblance to actual events or persons, living or dead, is entirely coincidental. Any mentioned brand names, places, and trademarks remain the property of their respective owners, bear no association with the author or the publisher, and are used for fictional purposes only.

Cover Design & Typesetting by Hannah Nichols
Ebook Conversion by Anna Riebe Raats
Edited by Katie Cruice Smith

AMBASSADOR INTERNATIONAL
Emerald House
411 University Ridge, Suite B14
Greenville, SC 29601, USA
www.ambassador-international.com

AMBASSADOR BOOKS
The Mount
2 Woodstock Link
Belfast, BT6 8DD, Northern Ireland, UK
www.ambassadormedia.co.uk

The colophon is a trademark of Ambassador, a Christian publishing company.

"In fluid dynamics, a breaking wave is a wave whose amplitude reaches a critical level at which some process can suddenly start to occur that causes large amounts of wave energy to be transformed into turbulent kinetic energy."[1]

1 Wikipedia, s.v. "breaking wave," accessed May 13, 2019, https://
en.wikipedia.org/wiki/Breaking_wave.

Calm Waters

Eve looked in the mirror. Her image reflected back, along with that of her sister, Juliette. Not just her sister—her twin sister. Eve loved her sister fiercely. They adored each other. Often, they didn't require words to communicate. They could look at each other and know what the other was thinking. It was quite handy when it came to boys, but it exasperated their parents when they couldn't get a straight answer out of them. The girls had an unbreakable bond and an unspoken code never to rat on each other and never to let anyone come before your sister.

Despite being twins, Eve and Juliette were like night and day. Eve was born first, five minutes before her sister, to Abby and Harvey Nicholas. Born with fiery red hair and green eyes, Eve didn't possess the Irish temper one would have thought. She was calmer and more conservative than her sister. She spent time with the hippie crowd, much like her sister, but thought many of their ideals were too radical for her own personal taste. Her twin considered her fairly dull and straight-laced. Eve liked it that way. She had fun and protested with her sister, but she did it within the limits of the law and always kept a level head about it.

Her sister was not the same. Juliette's personality was much like her hair—crazy, untamed curls. Black, kinky curls. But she had the same

7

green eyes as her sister and father. Juliette had gotten the temper and the wild demeanor of Irish lore. She believed completely in spreading love and peace and thought having fun was the only important thing in life. She had become the unofficial head of a band of hippies at their high school, and more kids joined their crowd all the time. She loved the idea of protests and holding sit-ins as a way to fight for the things she believed in. Eve thought she was too extreme, but never dared to hold her back from what she believed in.

Their senior year of high school wasn't over yet for the summer, but that didn't stop the girls from enjoying the beach on sunny afternoons. They loved living in Myrtle Beach from the moment they had moved there nearly seven years before. Even with their fair skin, both girls enjoyed the sun. Eve always donned a hat and carried an umbrella for shade, while Juliette baked under the sun's rays. Eve always told her she would come out looking like bacon one day, but Juliette didn't care.

They were used to being approached by boys as they sat on the beach. Juliette was the more daring twin, of course, and would flirt endlessly while showing off her skimpy bathing suits. Knowing her parents would disapprove, Juliette had cleverly modified her suit to include a mid-section panel she could attach when she was around her family. But when her minister father and conservative mother weren't around, the panel was gone, as were her inhibitions. Eve stuck to her favorite blue one-piece suit. No frills, no fuss—just like her.

One balmy spring afternoon, while lounging by the waves, a fellow Juliette knew approached and asked if he could treat her to a Coke. He wore a pair of blue swim trunks, and his sun-bleached hair went down his back and was coated with sand. Juliette invited Eve out of politeness, but Eve knew her sister would prefer to be alone with the attractive man she introduced simply as Larry. She declined, raising her book to show that she was too interested in it to get up. As her sister walked away with Larry, Juliette turned around and quickly gave Eve a look of thanks and motioned that she would bring Eve a Coke back with her as a thank you gift. Eve just smiled and returned to her book.

A few minutes passed, and Eve saw a shadow come over her. Thinking her sister had cut her soda date short, Eve didn't bother to glance up before speaking. "Did you bring me a Coke?"

"I didn't know I was supposed to bring one," a deep voice answered her. It wasn't Juliette. It wasn't any voice she knew at all.

Eve scrambled from her stomach to a sitting position and raised her hand over her eyes, so she could see. In front of her stood a tall, black man who was smiling down at her.

"I'm so sorry," she said as she blushed. "I thought you were my sister coming back with a drink."

"I can't imagine any sister of yours looking like me, Miss," he replied, flashing his pearly white teeth as he smiled. He tipped a faded baseball cap in her direction. "I don't mean to interrupt you, but I was trying to figure out which way the Sea Horse Restaurant is. I'm meeting my sister there. Can you point me in the right direction?"

Eve smiled as she relaxed in front of the stranger. He must be a tourist visiting the beach for the summer. "Of course. We locals know where everything is. Keep heading south like you are for about another half-mile. It's right on the beach. Your sister must visit often if she knows a local joint like the Sea Horse."

"My sister, Dee, lives here. I'm staying with her for the summer," he replied. "Maybe I'll see you around more if you're from nearby. My name's Jesse." He extended a muscular arm toward her and put out his hand. Eve shook hands with him and grinned. He was a good-looking man.

"Jesse. Nice to meet you. My name is Eve. I'm always around. If you happen to see me again, come say hi." She stood as she introduced herself and took the floppy hat off her long, red hair and tousled it a little. *What am I doing? Am I flirting? Flirting with a black man, no less?*

Jesse smiled back at her, the breeze catching his white shirt and wrapping it around his arms. Eve could see strong biceps underneath the cotton material and did her best to avert her eyes. "Eve," he repeated. "The first woman God created, and she was never more perfect." He smiled even bigger before saying, "Maybe I'll bring you a Coke next time, Eve."

And with that, Jesse turned and continued south along the beach. Eve watched the man saunter away from her. She felt self-conscious as she studied the way his dark arms swung in rhythm with his muscular legs as he walked across the white sand with little effort. Her heart had caught in her throat. What on earth was happening to her? Why was she so attracted to this man? So attracted that she felt the pull to run after him and throw her arms around him.

"So silly," she scolded herself. "It's just this book I'm reading. Why did I ever start reading romance novels on the beach? The storyline and the heat are getting to me," she mumbled as she settled back down under the umbrella. She glanced up the beach where her sister had disappeared and saw her returning, two sodas in hand. *Good, a drink will cool me down and bring me back to my senses.*

Juliette sat down and handed Eve a bottle with a straw in it. "Why do you look so bothered? You aren't angry that I went with Larry, are you? He's a loser, anyhow."

Eve glanced back behind them, looking for Jesse, but he was gone. "No, not that. I was just giving directions to a guy. He was heading to the Sea Horse."

Juliette's eyebrows rose as she took a sip of her drink. "A good-looking guy?"

Eve smiled as she drew her knees up to her chest. "Yes, a good-looking guy. A good-looking black man, actually."

"A black man? You were flirting with a black man? That's groovy, Evie, very radical."

Eve giggled at her sister, ever in favor of things against the grain. "I didn't say I flirted. I just gave Jesse directions."

"Jesse?"

"Mmm," she confirmed as she took a long sip on her straw. "And, Jules, I'll admit, I did flirt a little. I think it's these trashy romance novels that made me do it."

"No, Eve, it's your carnal desire as a woman in her prime. It's the need to reach out and love a strong man!" Juliette reached out to her sister and grabbed her arm for effect.

"Juliette!" Eve exclaimed. "I'm all for world peace and sit-ins, but I do not participate in free love. And neither do you. You're only eighteen. And Dad's a minister, for heaven's sake. You're not that stupid."

Juliette frowned. As much as she longed to participate in the radical lifestyle of her more adult counterparts, her sister was right. At eighteen and not quite out of high school, she wasn't ready to freely love anybody—at least not like that.

"Well, I'm just glad you flirted. And with a strong, black man, too! That's very in-style."

Shaking her head, Eve smiled at her sister. "Come on. It's getting late. Let's head home to eat. Only two more weeks of school until we graduate. Then we're free."

The girls gathered their things and slipped their sandals back on. They shuffled out of the sand and up the road three blocks to their house. The two-story beach house was like many of the homes just off the shore. It was raised up a story on stilts in case of a flood. It was high enough to park the car underneath, with a set of whitewash stairs leading into the house. The exterior of the house was a cheery yellow that was weathered from the salty wind and water. White wicker furniture sat inviting anyone to come and sit and listen to the tide from a few blocks away.

Inside the house, their mother, Abby, was helping their younger sister, Alisa, with her homework while dinner cooked. The smell of roast beef and herbs, potatoes, and fresh vegetables wafted through the thin, long kitchen and into the rest of the house.

Abby Nicholas was a striking woman of just over forty years. Her curly, dark hair had given way to some gray, which she claimed was the result of raising five children. She preferred to keep it natural, rather than color it. She said it was how God made her hair, and it had taken her a long time to accept it—she wasn't going to change it now. She wore clothes befitting a mother of five—a simple pencil skirt and a cotton tank top that showed off her trim figure. The twins thought her style was out of date, but their mother was always graceful and elegant.

Upon seeing the girls come home in their bathing suits and towels, Abby spoke up. "Girls, get dressed for dinner, please. Your father has invited some guests to dine with us. We will be eating at six o'clock."

They mumbled their replies and headed to the room they shared. Two twin beds sat opposite each other in the second-floor bedroom. Eve's bed sat to the right, covered in a simple blue sheet. A light and a stack of books were on her nightstand, her wall bare. Juliette's side of the room was covered in drawings and posters. She had tie-dyed her sheets a few months before, much to her mother's dismay. Between the beds was a large window where they could barely see the ocean between two neighboring houses, but it still counted as "ocean view" as far as they were concerned.

Eve frowned at the idea of dinner company. No doubt someone her clergyman father would want to impress. A new parishioner, perhaps? Or maybe someone from high in the ranks of the church world.

Eve thought she believed in God. But she did have a hard time believing that a loving God Who brought her parents through so much turmoil could also keep the world in a continuous state of warfare. If God loved all people, why were black citizens so discriminated against? Why was there still segregation across the country? How could a loving God allow such terrible things to happen to people? Eve struggled a lot with how to handle the idea of faith. She went to church on Sunday, and she prayed when she thought it necessary. But she wasn't sure she wanted a relationship with a God Who could be so cruel.

Juliette's take on faith was more extreme than her sister's. She also wondered how a God her father claimed loved her so much could at the same time hate others. "But He loves all people," her father had told her. Then why are women oppressed? Why are black men and women beaten and hated just for being born a different color? She didn't think her father's God loved anybody but rich, white men. She went to church with the family, but Juliette had long since given up on praying. She didn't want anything to do with such an unreasonable Deity. She preferred to honor nature and people instead.

Regardless of their views on their parent's apparent faith in God and Christianity, Juliette and Eve dressed to impress for their father's sake. Juliette put on a long, flowing dress that was claret in color. The top of the dress had been deemed too revealing by their mother previously, so Juliette knew to put a light, cap-sleeved sweater over it to keep it modest. She used a pick to tame her sea salt-smelling black curls into place, wishing she had time to iron her hair flat, but also loving that it gave her a bit of an afro—a look popular with the black people she knew.

Eve was more careful in her dress. She chose a dark green tent dress that was all the rage. The collar was high around her neck and the sleeves longer than she would have desired for such a warm evening, but she knew her parents would approve. The hem of the dress hit right at her knee when she was sitting, so stockings were in order as well. Eve ran a brush through her hair and tried to give it a little height and body before bounding down the stairs just before the chime of six.

Their guest was sitting in the living room when she got downstairs. Her sister sat opposite a young man who looked to be close in age to their cousin Pete. Pete had been raised by her parents after his own parents died when he was an infant. A tragic tale, to be sure. But as Eve descended the stairs, she heard other voices coming from the kitchen, and her mother appeared with a woman close to her own age.

"Ah, Eve, there you are," her mother called out. "Mrs. Herbert, this is my eldest daughter, Eve. Eve, this is Mrs. Herbert and her son, Buzz.

They're new to the beach and came to Respite Baptist for the first time last week. I don't know if you got a chance to meet them."

Eve put her church face on. "I didn't. But I'm happy to meet you now, Mrs. Herbert." She turned to the young man. "Buzz, was it? Nice to meet you." Buzz Herbert stood and shook her hand. He wasn't particularly attractive, but he wasn't unattractive either. His sandy blond hair was parted too far to the side to be hip, and his bottle-cap glasses hid his blue eyes. Eve eyed him with uncertainty.

"Eve. Nice to meet you. I've already met your sister, Juliette. Though I have to admit, I wouldn't ever think you two were sisters if I met you on the street," he admitted.

"Not just sisters, Buzz," Juliette said with her flirty voice. "Twins." The girl could, and would, flirt with anybody.

"Twins! Wow, I would have never guessed." He laughed nervously as he looked from Juliette back to Eve. Something about him wasn't quite right, Eve thought as gooseflesh came over her arms.

She was uncertain about him but knew her parents would want her to make him welcome to the community, so she smiled back at him. Juliette knew only that he was a man whose muscular arms were apparent under his oxford shirt. She flirted endlessly. Neither girl would ever fight over him if they wanted him. Eve immediately decided that her sister could have Buzz Herbert if she wanted him; he wasn't her type. He wasn't Juliette's type either, but that didn't usually matter.

After a few pleasantries about the weather were exchanged, Harvey Nicholas came home just as dinner was being set upon the table. Eve had always known her father, who was tall and strong, to be a wonderfully caring man. Not only was he a minister, but he was also her brother's baseball coach. Despite an injury from the Second World

War, her father was still active physically. Behind Harvey, her brother, Joseph, came running in and up the stairs to change before dinner.

All during the meal, Buzz Herbert was very polite. Almost too polite, Eve thought. There was something amiss about him, like he was hiding something. But Juliette seemed interested, and their parents were approving of her interest in a boy who attended their church. Eve wasn't at all surprised after the meal when Juliette whispered to her that Buzz had asked her on a date for the following weekend.

Always Jules, and never me, she thought. *Oh well, I didn't care for him anyhow. But still, it would be nice to be asked out. I wonder if I'll see Jesse again this summer . . .* Eve stopped herself short. Jesse from the beach? Where did that come from? She was more smitten with him than she had realized. He was a good-looking man. Maybe they would meet again.

Crashing Waves

"A DOUBLE DATE? COME ON, Dad," Juliette whined. She hated having to drag her sister with her like an unwilling chaperone.

"You know the rules," Harvey reminded her. "If you want to go to a beach party, you have to go with Eve or in a group."

"But he's been to the house, Dad. He goes to the church. You know him!"

Harvey Nicholas didn't budge. Not where his daughters were concerned. "You go with Evie, or you don't go, Juliette. I won't risk anything happening to one of my girls. If you were just going to a movie, then that would be one thing. But you just don't know what could happen at one of those parties."

Juliette's date with Buzz Herbert was the next night. He had invited her to a party on the beach. Surely Eve could find someone to take to a party, right? It couldn't be that hard.

She eyed her father's unwavering stance. "Fine, Dad, I'll see if Eve is busy tomorrow." She kissed her father and ran for the stairs. No matter how old-fashioned he was, Juliette loved her father.

She burst into her room to find Eve with her nose in a book. "Evie," she whimpered as she curled up next to her sister.

Without looking up from the page, Eve sighed. "What do you need now, Jules?"

"Dad is being so mean. Buzz Herbert asked me out to a party tomorrow, but Dad won't let me go without you. Don't you want to go to this party tomorrow? It's at the Sea Horse. Well, below the Sea Horse on the beach, so you'll probably know a lot of people there. Please?"

Her sister sat up and looked at her. Without hesitating, Eve replied, "The Sea Horse? Maybe Jesse will be there. Sure, I'll go. What time?"

Juliette jumped up and clapped her hands. "Yay! Buzz will pick us up at seven. Tell Daddy that you're meeting this Jesse guy there, okay?"

"Okay," Eve said. Juliette knew her sister would do anything for her, but she was surprised she didn't have to convince Eve to go to this party. It usually took a little more to persuade her to attend a beach party, but the notion of seeing the man she had met at the beach the week before piqued her sister's interest. That was enough for her.

Juliette and Buzz had spoken at Respite Baptist Church the Sunday before, and Buzz had whispered to her about a party the following weekend. Although he looked every bit the square, Juliette had a feeling that Buzz was just as fun-loving and free-spirited as she was. Maybe he also put on an act for his mom. He had to, if he invited her to a party at the Sea Horse. They were known throughout Myrtle Beach for their summer parties.

Maybe Buzz wasn't her soulmate, but at least he was a nice-looking guy to flirt with who would buy her dinner and a Coke. He could certainly be Mr. Right Now for the summer, she thought.

The next night, Juliette was dressed and ready well before her sister. Her curly black mane had a bright plum-colored scarf woven into a braid around her hairline. It matched her plum dress perfectly. She favored dresses with long, flowing skirts that swept the floor. Juliette also favored thin shoulder straps and plunging necklines that her parents disapproved of. She was an expert at covering herself with sweaters in front of them and shedding the additional clothing once out of sight.

She waited as her sister pulled a brush through her straight, red hair. How they could have such different hair was a mystery, to be sure. Hers wild and black, her sister's tame and red. Eve's hair stretched down over her shoulders and rested on the black dress she wore. It was simple, if not a little dull. The hem of her skirt modestly hit her knee; the neckline hugged close to her throat. It looked like a potato sack, Juliette thought. Oh well, at least Buzz's eye wouldn't stray to her striking sister tonight.

Once at the party, Juliette and Buzz left Eve to her own devices. Juliette gave her sister a quick kiss on the cheek before slipping off to a corner to talk to Buzz.

"You're the best, Evie. I'll find you later," she whispered. Eve only nodded and released her sister to have fun. Juliette watched her sister sit on a log by the crackling bonfire before turning her full attention to Buzz.

She had been right about him. He wasn't the same person tonight as he had been around their parents. At twenty years old, Buzz was attending college in Columbia and was back with his mother for the summer. His hair was now parted in the middle, his bottle-cap glasses nowhere to be seen. He wore a white button-down shirt with the top three buttons undone and a brown suede vest over top of the shirt. His denim jeans were well-worn and had small holes near the knees. His language had also changed from mild-mannered to completely hip. This was a man who knew how to get what he wanted from anybody.

"Whatcha drinkin', Juliette?" he asked, as he ran his hand along the back of her neck. The slight tickle made her smile.

"I'll have whatever you're having, Buzz," she replied. She gazed out into the ocean, while Buzz slipped away to get beverages.

She had slipped her shoes off already and dug her toes into the wet sand. She sat down, her legs curled behind her. Juliette arranged her skirt so that it was up around her knees; she pretended not to notice the portion of her thigh that was exposed. Her slightly tanned skin shone in the moonlight as the waves crested and broke a few feet away.

Juliette glanced behind her to see if she could see Eve back by the fire. She spotted her sister right away, talking to a group of people from school. *Good, she's not alone,* Juliette thought. As if sensing her, Eve looked up toward Juliette and gave her a small wave. Juliette smiled big for her sister just as Buzz came back to her.

"Here we are," Buzz said, his knees falling softly into the sand. He handed Juliette a cup, while he took a sip from his own. "This is one radical place, let me tell you. People everywhere. Is it always like this during the summer?"

"As long as I've been here, it has. Parties every weekend and all summer long." Juliette smiled as she tasted her drink. The flavor surprised her for a moment; it wasn't something she recognized. But she didn't want Buzz to notice her reaction, so she quickly took another sip.

"How long have you lived here?"

Juliette sighed, grateful he hadn't noticed her reaction to the drink. "Oh, about seven years now," she said, placing her cup in the sand and resting her hand on Buzz's arm. "My father came here to start the church. I wasn't too excited about moving away from our friends in Greenville; but when Eve and I discovered just what Myrtle Beach was, we were flipped out! We love it here."

"Well, I'm glad I met you here," Buzz said, inching closer to her. "You and your sister aren't much alike, are you?"

Juliette giggled. "She's five minutes older than me, but it might as well be five years. Or fifty years. She's so dull sometimes. I wish she would liven up a little, let loose. Did I tell you she doesn't believe in free love? Who, in this day and age, wouldn't believe in free love?"

Buzz's arm went around Juliette's shoulder. "Do you believe in free love? Truly free love?"

"We should all be free to love whom we please. Everyone deserves free love. Everyone. Men and women, white and black, rich and poor, young and old," she stated with as much resolve as she could muster. Her head was feeling a little wobbly. Perhaps another sip of her drink would help.

When she had a hard time setting the drink back down, however, Buzz helped her out. "Whoops, are you alright?" He set her glass down and steadied her hand. "Maybe we should take a little walk and enjoy the fresh air."

"That sounds groovy," Juliette replied. "Just let me tell my sister . . ."

Buzz hurried to his feet. "I'll do it. I'll be right back."

As Juliette slowly stood, she could see Buzz talk to Eve. He pointed to Juliette and motioned north up the shoreline. Eve smiled and nodded. *Good,* Juliette thought, *she's not going to tell me not to go. I think I could use a walk; my head feels like it's floating away.* She watched as Buzz jogged back over to her. He took her hand and led her south toward the pier.

"Oh, Buzz, thanks," she managed to say. "Let me be honest—I don't feel great. I think I need to clear my head. What was that drink, anyway?"

Buzz answered her, but she couldn't hear him. They had gotten closer to the water, and the sound of the surf and the wind drowned out his voice.

They walked slowly toward the pier in the darkness of night. Juliette could barely see to put one foot in front of the other; and her head was spinning, making walking even harder. When she could see the legs of the pier in front of her, she put her hands out and leaned on a wooden beam. She rested her head on her arm and caught her breath. Was she coming down with something? She didn't feel this bad before they left for the party.

"Let's come over here and sit down, Juliette," Buzz offered. "When you feel a little better, we'll head back; and I'll take you home."

"Oh, but Eve won't be ready to leave. I'll be fine. We can just hang out here for a while, if you don't mind." Juliette lowered herself onto the cold, wet sand. She shivered in the damp air, wondering where she had discarded her sweater.

As if he had read her mind, Buzz produced a light blanket from somewhere and wrapped it around her shoulders. "Here you go," he said. "This should take the chill off you. Your dress is too thin to keep you warm." He ran his finger up her bare arm and onto her shoulder. Juliette got goosebumps.

"I'm sorry I'm such a drag, Buzz. I was fine before; I don't know what's wrong," she said, peering into the darkness. She could barely make out Buzz's face in the moonlight. They were well-hidden below the pier.

"That's fine, baby. I'm not going anywhere. Now, tell me more about your ideas of free love." Buzz brushed his hand over her shoulder, her curls bouncing at the touch. It made Juliette shudder, and a notion of fear flashed in her head.

Juliette, calm yourself, she reasoned in her mind. *Buzz knows your parents. You've met his mom. Even if you don't believe in all that churchy stuff, bad people don't go to church.* The fleeting thought was gone, along with most of her rationale.

Soon, Buzz was kissing her neck, whispering that he completely agreed that everyone deserved free love. Several guys had kissed her neck before, and Juliette instinctively angled her head to give him more room. When he slid the blanket off her shoulders and lowered her onto it, Juliette couldn't resist him, though she tried.

Her arms wouldn't work properly, and her attempts to get out from under Buzz were feeble and useless. Panic filled Juliette's head. *No, stop!* She screamed in her head, but nothing was coming out of her mouth. No screams, no protests. *Stop, please! Stop! Where's Eve? Where's anybody? Someone, anyone, help me, please!* Silent tears slipped down her cheeks.

Eve didn't like Buzz Herbert at all, but her sister did. He had told Eve that he was going to take her sister for a walk, since it was such a beautiful night. But he had motioned north to her, and Eve watched him lead Juliette south instead. Something about that didn't sit right with Eve. Still, Juliette would be livid if Eve appeared out of nowhere while she was on a date, so she stayed still for the time being. If she didn't see Juliette soon, though, she would follow them.

While she walked toward the water and peered south, she heard her name called out from behind her. As she turned around, Eve saw Jesse coming toward her.

"I knew I would see you again, Eve," he said. "Remember me?"

Eve blushed, all thoughts of her sister vanishing. Of course, she remembered Jesse. She had agreed to come to the party based solely on the thought of seeing him again. She would never tell him that, so instead she played coy. "Jesse, right?"

He smiled at her. "Yes, we met last week. Jesse Washington. I believe I owe you a Coke."

Eve returned the smile, thankful for the night sky to mask her flush. "Ah, yes, you did promise me a Coke. I'd love one if the offer still stands."

Jesse Washington held his hand out for Eve, and she took it as she got closer to him. Feeling his strong hand envelop hers gave her a chill.

At the bar, he handed her a bottle of Coke, as he took one for himself as well. "God's first woman looks as radiant tonight as she did the first time I laid eyes on her," he said. His dark eyes twinkled in the light.

"Oh, you're a smooth talker, aren't you, Jesse Washington?" Eve smiled back as she tossed her glossy tresses over her shoulder. "Do you come to the Sea Horse often?"

"I'm working construction right up the road, so I frequent the Sea Horse a lot for supper. Especially since I first met you," he admitted. "I've walked up and down the beach every day since then, hoping to catch another glimpse of the most beautiful woman I've ever seen." Eve felt herself turn crimson at the compliment. "I'm glad I finally got a chance to see you again, Eve . . . "

"Eve Nicholas," she said. "I'm glad to have run into you again, too, Jesse. I've wondered about you since I saw you on the beach."

They made small talk for a few minutes before Jesse asked, "Did your sister ever bring you back that Coke?"

Eve gasped. She still hadn't seen her return after Buzz had led her off. "Oh, Jesse! She walked off almost an hour ago. I'm sorry. I need to find her." Eve stood, nearly toppling her stool over, panic in her eyes. Something wasn't right; she could suddenly feel it.

Jesse did not ask questions. "I'll come with you," he said, getting to his feet. They weaved through the crowd and back out to where Eve last saw Juliette. When they got to the spot, Jesse picked up a cup left behind in the sand. "Does your sister drink?"

"Nothing more than the occasional beer. What's in that?"

"I'd say a mix of any number of alcohols, and I can see something frothy around the top of the liquid. I've seen this before. Eve, I'm afraid your sister may have been drugged. Who was she with?"

"Oh no, we have got to find her! She was with a guy she met last week. A guy from church, no less! When Buzz said he was going to take her for a walk, he motioned north; but they walked south toward the pier," she explained. "He looked devious, to be honest. I have never felt much trust for him. But Juliette looked happy, and she waved at me. And I don't think they've come back yet." She looked into Jesse's eyes. She barely knew him, but she felt like he could trust him. "I'm scared, Jesse."

"We'll find her, Eve; don't worry," he said, taking her hand and leading her down the shore toward the pier.

Jesse was the first to spot footprints—Juliette's bare ones and Buzz's heavier, sandaled step. The set of prints wove up and down the sand from the water to the dunes and back, not straight like those of people taking a stroll in the moonlight. These footprints looked like those of people who were whacked out. He looked at Eve, worry apparent in his face. As they approached the pier, Juliette's prints started to drag; lines from her toes cut through the damp sand. Eve's panic level rose as the set of steps came to a pause in front of a beam.

The set of footprints mingled together before wandering under the pier as if in a sloppy duet. Fear gripped Eve. Juliette was hurt—she could feel it. Something had gone terribly wrong.

"Hurry, Jesse! Under the pier," she practically yelled. They bolted into the darkness, Eve calling all the way, "Juliette? Juliette, where are you? Please, God, let me find her!" She thrust her arms out in front of her, stumbling to the ground. Tears stung her eyes, but she couldn't afford any more impairment to her vision; she had to find her sister.

Finally, Eve heard sounds coming from under the pier. She held still, and Jesse inched behind her. She heard the noise again, followed by a weak voice calling for help. Without hesitating, Eve lunged toward the voice. In the pitch dark, she crawled on her bare knees as the opening became smaller, feeling all around. At last, she grasped a hand.

"Eve?" Juliette asked, her voice frail and fearful.

Tears flowed down her cheeks as Eve answered, "Thank the Lord! I'm here, Juliette. Don't worry. Evie's here. We're going to get you out of here." Eve turned to Jesse and grabbed his arm, pulling him forward.

Jesse moved in front of Eve and gently pulled Juliette out to where there was more room, and he lifted her gently. Her head nestled onto Jesse's shoulder; her clothes hung like wet rags; a thin blanket covered her. Jesse made sure she was fully covered and carried her out from her hiding spot. Eve clasped her sister's limp hand.

"Oh, Juliette. I'm so sorry, I'm so sorry. I should have come after you right away. I knew that Buzz Herbert was trouble. Did he hurt you, Juliette?" Eve cried softly as she hovered near her sister.

"Evie . . . " Juliette whispered. "Help . . . "

"I'm here, sweetie. I'm right here. This is my friend, Jesse. Remember me telling you about him last week? We found you, Jules. Just tell me what happened."

As the trio emerged from under the pier, Jesse laid Juliette down just outside the direct rays of an overhead pier light. "Eve, you're going to need to clean her up," he said as he stood and turned his back to the girls.

Eve hunched down over her twin. Juliette's dress was pulled down, her chest exposed. Her arms had been tied up in the dress. Purple bruises were already coloring her body. Eve quickly pulled the dress back into position. She then looked at her sister's legs. Small cuts from where shells had pierced her skin covered her legs, and Eve pulled the dress back down over Juliette's knees and ankles. It was then she saw the stain. Even on the dark plum material, a blood stain was apparent on the back of the dress.

"Oh, Juliette. Oh, no." She sobbed as she stroked her sister's sand-laden hair. "I am so sorry. Buzz will pay for this. I promise you. Where is he? Where did he go?"

Juliette's voice was barely a whisper. "I don't know. When he . . . Something spooked him, and he ran away. I think I passed out until I heard your voice." Tears began to pool in the corners of her eyes. "Evie?"

"Yes, Juliette?" Eve got closer to her sister, lying next to her in the sand, her hands rubbing her sister's arms to keep her warm.

"Eve, he raped me," she whispered, her voice barely audible. The tears flowed freely from Juliette's bloodshot eyes. Her entire body shook as she admitted what happened to her. Eve sat up, brought her sister's head into her lap, and rocked her softly as they both cried and grieved.

Lord, how could this happen? Eve shot up an angry petition to God. *How could You let my sister get raped? How could You do this? I have my doubts about You, anyway, and this does not help! How are You a good and just God if You let this happen? Do You hear me? HOW?*

Furious at God, at Buzz Herbert, at herself—Eve squeezed her eyes shut and willed the entire evening to disappear. She willed the clock to turn back to the afternoon when all was right in her little world. Now her sister's world, and hers along with it, was shattered.

Jesse knelt down beside her and whispered, "I'll go get my car. You stay here with her, and I'll get you home. Don't leave her side."

"I'll never leave her side again," Eve vowed. Jesse stood and glanced around to be sure the perpetrator wasn't still lurking around looking for another Nicholas girl to harm. Convinced nobody would come upon them, he ran off at full speed back to the parking lot to get his car.

"Eve?"

"Yes, Juliette? I'm right here." Eve stroked her sister's hair as she rocked back and forth.

"I think he slipped me something. He said a walk would clear my head, and we came here." She gulped a big breath. "Then before I knew it, we were in the dark; and he was kissing me. At first, I let him; but then when he started to do more, I tried to stop him, but I could barely move. I couldn't move my arms or legs. I couldn't even call for help. I tried to scream," Juliette sobbed. "I tried, but nothing happened. Nobody came, and he didn't stop, Eve. He didn't stop. And then he was just gone."

Eve's heart broke for her sister. For all her talk of free love, this was certainly not what she intended. Love was meant to be given freely, not taken forcefully. Eve's whole body shook along with Juliette's. Her body ached with her sister's. Eve would forever endure the guilt over not saving her sister in time. She would always bear a stain on her heart and conscience because of it.

After a few seconds, she spoke. "I'm here now, Jules. I'm here. I will always be here to help you. Jesse's coming with a car, and we'll take you to a hospital, okay?"

Turning her head, Juliette finally spoke with strength. "No! No, doctors. No poking and prodding. I don't want anyone to know about this. And if we go to the hospital, Mom and Dad will find out. Then what will they say? What about all their high and mighty church people? They'll all say that the Nicholas's hippie daughter got what she deserved."

Eve shook her head. "That's not true. Not a single person would ever say that. You did not deserve this, Juliette. Nobody would or could deserve this. You need to see a doctor. Please."

Headlights appeared above the girls. Eve huddled over her sister to protect her. Jesse ran down the beach to their side, ready to go. "Is she okay?"

"She will be, eventually," Eve answered honestly.

"Let's get her into the car," he said, then turned his attention. "Juliette, is it? I'm Jesse. Don't worry. I'm just going to help you up, okay?" Juliette nodded as Jesse put one arm under her back and the other under her knees. He lifted her effortlessly, while Eve got to her feet as well. "Are we going to the hospital?"

"She doesn't want a doctor, but I think she needs one."

Juliette lifted her head. "No hospitals, please."

Jesse made his way back up the dunes to his car. Eve swung the door open for Jesse and ran around to the other side to help get Juliette into the car. Juliette was stretched out across the back seat, her head in Eve's lap, as Jesse got behind the wheel.

"Where to, then?"

"I don't know," Eve confessed. "She doesn't want anyone to know, so I can't take her home like this. How can I explain a drugged, dirty, and blood-stained sister to my parents?"

Jesse sighed. "I'll take you both back to my sister's place." As he made his way through the narrow, sand-lined streets, Jesse whispered, "Is she asleep?"

"Yes, she is. Poor thing."

He whispered back over his shoulder, "I have a friend. He's at the beach this summer, but he's finishing up medical school. I can call him over to look at your sister. No hospitals, no parents. You can be with her the whole time."

Eve thought a moment. "Yes, call him the minute we get to your house." Jesse merely nodded. Eve realized that Jesse was doing an awful lot for two girls he didn't even know. "Jesse, thank you. For all of this. I know this is an awful lot for someone who just wanted to buy me a soda."

"I'm happy to help, Eve."

"Well, thank you. From me and my sister." Eve gingerly looked down at her sister's face, still peaceful and unharmed. Not like the rest of her.

As they drove, Jesse asked a few questions of Eve. "Is Juliette your only sister?"

"No, we have a twelve-year-old sister as well, and a brother who's almost fifteen. And my parents raised my cousin, Pete. He's twenty-three and about to be married."

"You two seem awfully close. Is Juliette your older sister?" he asked. He sounded genuinely curious.

"No, younger by five whole minutes." Eve chuckled. This was usually the twin's favorite game to play on people they just met. Everyone was always shocked to hear that they were twins.

Jesse was no different. "Twins? I would have never thought that you were twins," he said over his shoulder. "I didn't get a good look at Juliette, but isn't her hair dark and curly?"

"Very much so," Eve said, as she continued to stroke her sister's hair. "I was born first with fiery hair and a calm temperament. Five minutes later, Juliette arrived with the wild black hair and wild demeanor to match. It's my dad's favorite story about us. Mine, too, actually."

"Well, Eve. I'm sorry to have met your sister like this. But I am glad I'm able to help out."

"So am I, Jesse. So am I."

A Tumultuous Sea

HE PULLED THE CAR INTO the driveway of a small, older house. Jesse opened the door for Eve, and she lifted Juliette's head for Jesse to take hold of. He lifted her out of the car, Eve scampering behind him. Eve ran up to the house and opened the door for him.

"Is anybody here?"

Jesse shook his head as he went through the doorway. "No, everybody is at work still. They won't be gone too much longer, though." He laid Juliette, still unconscious, on the couch. "I'll go call my pal Patrick."

Jesse disappeared into another room for a minute. Eve bent over her sister and gave her a closer look. The light in the room allowed her to see the bruises on her sister's body better. If Juliette didn't want her parents to know what happened, she couldn't go home tonight. But her parents should know what happened. Eve wasn't sure what she should do—lie to her parents or betray her sister's trust?

When Jesse came back into the room, Eve asked to use the phone. "I need to call our parents," she told him.

"Will you tell them what happened?" He stood close to her, and Eve could see beads of sweat on his brow—both from the heat and from carrying Juliette.

"Not yet," she replied. "Juliette needs to tell them what happened. But we need to stay away from home tonight." She bit her lip, a nervous habit she had inherited from her mother. "If you don't think your sister would mind." She hated thrusting Jesse into the middle of everything, but she didn't know what else to do.

"That's fine," he said. "Go ahead; I'll stay by her." He assumed the position of sentinel standing post in front of Juliette's limp body.

Eve smiled at him and went into the kitchen. She picked up the phone off the wall and dialed her home number. Glancing at the clock, she saw that it was barely nine o'clock. It had been only two hours since they had left their house.

When her father answered, she did her best to hide the fear from her voice. "Daddy? Hi, Daddy, it's Evie. Listen, Ginger Fowler and her boyfriend broke up tonight, and she's really bad off. Do you mind if Jules and I stay with her tonight? We'll be home tomorrow." She paused as her father gave her permission to stay out. "Thank you so much, Daddy. You're helping us help a friend. You're the best. See you tomorrow." She hung up the phone and gave a big sigh of relief. At least they were clear until tomorrow.

As she came back into the room, there was a knock on the door. She glanced at Jesse, who nodded at her. It would be his medical student friend. Jesse opened the door as Eve took the position of guard over Juliette. He greeted a man at the door and bade him enter.

"Patrick, thanks for coming, man. This is Eve," Jesse introduced them.

"Hello," Eve said quietly as she assessed the man before her. Patrick was quite tall and thin, but she could see he possessed great strength. His whitish-blond hair was mussed on top of his head; his blue eyes shone with concern; and his lips pursed as he caught his first glimpse of Juliette.

"What happened to her?" He swept past Eve to Juliette's side. "How long has she been out?"

"Just a few minutes. She fell asleep in the car," Eve explained. "She was drugged, we think, Doctor . . ."

"McKenzie. Patrick McKenzie," he said as he checked Juliette's vital signs. She remained unmoved. "Is she hurt?"

"She's bruised on her chest and stomach," Eve said as she leaned in toward her sister. She glanced back at Jesse, who seemed to approve of Patrick McKenzie's skills as an impending doctor. "Do you need to see . . . ?"

"I should take a look." He sighed. "But you can stand right here and make sure she's alright." Eve nodded her appreciation before slowly uncovering her sister's bruises. She quickly grabbed a section of the blanket and spread it over her sister's breasts, lest she be compromised any further. He tenderly felt each thick, purple mark while looking over her skin. Eve uncovered her sister's legs to show him the scrapes on her legs as well. "Some of these scrapes are pretty bad. I'll need to clean them up. Jesse, can I get a few hot, wet towels?"

Jesse nodded and retreated into the house. As he did, Juliette finally stirred awake. "What's going on?" As she realized she was being examined, she protested, "Eve, I said no hospitals. Please, stop." She pushed Patrick's arm away from her as she backed herself from him.

"Juliette, we're not at a hospital," Eve explained, trying to calm her sister. "Patrick's a friend, a medical student. No records, I promise. I just want to make sure your cuts and bruises aren't too serious."

Juliette eyed her sister, then inspected Patrick. She didn't speak, but relaxed and allowed him to continue looking at her legs. "I'm sorry about all this, Juliette. We just need to clean you up some." He worked quietly; and when Jesse brought him the towels, he had requested, Patrick pulled out a bottle of antiseptic and poured it onto a towel. "This will hurt," he warned.

As he pressed the towel into Juliette's legs, she cried out and sat up. The blanket slipped out from under her. Patrick quickly snatched it up. "There's blood on this blanket. What happened?"

Juliette froze in place, but quickly blurted out, "Nothing."

Eve felt tears return to her eyes and slip over her cheeks. "She was . . . abused. Raped. I should have been with her. I should have protected her."

He turned to Eve, and his face softened. "Many times, there's nothing you could have done. Getting her help is the best thing you can do for her." He turned his attention back to Juliette. "Tell us what happened."

"He brought me a drink. It was nothing I ever had before, but I didn't say anything about it. I wanted him to like me," she said as tears trickled down her face like a waterfall. Eve held her hand tightly as they all listened. "He wanted to hear my ideas about equality and women's rights. He wanted me to tell him about free love," she sobbed. "And when I didn't feel good, he said a walk would help me feel better. He said he would tell Eve that we would be right back. When we got to the pier, I could barely stand, and he had a blanket all ready to sit on. The next thing I knew . . . " She closed her eyes and cried out. Eve held Juliette's head to her chest, shushing her and stroking her hair.

Jesse looked enraged. "He planned this. He had the whole thing planned. Drug the drink, get her away from the crowd." His voice was raised almost to a shout, the fury evident.

"Who did this to you?" Patrick demanded to know, his voice also full of anger. "Did you know him before tonight? We should call the police."

"That's enough," Eve snapped at the men as tears streamed down Juliette's face. "Please, just hurry. She's been through enough tonight."

Patrick finished cleaning the cuts on Juliette's legs. "If she wants to keep these hidden, she'll need to wear pants or long skirts for a while. I don't think any need stitches; but if they look infected, call me back, and I'll come check them out. The bruises, however, will last a while. You really need to see a proper doctor. Especially if he . . . violated you."

"No," was the simple response from Juliette. Eve wished she'd reconsider.

"Well, then, I'm done here. Call me back, Jesse, if she needs anything." Patrick packed up his bag and stood. "One more thing, Juliette. You'll want to keep an eye on the calendar."

"Why?" Eve asked before Juliette had a chance.

Patrick looked away from the girls, unable to meet their gaze. "In case you end up pregnant." He and Jesse walked out the front door together without another word.

"Oh, no!" Juliette wailed as she winced from pain. "I can't believe this is happening to me." Eve held onto her sister as they cried together.

When Jesse came back into the room, he lightly laid his hand on Eve's back. "Dee will be home soon," he said softly. "Why don't we move your sister into my bedroom for tonight? That way, she won't be disturbed, and I can explain all this to Dee when she gets home."

"Okay, that sounds good to me." Eve helped Juliette to her feet, and Jesse led the way to his room.

He opened the door for them, then disappeared for a few moments. He came back in with fresh clothes for Juliette to change into. "I figured you may want to sleep in something else," he offered.

"Thank you. I do want a shower, if I could," Juliette said weakly.

"Right next door," Jesse replied. "Please make yourself comfortable."

Both girls said thank you in unison, and Jesse left them. Juliette stood and took the clothes in hand. "I'm going to take a shower, then crash. What about Mom and Dad?"

"I called them and said we'd be staying with Ginger," Eve told her. "Don't worry. I won't tell them anything until you're ready to." She helped her sister into the small bathroom and started the water for her.

"Hot water, Evie," Juliette demanded. "I'm never telling them anything. Especially since Buzz Herbert—that despicable rat—is the son of a new parishioner. They'd never believe me over him, anyway."

"Mom and Dad would believe you. I know they would. They can help you."

"No." Juliette was firm.

"Oh, Jules! What if he's in church Sunday?" Panic shot through Eve's mind as she thought of coming face to face with her sister's attacker. Surely, nobody would blame her for seeking revenge on such a monster.

"He won't be there. He told me he was leaving town tonight to go to Tennessee to work with his cousin. Isn't that convenient?" Juliette glared at her sister, but wasn't angry with her, and Eve knew that. "Please, let me be. I don't need you hovering like Mom would."

"Okay, Juliette," Eve said softly. Feeling useless, she added, "Let me know if you need anything at all. I'll probably join you in a little while in bed, if that's okay." Juliette nodded, and Eve slipped out the door.

She went back out into the living room and looked around for the first time. It was sparsely furnished. The green couch Juliette had laid on sat against the wall opposite a small television. To its left was a gold recliner chair, and between them was a small table with a lamp.

The carpet was stained and worn thin. Pictures of Jesse's family sat propped up on a buffet behind the recliner. Jesse was sitting on the couch, waiting for her.

"She going to be alright?"

"I sure hope so." Eve sighed. "There's nothing else I can do. She's in the shower. Thank you so much for everything you've done for us. I think most anyone else would have gone running the other direction if put in the situation. But you didn't. Why not?"

She sat next to him on the couch, their knees touching. Jesse took her hand in his before speaking. "Nobody deserves to be treated and abused the way your sister was. And you and I are friends now. I always help a friend. Especially when one's as pretty as you are." Eve blushed madly.

"You're like a knight in shining armor, Jesse. I can never repay you."

"Well, I'm no white knight."

Eve knew exactly what he was alluding to. Maybe he wasn't interested in her because she was white and he was black. Mixed couples were taboo, though marriages were just made legal and weren't usually seen out in public. But that didn't matter to her. Did he not just come to her rescue? What did skin color matter when it came to matters of life and love? "I don't care what color my knight is," she said, looking down at her hand in his. "As long as he comes to the rescue, I will always be thankful."

With that, Jesse leaned toward Eve and brushed his lips against hers lightly. Eve felt her breath catch in her throat, her heart flutter, and her stomach flip. The kiss was so gentle, it was hardly there. But there it was, hanging between them. Eve fought the urge to lean forward and kiss Jesse back; but instead, she moved away.

"I'm sorry, Jesse. After what my sister has been through tonight, I better not," she said quietly. "It's not that I don't want to. I do really like you. I just . . . not tonight." She looked into his coal black eyes and hoped he understood.

A small smile came across Jesse's full mouth. "I understand. Maybe once all this has blown over a little, I can take you out. What do you say?"

Eve's face lit up. "I would like that very much, Jesse. I hope you don't mind if I go check on Jules. Or should I stay here and meet your sister?"

"No, go ahead. I'll handle Dee, and you can meet her tomorrow. I hope you two sleep okay."

Eve stood, unsure if she should kiss Jesse or shake his hand. Instead she nodded her head, her red hair falling over her shoulders, and retreated back to the bedroom to wait for Juliette to emerge from the shower.

Juliette stood in the shower and let the water pour over her body. *I don't care if I use up all the hot water. But wait, this isn't my house. Whose house is this? Eve said we are at Jesse's house. Was this the same Jesse Eve had flirted with last week? She said he was a good-looking, tall, black man, and this guy fit that description. Where had she found him? At the party? Oh, that stupid party. Why did Eve agree to go? Why did I agree to go out with Buzz Herbert? Evie had said she didn't trust the way he looked. Why didn't I sense that?*

She scrubbed the soap over her skin, ignoring the searing pain let off from the purple whelps. She scrubbed so hard that the dry, cracked soap nearly cut into her flesh. *Let it*, she thought. She had washed her hair twice and washed her entire body several times over, but she still wasn't clean enough. She could still feel the sand under her back; she could still smell the scent of Buzz's aftershave mixed with sweat and blood. The smell permeated Juliette's body, and she didn't think it would ever leave her. While the water flowed over her face, Juliette let the tears also flow. She sobbed, half hoping nobody would hear her and half not caring who did.

Thinking she could get cleaner at home in the morning, she shut the water off. Stepping out of the dingy shower, she grabbed a towel and gently dried her skin, being careful to avoid the bruises and cuts that covered her body. She helped herself to Jesse's sister's comb and kerchief and then dressed in the borrowed t-shirt and shorts. Feeling somewhat better, she cracked the door open, unsure if she should go back into the bedroom or see if her sister was still awake in the living room.

As she opened the door, she heard voices. She heard Jesse's masculine voice first. "Dee, listen, these girls are friends of mine, and they met up with some trouble tonight. I told them they could stay here until the morning."

"And why can't they stay in their own house? I don't want you accused of kidnapping two white girls, Jesse," came a female response.

Another male voice joined in. "Dee's right, Jesse. What if these girls try to claim something happened?"

Juliette gulped. Something did happen, just not with Jesse. Should she step in and reassure them? But she hardly knew Jesse in the first place.

He spoke up. "Trust me, they won't cause any trouble and will be gone in the morning. Eve and Juliette are fine women. Their daddy's a preacher. They're solid girls."

Juliette heard a snort come from the woman, Dee. "Preacher daddy or no, white girls don't belong here, Jess."

"Nah, she's different. She even said skin color don't make a difference to her. I know it does to everyone else in the world, but aren't we fighting now for equality? Doesn't that mean mixing the races a little bit?" Jesse retorted. "Listen, Dee. It's just for tonight. The one that got hurt, she's in the shower; the other one's sleeping already. I'll stay on the couch . . . "

Juliette stopped listening. It didn't seem that Dee was going to kick them out, and Eve was already in the bedroom. She snuck out the door and into the room to the left. The light was still on, and Eve was lying in bed with her eyes wide open.

"Are you feeling better?" Eve asked with concern, which made Juliette attempt a smile.

"A little, thank you," Juliette said, climbing into bed with her sister. "Can you hear them in here?"

Eve nodded. "I feel bad for making Jesse explain all this alone. But he really did come to your aid—our aid—tonight."

"Did he ask you out?" Juliette wanted to be mad at her sister, but was too tired and decided she could be mad at Eve once she was done being mad at herself.

"Kinda," Eve confessed. "He seems interested in me, and I do like him. But I told him that I needed to be with you right now. Maybe one day we can go out. But I am more concerned for you." Eve's green eyes bore into her, searching for answers that Juliette didn't think she could give.

"I'll be okay, Evie. Right now, I want to sleep. Then tomorrow, we can deal with this," Juliette said as her head hit the pillow below her.

She nestled up to her twin sister, putting her cheek against Eve's shoulder blade. "Thank you for finding me."

"I'll always find you, Jules," came the reply. Eve turned off the light, and they both tried to sleep.

For Juliette, sleep did not come. Every time her eyes started to close, she saw images of Buzz Herbert hovering over her, an evil grin on his face. She hoped Eve slept some for the both of them.

The next morning arrived too soon for Juliette, who watched the light outside the window grow brighter and brighter until it woke Eve.

Turning to face her, Eve's voice was heavy with sleep. "Juliette? How are you? Are you okay?"

Eve always mothered her. But now Juliette supposed she needed it a little. "I'm okay," was all she said.

"Did you sleep?" Eve sat up and rubbed her eyes. Her hair tangled around her head and neck as she attempted to push it out of her face.

"No, I didn't," she confessed. No use in lying; Eve would know right away.

Eve sat silent for a few moments, as if contemplating something. "What do you want to do?"

What do you want to tell Mom and Dad? is what she meant. She didn't have to say it. Juliette knew how her sister thought. She didn't want to do anything about telling her parents. She didn't want to do anything about seeing doctors or telling police. What she wanted to do was curl up in a little ball and wish herself away—or at least back in time twenty-four hours.

Juliette looked at her sister, who was staring at her, waiting for an answer. She didn't have an answer to give. "I don't know," she admitted. "I just want to pretend like this never happened."

"Jules, are you sure about that? Buzz needs to be held accountable for what he did to you," Eve said in a hushed tone. "You need to report him to the police, so he can be arrested."

"Eve, you know as well as I do that it's my word against his. He could claim that I got drunk and wanted to . . . to . . . " Juliette felt her cheeks grow warm as she flustered. "Well, at any rate, I don't think it would do any good, Eve. I just want to go home and start healing, okay? I just want everybody to act cool around me, like everything is normal." She paused before adding, "Please, Eve."

Eve nodded. "Alright, Jules. I'll act cool. I'll ask Jesse not to tell anybody either, okay? We'll just tell Mom and Dad that you were up all night comforting Ginger after a bad breakup. When we get home, you can sleep in your own bed for a while."

With a sigh of relief, Juliette relaxed a little. She thought back to what her father had said before about not knowing what could happen at beach parties. *Oh, Dad, if you only did know what could—and does—happen at beach parties. I should have listened to you.*

Sea Caps

EVE AND JULIETTE BOTH GRADUATED with honors. The outdoor ceremony was warm, but the humidity was what made them all sweat. Their mother said it was the kind of day that reminded her of her childhood back in the Appalachian foothills. Juliette's curls were frizzier than normal, and Eve's loose waves were also standing on end.

Eve walked up to the stage first, the collar of her black robe sitting uncomfortably along her neckline. She wanted to scratch it—or remove it entirely—but had to wait. Juliette stood behind her and briefly clasped her hand to Eve's.

Principal Manning called her name. "Eve Catherine Nicholas, magna cum laude." Eve stepped forward and approached her principal. She didn't realize that she was graduating magna cum laude. Now she knew why everyone had pressed her to apply to colleges. Maybe after some time off, she would think about enrolling in technical college. She still had no idea what she wanted to do with her life.

She smiled as the principal handed her the rolled-up paper. They had been told that this was not their real diploma; those would be mailed to them. *So why all the ceremony just for a piece of nothing?* Eve wasn't sure, but she smiled, anyway.

When she got to the other side of the stage, she waited before descending the steps. She turned to watch her sister.

"Juliette Christine Nicholas, cum laude," the principal announced.

Eve smiled at her sister, who did not smile in return. Juliette wore a stern expression on her face as she walked toward Principal Manning. *Please smile, Jules, please,* Eve begged in her head. *This is a happy time, Juliette, please.* But her internal pleading did nothing, nor did the smile she herself plastered across her face. Juliette took the paper and marched the rest of the way across the stage.

Despite her biggest smile and best hug, Juliette did not respond to Eve's prompting. When they sat back down, Eve leaned in to Juliette and whispered, "Please, Juliette. Mom and Dad will know something is wrong if you keep this up. If you want to hide this, you need to do a better job. I love you. I want you to be happy." A tear trickled down her cheek as she sat back up, her heart reaching out to her sister.

What she didn't see was the tear that also fell lightly down Juliette's own cheek.

After the ceremony, family and friends gathered at the Nicholas' home for a celebratory dinner. Eve had invited Jesse, so that he could meet her family. Pete was there with his fiancée, Linda, and several families from their church were also present.

Before the food was served, Eve's mother approached her and Juliette. "Eve, I see you invited a date. He seems like a very nice young man."

Eve beamed. She had come to like Jesse Washington more than she had expected.

Turning to Juliette, Abby asked, "Didn't you want to invite Buzz Herbert today? I haven't seen him since your date. Did it not work out between you?"

Juliette flushed bright red, and Eve tried to think quickly. "He wound up being a big bore, Mom," she said, glancing at her sister. Juliette merely nodded.

"Oh, that's too bad," Abby said as she wrinkled her forehead. "He and his mother seemed so nice. Mrs. Herbert is a sweet lady." Then she changed to a smile. "They can't all be as wonderful and handsome as your father." Abby looked across the yard to her husband, and the girls' gazes followed.

Juliette excused herself and went into the house. Eve wanted to run after her, but didn't want to seem anxious and decided to give her sister a moment alone. She looked back to her father. He was a handsome man, despite his forty-six years. He was a little gray at the temples, and a few lines had crept up around his eyes. Eve sighed as she watched her mother fold neatly into his open arms. Such a perfect pair, she thought. Her gaze shifted to Jesse, and he smiled when he looked up at her. As he made his way toward her, Eve couldn't help but imagine what the future might hold.

Juliette splashed her face with cool water and hung her head over the sink. *Too bad,* her mother had said about Buzz. *He seemed so nice,* she said.

Nice. Right, she thought. *He was a monster. An assuming, conceited, phony of a man. Not even a man,* she told herself. *More like a selfish pig, a waste of a human soul. And I let him. I just let him. Why didn't I fight back? Why didn't I scream and kick and defend myself?* Guilt and self-blame began to settle over Juliette. *Why didn't the God my parents pray to wise me up and get me out of there?*

I should just end it all and see if this God exists. She began searching the medicine cabinet for pills—anything to ease the pain she felt. Pain in her body that was still not subsiding. Pain in her mind over the turmoil she had been through in the past two weeks. *I know there's a bottle of something in here,* she thought as she rifled through the cabinet and moved on to the linen closet. She found nothing but aspirin and wondered how many she would have to take to make the pain stop. *Every last one,* she thought as her hand landed on a full bottle that had been forgotten in the back of the closet.

Footsteps came up the stairs. *Eve.* Juliette knew who it was just based on the way the feet fell on each step. Her sister would be coming to check on her. She needed to swallow the pills before Eve figured out what she was doing. Eve would try to stop her. Juliette fumbled with the cap, but found the bottle still stuffed with cotton. The footsteps came up to the bathroom door, and Juliette raced to pull the last traces of cotton from the bottle.

"Jules?" Eve's voice was soft and tender.

"Go away," Juliette demanded. Unlike her sister, her voice was harsh and low.

"Juliette, what's wrong?" Eve's voice was alarmed; she knew something was amiss. "Are you okay?"

"Go away, Eve," Juliette said, her voice livid. She felt sweat bead up on her forehead. She just wanted the pain to go away. She turned the water on and poured the pills out into her hand.

But before she could toss them all into her mouth, Eve opened the door, knocking her elbow. The pills scattered all over the floor. Juliette looked up at Eve like a deer caught in headlights. Eve looked just as horrified.

"Juliette, what are you doing?"

Juliette immediately started to bend down to pick up the pills, but Eve caught her by the shoulders. Eve pulled her up to eye level and looked at her—green eyes to green eyes. Juliette could feel her sister's thoughts. *What's going on?* she seemed to be saying. But Juliette knew that Eve knew what was going on.

"How could you, Juliette? What are you thinking?" Tears fell down Eve's cheeks as she pulled Juliette close and embraced her tightly.

Juliette could feel tears flooding her cheeks. "I just want the pain to stop, Evie. I don't want to hurt anymore," she cried.

"Shh, I know," Eve said in her mothering voice. "But taking fifty pills is not the way, sweetie. Talk to me; I'll help you. But please don't leave me, Jules. I can't survive without you. Maybe we should talk with Mom and Dad."

"Absolutely not, Evie. I can't. You promised."

"This is not the answer, Juliette," Eve whispered. "This is more than I can help you with. I don't know how to help, but someone else might."

"Call it momentary insanity, okay? I wouldn't have actually done anything," Juliette tried to reassure her sister. The look on Eve's face said she was not fully convinced.

Both girls picked their heads up when they heard the front door swing open. "Eve! Juliette! Dad says come on," Alisa yelled up the stairs. "So, come on, we're all hungry and waiting on you."

"We'll be right there, Alisa," Eve called to her younger sister. "We're just having a twin moment." When the door closed, she turned back to Juliette. "Let's clean this up and go downstairs, okay?"

Juliette nodded. "Okay," she said quietly, her whole body shaking. Eve bent down, scooped up the pills, and quickly tossed them into the toilet. After picking up a few strays, she flushed every last one. Before going back out to their family, Eve fixed Juliette's hair and wiped her face with a damp cloth.

"No more pills, okay?"

"Okay. I'm sorry," Juliette said. Her body felt limp and lifeless, but she knew she needed to make an effort for her sister's sake. And her parents.

"We can talk about it later, okay?" Eve smiled at her, but her face shone with concern.

"No, I'm alright, Evie. I'm sorry," Juliette relied quickly. "It was momentary insanity." She attempted a half-smile.

The girls went back out to their family and friends to celebrate their graduation. Juliette vowed not to even consider taking her life again. Her family loved her, her twin especially. Despite the pain she felt, it would pale in comparison to the agonizing pain Eve would feel if she were gone.

Lapping the Shore

EVE HAD BEEN OUT WITH Jesse Washington every night that week. They were stared at—mixed race couples just weren't seen around town, even with the thousands of tourists who descended upon Myrtle Beach in the summertime. But Eve didn't care. Jesse was a wonderful man, and she felt lucky to have found him, especially after he came to her aid when Juliette was attacked. In fact, Eve thought she might be falling in love with the man.

This evening was no different. Jesse came by the house to pick up Eve. He even came inside and chatted with her mother for a few minutes. Eve was thrilled that her parents didn't seem to mind the color of his skin, though they had told her others would not be as accepting. As she finished getting ready, she heard Jesse ask Juliette if she wanted to come along. Eve pressed her ear to the door, not meaning to eavesdrop, but curious to hear what Juliette would say.

"It's just a burger and a movie, Juliette," Jesse said. Eve could hear the smile in his voice. He was so sweet to try to include Juliette. She had hardly been out of the house since the night of that terrible party.

"Thanks, but no," Juliette replied.

"Are you sure?" Jesse prodded, hoping to get her to change her mind.

"Yeah, I'm sure," Juliette said with a sigh. "You and Eve have fun." Eve heard her sister start ascending the stairs. At the bathroom door, she paused. "He's a really nice guy, Eve. Have a good night." Eve didn't respond, and she heard Juliette slip into their shared room, the door closing behind her.

Eve took a heavy breath, unsure how to further help her sister. There had been no more scares since the day of their graduation. She hoped Juliette was feeling better. She opened the bathroom door and headed down the stairs. Her mother pulled her aside immediately, concern on her face. "Eve, what's wrong with Juliette these days? She's barely gone out since you two graduated. Is she okay?"

Eve hated lying to her mother, but knew she had to protect Juliette. "She's fine, Mom," she said and smiled. "I think she's just a little overwhelmed at what to do next. She's been thinking a lot about what to do with her life." *Not a complete fabrication,* Eve thought. Juliette was wondering what to do with her life, just not in the way her mother was thinking. Abby smiled at her and patted her arm, satisfied with the answer.

"Well, then, Jesse's waiting," Abby said. "Just . . . Evie . . . just be careful."

Eve raised an eyebrow. "Careful?"

Abby's cheeks flushed much the way Eve's did. "I know people are talking. White girls and colored boys just don't date in this world, Eve. I know that God doesn't see colors, and your dad and I are doing our best to follow Christ's example, but it's hard. I don't want to see you hurt. Not by the world or by him. He could lose his job; you two could be shunned from the community simply by being seen out together."

Eve attempted a smile. So, her mom knew that tongues were wagging about the preacher's daughter and the black man. She had heard what was being said herself. At least Abby was gracious about it. "It's okay, Mom. I don't care if people talk about me," she said, secretly adding *as long as they don't talk about Juliette* in her head. "I'll be home later."

She made her way into the living room, where Jesse was waiting patiently. He stood as she entered the room. He was a truly good-looking man. He was at least six inches taller than her. His black, curly hair cut close to his scalp. He said an afro didn't bode so well for men who worked in construction, despite the look's rising popularity. Jesse's eyes were large and as dark as night, his eyelashes curling at the ends. He had a wide nose, a strong chin, and dimples to boot.

But his smile was what captured Eve. Jesse's smile was a mile wide at its fullest. His lips were full and round, and his teeth were white as snow. Everything he said, Eve listened to. Anything he ate, Eve paid attention to. Whenever Jesse smiled, Eve's heart skipped a beat; her knees went weak; and she felt like she could be with him forever. Even though she was only eighteen, she could hardly wait for forever with Jesse to happen.

They made their way to a favorite diner frequented by locals and tourists alike. As they walked through the door arm in arm, several heads turned to stare at them. One older woman gasped. A hushed whisper could be heard in the crowded eatery. *What is so wrong about mixing races?* Eve thought. Looking around, there were tables of whites and tables of blacks; but no groups mixed, no "checkerboard" couples to be seen. Not tonight and not ever. Eve wanted to shout to all of them that they were being blatantly prejudiced, but then they would know they had gotten to her. She didn't want that, so she kept her mouth shut. Eve held her head high and gazed up at Jesse, a huge smile on her face.

Jesse, ever perceptive, seemed to know just what Eve was thinking. He smiled at her and bent down and casually brushed his lips across her cheek. It was a simple gesture, but intimate enough. And the sight of his chocolate brown lips on her porcelain skin made many people turn away and gasp. What Eve didn't see were those gazes that become even more intent on watching them.

The diner wasn't segregated by force, but the patrons with skin the color of burnt milk and darker seemed to stay toward the back of the dining room. Those with creamier skin sat toward the front. Lucky for them, there was a table open right between the two areas; they took it with a smile. Eve sat toward the back, Jesse toward the front.

"Can you imagine if you had walked in here with me and Juliette?" Eve whispered across the red-topped table. "They would have laid an egg!"

Jesse laughed. "Yes, but would that have been a white egg or a brown egg?"

A laugh escaped Eve so loud that she heard spoons fall into coffee cups as people turned again to stare. She wasn't usually comfortable with attention like this; this was Juliette's specialty. Eve felt like she was partaking in a protest that only she and Jesse knew about, and it was exciting. She enjoyed having people stare at her and Jesse. *Let them,* she thought. *This is what free love means. It means if you love someone different from you, those differences shouldn't matter. The only thing that matters is that we feel the same way.*

But did Jesse feel the same way about her as she did him? He had to. Over the past few weeks they had been together, he was attentive, polite, captivating. He had met her entire family, and she had met his family who lived nearby. This was going somewhere. Had her mother not told her that she knew right away that she would marry her father? Within a few weeks, her mother had said. Maybe it ran in the family to know who your soulmate was after only a short amount of time.

Eve ate quietly while looking at Jesse's smile and pondering whether or not this was true love. Every time she saw him, her heart fluttered. Wasn't that a sign of love? When he took her home in the evenings, she felt her heart miss him. Wasn't that a sign of love?

As the sullen waitress took their plates away, Jesse leaned in toward her. "Are you okay, Eve? You've been awfully quiet tonight. Is it bothering you that people are staring at us?"

Clearing her head, Eve quickly spoke up. "No! Not at all. I'm here with you, not them. Let them stay in their square, narrow-minded, little bubbles." She smiled at him. "I'm sorry. I've just been thinking is all."

"Okay, then. Let's say we get out of here, and you can tell me what you're thinking about." Jesse stood and reached his hand out to Eve, who took it gladly. Her brown, linen dress trailed behind her as she followed him to the front of the restaurant.

Before they made it to the door, however, two men in blue jeans and t-shirts rose and blocked their path. Jesse smiled. "Sorry, guys. Excuse us."

One crossed his arms and nodded toward Eve. "Not with her. You should be with your own kind, black boy. Leave the girl, and get out of here."

Eve was shocked. What did these two think they were doing? And what would Jesse do about it?

Jesse's smile faded with the crass language. "Sorry, boys. The lady and I came in together, and we'll leave together." He made a motion to step between the two men, his hand still clutching Eve's. But the troublemakers stepped closer together, blocking them entirely.

The entire restaurant had turned to watch the scuff between black and white, tradition and forbidden. Eve again stood tall, proud. She wouldn't let them treat Jesse and her like this!

She stepped up next to Jesse. She spoke quietly, but everything else was silent so each of her words resonated throughout the diner. "I don't know who you think you are, but you're not doing anybody in here a service. If you don't mind, I would like to continue my date. Step aside."

A murmur rose throughout. Everybody stared at Eve and Jesse, watching to see if the two men would allow them to pass together. After a tense moment, one stepped to the side. His mission to make a scene was completed. Jesse put his arm around Eve and led her to the door.

As Eve passed the man to her right, he spit on her and scowled. He called her a foul name she would never repeat.

Time stopped. Eve turned on her heel and looked the man right in his steely grey eyes. She reached up her hand and slapped him as hard as she possibly could. "You, sir, should wash your mouth out with soap," she hissed. Then she turned on her heel and strode out the door with Jesse by her side.

They got into the car without speaking and sped away, the plans forgotten and their just-eaten dinner churning in their stomachs. About a mile down the road, Jesse pulled off into a parking lot and turned to Eve.

"Are you alright?"

She was shaking, and her hand hurt. She was angry and scared and exhilarated at the same time. But mostly she was angry. "I'm . . . I'm . . . I'm angry. I'm furious! I didn't ask to be saved by those two. I have never met them before. Ever!" Jesse just looked at her while she struggled with her emotions internally. "Why aren't you mad?"

"I am, but this is my life, Eve," he said calmly, quietly. "Everywhere I go, I am faced with racist people who treat me like dirt. No matter where I am, someone is staring at me as if I might rob them or point a gun at them. White women avoid me on the street and pull their children closer. It's just how it is."

"But why, Jesse?" she implored. Who could be afraid of so gentle a man? Who wouldn't want to be friends with someone who smiled the way Jesse did?

"Because that's how it is, Eve. White people always seem to be afraid of black men, no matter what."

"I'm not. My family's not." Eve felt tears slip over her cheeks. She had no idea day-to-day life was so difficult for Jesse. For any person of color, for that matter. She knew only her middle-class, white-bread life.

Jesse pulled her close to him and put his arm around her shoulder. Despite the summer heat, Eve was chilly, her bare arms cool to the touch. "It's okay. You, your sister, and your family are showing the white world that it's okay to work with and love black folk. And my people are holding peaceful protests for integration. One day, it will work. My parents used to tell me about what it was like during World War Two and how they were treated then. Things are getting better every year. Maybe not as fast as black people would like, but better anyway. And great black thinkers like Dr. Martin Luther King, Junior, are making great strides in black equality and power. Don't you remember his dream speech?"

"Yes, I do," Eve said with a small sniff. "But it seemed so distant, so far away. But now it seems like racism is on my doorstep."

"Well, if we're not careful, Eve, it will be," Jesse warned in return.

Eve pulled back and looked at him. "What do you mean?"

"You saw how those two acted back there. White men don't like black men dating their women. I'm afraid if he knows who your family is, you all could become targets for vandalism and other crimes against black sympathizers." Jesse lowered his head, and Eve could see just how upset he really was. "Let me take you home."

"No, Jesse," she pleaded. "I don't want to go home, please. Can't we go somewhere quiet? Where nobody will argue with us about being together? Besides," Eve added, "I've wanted to talk to you, anyway."

With a smile, Jesse nodded and put the car back into drive. He drove down the sand-banked street until it came to a stop close to the inlet. They removed their shoes and grabbed a blanket so they could sit and watch the sky grow dark above them while the waves crashed near their feet.

Their portion of beach was isolated and deserted. Eve breathed a sigh of relief to find that no one would impede their evening anymore. Surely, the sand and ocean would not protest their date. Eve knelt in the sand and loved feeling the cool, damp granules under her knees. She helped Jesse spread a large, fluffy blanket out for them to sit on. Eve didn't mind the sand between her toes, but Jesse didn't care for it. She twisted the skirt of her dress around her knees and tucked it between them to allow herself to sit gracefully without exposing too much flesh.

She curled up next to Jesse, laying her small, pale hand over top of his large, brown one. He laid his other hand on top of hers, enveloping it completely. She loved how they fit together. She loved Jesse. She knew it now, after what had happened at dinner. She loved him and wanted to fight for him and their relationship and all mixed-race relationships.

After watching the sky to the east grow dim, Jesse turned to her. "What did you want to talk about, Eve?" He turned his gaze on her, his eyes shining, his mouth moist.

Eve couldn't help herself. She reached her head up to his and kissed him. Yes, they had kissed before, but not like this. Eve felt the passion, the longing, pour out of herself and into her lips. And she could swear she felt the same come from Jesse. As they kissed, waves rose and met the shore in front of them, making Eve feel slightly dangerous and lightheaded. Jesse's hands cupped her cheeks, firm but not rough. Eve pressed herself into Jesse more, her torso turning toward him. When they broke apart, Eve could feel the breeze swirl between them, and she longed to be closer still.

With her breath heavy, she looked at Jesse. "I love you, Jesse. I love you, and I have to know that you love me." Never had she been so bold in action or in word.

When Jesse didn't jump to profess his love in return, panic filled Eve's heart and head. But then a slow smile spread on his face, and a sheen came across his eyes. Jesse gently cupped her face again in his hands. "You know I love you, Eve. From the moment I first saw you."

Eve felt as if her heart was bursting; a dam full of emotions let loose. She felt sparks fly from inside her. Her fingers tingled; her skin felt electric. Jesse loved her. She knew it. She popped up to her knees and wrapped her arms around Jesse's muscular neck, kissing him anywhere she could. She smelled his aftershave and could taste the salty sand on his neck.

In return, Jesse's strong arms wove around her back, his hands splayed out as if claiming her for his own. He breathed her in, smelling her heathery scent mixed with the salty sea air. He moved his hand to stroke her hair, the copper strands glistening in what sunlight remained. He held her back and looked into her eyes, and Eve thought she might shed tears for the way he looked at her.

Jesse pulled her hair from her face and then whispered, "Let me show you how much I love you."

Warmth turned to heat as they came together, the moist sand under them, the ocean carrying their promises on the breeze.

Summer Breeze

AS DUSK FADED INTO NIGHT, Eve curled up close to Jesse. She held her discarded dress over her body to keep the breeze off her damp skin. Jesse's chest remained bare, and Eve laid her head on it to hear his heartbeat. Each thump seemed to echo her name. *Eve-Eve, Eve-Eve, Eve-Eve.* She shifted so that she could see his face and traced her finger along his jawline. Jesse was such a handsome man, and he was all hers. She was in utter amazement over how a man like him could love a girl like her.

She smiled at Jesse and snuggled close to him. "I don't want this night to end."

"If we're here much longer, we'll see morning," Jesse said and laughed. "I do need to get you home."

"No, Jesse, let's just stay here."

"I don't think that will go over well when tourists show up at daybreak." He chuckled. "We will be together again soon, baby. Don't you doubt it. How about I come by on Thursday?" He reached for his shirt and started to put it back on.

Eve followed suit and redressed quickly. "Thursday? That's so long."

"I've got a busy week ahead at work. We're building a new restaurant down here, actually. I'll be on the inlet all week."

"Oh, okay," Eve said, disappointed. Jesse kissed her and promised they would be together again soon.

They loaded the car, and Jesse drove Eve back home under the cover of night.

As he drove, Eve thought of Juliette. This was something she would want to share with her sister, her confidante, her closest friend. But would Juliette understand after what had happened to her a few weeks ago? Maybe she shouldn't tell her. But how could she not?

Jesse could see that she was upset. "Are you okay? Eve? Did I hurt you?" He was obviously concerned.

"No, not at all. I was thinking about Juliette. I don't know if I can tell her about this." A tear slipped down Eve's sandy cheek and splashed onto her dress.

"Do you have to tell her?"

Jesse just didn't understand how sisters were. "We tell each other everything. We have no secrets," she said. "But I just don't know if she'll understand after all she's been through. I don't know that she'd understand that we did this out of love."

"Give her time, Eve," Jesse said in a smooth voice. "In a week or so, maybe she'll be ready to hear it. Is it a secret if you plan to tell her later?"

"I guess not." Eve shrugged. She was silent the rest of the ride home.

When he pulled into the driveway, Jesse kissed her, and she jumped out of the car. She carefully opened the door and slipped inside. She went to the bathroom and sponged her body down to get rid of most of the sand and salt. She braided her hair and went to her room, hoping her sister would be fast asleep.

Juliette jumped when the door opened and her sister quietly snuck in. She flicked on the light next to her bed. Eve stopped in her tracks and backed against the door. She looked flushed, almost secretive.

"Juliette, I thought you would be asleep by now," Eve said to her with a deep breath.

"And I thought you would be asleep in the bed beside me," Juliette replied with a hint of bitterness in her voice. "Did Mom hear you?"

"I hope not." Eve crossed to her dresser and pulled out a nightgown. She quickly disrobed, trying to keep her body in the dark corner of the room. Juliette eyed her; something was amiss. Eve wasn't shy around her when she was changing clothes. Why was she now?

She swallowed hard. Would her sister, her twin, not tell her what was wrong? Had Jesse hurt her the way she had been hurt? She searched Eve's face when she turned back to face her.

"Eve? Is everything okay?" Juliette's protective side was starting to come out. If Jesse had broken her sister's heart, she would mend it the way Eve had mended her broken body.

But Eve smiled—albeit, a feeble smile. "I'm fine. We ended up going to the beach, and I just got a little sandy is all. I didn't want to wake anybody by taking a bath so late. I feel like I'm covered in sand." Eve laughed a little and sat in her bed. She wiped at her feet to rid them of any extra sand.

Not convinced, Juliette pushed a little harder. "Is that all? You look like something's troubling you. Is everything okay with Jesse?" Even the idea of the beach was still hard for her. The thought of being covered in sand gave Juliette chills, and she felt fear rise up in her body.

With a genuine smile, Eve bounced into Juliette's bed. She wasn't frightened the way Juliette was. Eve was happy, joyful. "Oh, Juliette. Is it ever!" Eve hugged her and held her close. "Jules, we're in love. He actually said he loves me. Isn't that . . . well . . . Juliette, I think he's my soulmate!"

Stunned, Juliette now knew why her sister was being so shy before. Eve didn't want to hurt her feelings. While Juliette was happy for Eve, she was hurt. She felt betrayed. After what had happened to her, her sister had the nerve to go and fall in love? Juliette didn't think she would ever date again, and here was her sister crazy in love. But she knew she should act happy.

"Love? Really?" She searched Eve's eyes and saw nothing but adoration for Jesse in them. *Oh, Eve, you* are *in love.* "I'm so happy for you, Evie." Juliette smiled softly and held her sister's hand.

"Are you really? I always thought we would be in love at the same time. We've always done everything the same."

Juliette thought for a minute. "I am happy for you. Anything that makes you happy makes me happy." It was the truth; Eve's happiness meant the world to Juliette. Especially when she didn't think happiness would ever find her again. "Now, it's late, big sister. Go to bed."

Eve returned to her own bed, and Juliette turned out the light. She laid motionless, but again, sleep did not come. Sleep evaded her most nights now. Her parents were starting to take notice. At least it was summer, and she no longer had to wake up for school. But she couldn't continue as she was for much longer. Guilt over her stupidity at trusting Buzz encompassed her. Pain over what he did engulfed her.

Will this pain never cease? The bruises are nearly gone, the cuts almost healed; but my mind, my soul, are forever wounded. Pain circles me everywhere I go; grief washes over me with every step I take. And to top it off, there's still a chance I could be pregnant. I can't believe Eve has fallen in love and left me behind. I know Jesse Washington is a nice guy; but if she's in love, she'll leave me behind. What will I do now? I can barely talk to men anymore, let alone think about dating. And so, my pain increases when I think that I will never feel the love that my sister now feels. Dad preaches that jealousy is a hateful thing. I may not believe in the God he claims said that, but I can't argue with the logic. I don't like feeling jealous of Eve. I wish I could heal—heart, mind, body, and soul.

Juliette finally fell into a fitful sleep, tossing and turning for most of the night. She woke and wrestled with herself over the jealousy and pain she felt, then fell back to sleep, only to wake again minutes later.

Morning came too soon for Juliette. Her mother had signed her up to work at the family bakery that morning, so Juliette got up and dressed in a pair of slacks and a high-collared, fitted black shirt. She put a bright fuchsia scarf over her hair, so she could avoid wearing one of her mother's hairnets.

Only a ten-minute drive away was Abby's Sweet Treats. Her mother had opened the bakery five years before when she realized she needed something else to do while all her children were in school. Her father encouraged her to go back to what she loved—baking. A month later, Abby's Sweet Treats opened its doors. Juliette's mother was immensely talented and made anything from muffins to wedding cakes, breads to pastries. Aside from raising five children, Abby found her pride and joy in the bakery.

An hour before opening, Juliette and her mother set to work. With little direction, Juliette knew exactly what was expected of her. Getting a muffin base started in the mixer, checking any special orders for the day. Making sure she knew if any deliveries had to be made. She wiped down the counter and set up displays for doughnuts, bagels, and muffins alike. As she worked, her mother handed her a steaming hot cup of coffee, black with sugar, just how she liked it.

"You look happier today, Juliette," her mother said as she inhaled the aroma of the coffee. "I've been worried about you."

Juliette's back stiffened, and her face turned red. "Don't worry about me, Mom. I've just had a lot on my mind."

"Can I help? You know you can always talk to me," her mother said, her voice full of love and understanding.

Could she tell her mother the truth? Not here, not with the store opening in a few minutes. *Maybe one day, Mom,* she thought. *But not today.* "I know. I think I'm happy because Eve seems so happy."

"Really?"

"Jesse seems to be very into her. They're a groovy couple, don't you think? Quite hip," she said with a smile, albeit a fake one.

Abby sighed. "They do seem to like each other quite a bit. And Jesse is a nice young man. But I worry for them if they think this relationship will be long-lasting. It's just not accepted for races to intermix. I know you think there's nothing wrong with it, and perhaps there's not, Juliette; but they will face a lifetime of stares and comments and even hatred wherever they go."

"Times are changing, Mom," Juliette reminded her mother. "Look at Doctor King. Has he not made great strides in the black movement for civil rights? I bet in a few years, he could run for president and win."

Abby gave Juliette her sympathetic smile. Juliette knew her mother well enough—she thought her sentiment was nice, but didn't think she was right. "Well, let's get those muffins out of the oven and unlock the door. I have someone picking up an order at 7:30 sharp."

Juliette went to the back and placed fresh blueberry muffins onto the cooling rack. She had about ten minutes before they and an assortment of other baked goods would be picked up. She looked at the order sheet. A dozen blueberry muffins, half a dozen cinnamon, half a dozen banana nut, and two loaves of pumpernickel bread were on the list. Two gallons of orange juice were also on the order. The juice had been prepared the night before by her mother's loyal employee, Fred. She pulled the two gallons out of the fridge and placed them inside a doubled-up paper bag. She collected her muffins and bread and wrapped them up as well. She brought everything out to the counter just in time to see the door swing open and a man walk in.

Juliette was spellbound from the moment she saw him. In strode a tall, handsome man. He was black; but his eyes were almond-shaped, and his hair was in tiny braids along his scalp. His skin was light for a black man, and it reminded Juliette of clay on a potter's wheel. He wore sunglasses on the top of his head and a brown, suede jacket on his lean frame. When he saw Juliette, he smiled, his eyes creasing and his high cheekbones becoming more prominent. He was the most gorgeous man she had ever seen.

His smile made her weak in the knees. "Hi, there. My name is Booker Winston. I have an order to pick up."

Booker Winston. Juliette forgot all about Buzz Herbert, all about her oath to never date again. Booker Winston was all that she saw. "Hello," she managed to say. It took him raising his eyebrows for her to realize he was there as a customer. "This must be for you," she said, her voice high and barely audible. She pushed the bags forward and rang his order up on the cash register.

"Thanks so much. Here you go," he said, handing her some cash. His fingers brushed against hers as she took it. Juliette could have sworn she saw sparks ignite, so hot was his touch. "This is a wonderful little bakery. I own the Blue Rooster restaurant down the street. I worked out a deal with the owner here to sell some of her muffins to my customers. Do you know where Mrs. Nicholas might be?"

Juliette smiled. "That would be my mother. Let me get her for you," she said. *Drat, why did I mention that she was my mother? That makes me seem so juvenile. Oh well, I'm in no position to be dating anyway. I'd never be able to trust a man again.* She excused herself and got her mother from the back. "Mom, there's a Mr. Winston out front to see you."

Her mom wiped her hands on her apron and hurried to the front. Juliette followed her and took the orders of the couple who had just walked in for breakfast. The bakery had only five tables, but most customers took their goods to go. Only the ones who wanted coffee stayed to eat their doughnuts and scones. While she got coffee, she listened in on her mother's conversation with Booker Winston.

"Thanks so much for all of this, Mrs. Nicholas. I'll spread the word about your bakery if you'll spread the word about the Blue Rooster," he said.

"I was thinking—why don't we offer an exchange? We can each make up some handbills—you can pass out mine, and I'll pass out yours. Maybe a ten-percent-off deal or something?" Abby Nicholas had a mind for business, that was for sure.

Mr. Winston smiled. "I think that's a great idea. I'll draw some up and bring them by next week."

Abby clapped her hands together and smiled. "Wonderful! I'll send Juliette over with some for you, too." She motioned to Juliette, who had just handed coffee to the waiting patrons.

Juliette smiled and walked to her mother. "I'd be happy to take anything over to your restaurant."

"Good, because I plan to use your breads in some of my recipes," Mr. Winston said with a smile. "You're welcome over any time, of course. Juliette, was it? You can come anytime as well."

"Thank you, Mr. Winston," she said, trying not to sound too eager.

"Please, Juliette, call me Booker," he said and winked at her.

Juliette felt like a little girl with her first crush all over again. Booker was amazing to look at. But she knew that looks could be deceiving, and a shiver ran through her body. Recalling how she was treated weeks before by someone she liked, her skin grew cold, and her smile disappeared. She nodded and turned away before Booker or her mother noticed just how blanched she had become.

When she had regained her composure, Booker was gone. With no customers in line, she went to the back of the store to her mother. Abby looked Juliette up and down. "He's a good-looking man, isn't he?"

Juliette could control her blushing better than her sister and acted as cool as possible. "I suppose," she said without commitment.

"I saw your face when he said to call him Booker. It's okay if you like him, Juliette," her mother said. She had noticed her face, but Juliette was glad she didn't realize why her face had changed. Her mother continued. "I know your dad and I aren't too keen on the idea of your sister dating a black man. But we're not stopping her, and we wouldn't stop you either."

Juliette smiled. *Oh, Mom. I love you. If only you knew why I couldn't . . .* "Thanks, Mom. But I doubt Mr. Winston would be interested in me. He's much older, isn't he?"

"He's the same age as Pete. A little older, yes, but your father is older than me by a few years as well."

The bell above the front door chimed. New customers were coming in. Juliette smiled at her mother and excused herself. She worked by rote the rest of the morning.

Inside, she struggled and argued with herself. One side saying she couldn't date. She had been violated, her innocence stolen. Her trust in men could be ruined forever if she let it. And maybe she should. Several others had tried to get her to sleep with them but stopped when she firmly said no. Would others be so nice? Or would they be cruel like Buzz? Maybe they could tell now that she was no longer a virgin. Maybe guys had some way of knowing. Juliette began to wonder if the word "harlot" was stamped across her forehead, and she grew hot and dizzy.

Juliette ran to the bathroom, thankfully it was past lunch and the bakery was empty. She closed the door behind her and exhaled. Splashing water on her face, a thought came to her mind.

I'm three days late. Am I pregnant? Is this a symptom? On television, pregnant women faint all the time. Please, I can't be pregnant.

She sat on the toilet for a minute and suddenly realized that her worst fears would not be coming true . . . *Finally!* she thought. *Thank goodness, I'm not pregnant! I'm not pregnant!*

After fixing herself up and checking again to be sure she was not pregnant, Juliette bounded out of the bathroom. The rest of the day rushed past; and before she knew it, it was time to go home. She smiled the entire car ride home, eager to share with her sister.

She ran into her room and found Eve curled up with a book. "Eve! Eve!"

Shielding her eyes with her arm, Eve looked up. "What's wrong, Juliette?"

"Nothing's wrong. Finally, something is right." Juliette beamed. "Eve, I'm not pregnant. I can finally start to put this behind me."

Eve sat up and smiled at her. "Are you sure? Everything's okay?"

Juliette hugged her sister tight as a few tears escaped her green eyes. "It's over, Evie. I was a few days late, but I'm sure now. I thought Buzz might be with me forever, but he won't be." Pulling back, Juliette and Eve smiled at each other.

"I'm so happy for you!" Eve shed a few tears as well, her tears growing into sobs.

"Why are you crying so much? I'm the one who should be so relieved!" Juliette laughed as she pulled the flour-covered scarf off her head and tossed it onto her bed.

Eve looked at her, her eyes matching Juliette's in color and tears. "I know, but I've been so worried about you, Jules. I am just so thrilled that now maybe you can start to heal in here," she said, laying her hand over her sister's heart. Juliette was overcome with emotion at her sister's tenderness.

They embraced again, both girls crying. After a minute, Juliette wiped her tears away. "Let me tell you about this new restaurant I heard of." She grinned at her twin sister as she told her about Booker Winston and his almond-shaped eyes and braided hair.

Fireworks on the Sand

THE FOURTH OF JULY WAS as hot as ever, and Eve was not enjoying the heat as she normally did. Being outside for more than a few minutes left her feeling unsettled and queasy. She thought she wasn't drinking enough fluids and downed Cokes and water whenever she could. They always helped her feel better. But she didn't like that the heat was affecting her so adversely.

While working in the bakery with her sister that morning, a familiar face stepped in. Patrick McKenzie, the medical student who had helped her sister the night she was raped, was standing before her. He ordered a blueberry and strawberry muffin, the Independence Day special, and then smiled at Eve.

"I didn't know you worked here, Eve. I would have checked on you and your sister before had I known." He took a bite out of his muffin, and Eve could see the smile spread across his face at the taste. "How is Juliette?"

Juliette appeared from the back at that moment and responded, "I'm fine. Who's asking?" When she saw Patrick, she scowled and furrowed her brow. "I'm sorry. Have we met?" She didn't remember Patrick from the night nearly six weeks ago.

Eve excused Juliette and herself, taking her sister aside. She pulled Juliette around and whispered, "Don't you remember him?"

"No, should I?" Juliette's face revealed that she really had no idea who he was. "He's a looker, though. I wish I did remember him."

Eve frowned, a crease forming in her forehead. "No, you don't, Jules. Patrick is the medical student Jesse called when . . ."

Her sister's face fell. "Oh," was all she said. Eve could see the memories come back to her sister. The bruises, the scrapes, the young medical intern who had examined her and learned what had happened. "He won't tell . . . ?"

"No, we swore him to secrecy, I promise," Eve reassured her, glancing up at the blond man.

Juliette turned to face Patrick, her face calm and sweet. "I'm just fine, now. I'm sorry I didn't recognize you."

"That's alright," he said. "Um, it's been over a month; nothing else has come up?"

Eve knew right away what he was talking about. And she was thankful that Juliette would not be forced to bear the seed of a rapist.

Juliette shook her head, her black curls bouncing all over. "No, everything is clear," she said with a smile. A genuine smile that Eve was always thrilled to see these days. Juliette was still not back to her old self; but since discovering that she was not pregnant, each day had been a little better than the last.

Patrick nodded. "Good." He took another bite before adding, "Eve, will you see Jesse today?" Eve nodded and smiled at the thought of watching fireworks with Jesse. "Will you tell him to give me a call about hitching a ride back south next month?"

Eve's smile faded, but she replied, "Of course. I'll tell him to call." Patrick paid for his muffin and left, the door jingling behind him. But Eve was confused. How far south was Jesse going? And when was he going to tell her about it? He had not mentioned to her about taking a trip anywhere.

She was brought out of her thoughts by Juliette. "He's a looker; too bad he knows what happened to me." Her sister grimaced, convinced that no man was trustworthy anymore.

"He was very sweet that night and very worried about you."

"Well, each day is a new day," Juliette told her. "You know, yesterday I didn't even think about what happened at all. I was so surprised when I realized it."

Eve smiled at her sister and was about to speak further when her mother came out. "What did you realize, Juliette?"

The girls froze. What had their mother heard? Had she noticed them talking to Patrick? Eve felt Juliette grab her hand in fear. Their mother looked at them, a content smile across her face. If she suspected anything, Eve thought, she wouldn't look like that.

Her sister thought faster than she and spoke up. "I realized just how many single guys come in here, Mom. I may want to start working more." She laughed at her mom, who smiled in return and shook her head. Eve squeezed her sister's hand and let out a sigh of relief. Juliette sighed in return and released her hand.

Eve was thinking about how fortunate her sister was in avoiding an unwanted pregnancy after Buzz had defiled her. Abortion was illegal and certainly immoral. But Juliette was too young to raise a child, and Eve didn't think her sister could handle giving a child to someone else to raise.

Even with a shaky belief in her parent's God, Eve thanked Him when her sister announced that she had started her monthly courses. Both girls had wept with joy that Juliette could finally begin to heal from her ordeal.

A timer went off in the back; a cake was ready to come out of the oven. Eve said she would get it, as her mother was elbow-deep in dough and her sister was ringing up a customer. She opened the hot oven with gloved hands and pulled the round cake pan out. The aroma of the hot, golden cake wafted out to greet her. But the smell didn't sit well. She set the cake on the counter and ran to the bathroom just in time.

Her entire breakfast gone, Eve washed her face with a towel and let it rest on her neck. She rubbed her finger over her teeth and tongue to try to rid herself of the stench of vomit. *Maybe I'm coming down with a virus,* she thought. *I haven't felt well all day. I hope this doesn't ruin my plans with Jesse tonight. Besides, I have to ask him about this trip he might be taking with Patrick McKenzie.*

She came back out into the kitchen and looked around. She didn't look missed; perhaps nobody had noticed her quick dash to the bathroom. She felt better now and decided she could work the hour left until the bakery closed for the holiday.

At home, Eve and Juliette sat in their rooms, Juliette's nose immersed in a book, Eve looking for the right outfit to wear out that night. Juliette had taken to reading more lately, a habit Eve didn't mind. She had calmed down a lot over the summer and seemed to really be pondering her future. Eve wasn't sure if it was the events with Buzz Herbert that caused the change or something else, but Eve was glad her sister wasn't partying like she used to.

Eve pulled a pair of tight jeans on over her hips and tried to button them, but to no avail. She tried again. "Jules, did these pants shrink?" She stood in front of her mirror and pulled the button together a third time without success.

Juliette looked up. "I wore them last week, and they fit," she said. "Is it that time of the month? I always bloat when it's that time, and things feel tight."

Eve thought. "It must be coming," she frowned. "I do feel bloated and a little off." She discarded the jeans and went back to her closet to find something else to wear.

She pulled out a blue mini dress she had gotten a few weeks before. It had wide shoulder straps and a ruffle that ran down the length of her breastbone. The hem hit her knees, which her parents approved of, but Eve had figured out how to pin the hem under so it was a good three inches shorter. When modified, the skirt showed off her thighs. It wasn't a look she normally went for; but Jesse had said he liked her legs, so she wanted to show them off for him.

It had been a month since they had slept together. Eve wasn't sure if it would happen again, as the opportunity hadn't presented itself. But Jesse had professed his love for her nearly every day since, and Eve longed to be with him.

She looked at her sister. Maybe it was time she told Juliette what had happened. Would her sister be happy for her? After a month of keeping it private, Eve couldn't contain herself any longer; she had to tell Juliette.

"Can you keep a secret?" She sat on her sister's bed, a smile spread across her lips.

"Eve, you have kept my darkest secret. You know I'll always keep yours." Juliette set her book aside and leaned closer.

Oh, sister, please be happy for me. Eve took a deep breath. "I'm sorry I haven't told you sooner, but it didn't seem like the right time. But about a month ago . . . do you remember me telling you that Jesse said he loved me?"

Juliette smiled; she loved Eve and was happy when Eve was happy. "Yes, I remember."

"He didn't just *tell* me he loved me." Eve bit her lip and blushed like mad. She looked into her sister's eyes, hoping she would understand her meaning, but Juliette looked confused. "Juliette, he didn't just tell me; he showed me."

Juliette's smile slowly faded as she considered what Eve was saying. "I don't think I understand . . . "

Eve wished she could now change her mind about telling her sister, but she was too far in. She had to spill her secret. "Jesse and I slept together, Juliette. We made love that night."

Juliette's face paled. Eve winced. Would her sister pass out or explode? "You did what?"

"We—"

"No, no, I heard you, Eve," Juliette nearly spat out the words. "You slept with him? A month ago? You slept with him, and you're just now telling me?" She stood and put her hands on her hips. A sure sign of the wrath to come.

"I'm sorry, Jules. Everything was so fresh for you. I didn't think it was the right time to tell you." Eve felt tears spring to her eyes and slip over her lashes.

"You're right; it wasn't the right time. And now's not either. I can't believe two weeks after I was attacked and raped, you traipsed off and slept with Jesse." Juliette scoffed for a minute, her mind reeling. Eve felt horrible; she had never seen her sister so upset with her. She should have known. "That night you were on the beach. You had sand everywhere. You did it on the beach, didn't you?"

Eve nodded. She had never thought about the connection to the beach. For her, it was romantic with a thick blanket and a sunset tryst. For her sister, it has been dark and cold in more ways than one. She looked down at the floor below her, her mind reeling. Finally, she spoke. "I love him, Juliette. I just want you to be happy for me."

"How can I be happy for you? Not only did you have sex on the beach two weeks after . . . after . . . " she cried out. "But to not tell me?"

Eve looked up, tears flowing freely down her face. "If the tables were turned, would you have told me?"

"But the tables aren't turned, are they?" Juliette glowered. A sob escaped her, and her own tears washed freshly over her. It broke Eve's heart. "I was the one raped, and you're the one playing harlot to your boyfriend."

"I am not!" Eve called out to her sister as Juliette slammed the door behind her. She heard her sister run out of the house and could hear angry footsteps below her window. Juliette was heading south. *Maybe some fresh air would help her calm down,* Eve thought.

Thirty minutes later, and Juliette wasn't home yet. Eve had freshened up, applied a light layer of lip gloss, and was ready to celebrate Independence Day with Jesse. She needed to speak to him desperately. She smoothed the blue dress over her knees, pins ready to turn it up once they were out of the house. She slid her fingers through her thick, red waves, imagining Jesse doing the same.

She heard the doorbell downstairs, and Joey called out, "Evie! Jesse's here!"

She made one last check in the mirror, hoping she no longer looked like she had been crying. Satisfied, she went downstairs. "Thanks, Joey. Tell Mom and Dad I'll be home late."

Joe, ever the teenager, rolled his eyes and responded, "Tell them yourself."

Ignoring her brother's rudeness, Eve smiled. "Thanks, Joey!" She looked at Jesse and smiled. "Ready?"

He held his arm out for her, and she gladly took it. They left the house and got into Jesse's red 1961 Dodge Lancer. It wasn't a great car, but it was a car nonetheless. Before sitting down, Eve skillfully tucked the hem of her skirt up. She had it pinned into place before Jesse slid behind the wheel.

Without speaking, Jesse eyed Eve's legs, then her face, and smiled. Eve knew he was pleased. *Maybe tonight will be a repeat of last month,* she thought as the car turned out of her driveway and down the road.

They dined alfresco at a seaside Italian restaurant with a table looking over the ocean. Instead of sitting across from each other, Jesse had pulled Eve's chair next to his, so they could look at the ocean together. Between bites of shrimp fettuccine, Jesse caressed Eve's leg, running his finger along the underside of her shortened hem. It gave her goosebumps, and she longed for dinner to be over. She still wanted to talk to him, and now she really wanted to kiss him.

Back in the car, Jesse suggested going to his sister's house.

"Won't Dee and her husband be there?" Eve liked Jesse's sister and brother-in-law well enough, but hoped a family-style holiday was not in the plans.

Jesse smiled at her without taking his eyes off the road. "Actually, Dee and Ed are in Georgetown with his family. They won't be back until tomorrow." Eve could hear the anticipation in his voice. He was just as eager to be alone as she was.

Trying not to sound too impatient, Eve looked down at the frill of her dress and said, "That's nice. I would like to talk to you in private."

"Just talk?"

"Well," Eve said, feeling the blush rise on her cheeks. "We can start off talking. I do need to tell you something."

Jesse laughed, the sound light and infectious. "Good, I need to talk to you as well." He turned down the now-familiar road to Dee's house.

Eve wondered how much longer he would be living with his sister. *Maybe the reason he was going back south was to look at houses. He was only twenty-one, though. Perhaps he should look at renting an apartment near the beach. Having a quiet place to themselves all the time would be nice,* Eve thought.

Inside, Eve sat on the couch. She knew not to sit on the left side; it was flattened by years of use. But the right side was still plumped and cushioned. Jesse sat in the chair beside her, his back against the chair, his knees turned out. He closed his eyes and sighed deeply.

"Happy to relax?" Eve smiled at him, ever drawn to him.

"Happy to be with you," he said as he opened his eyes and glanced her way. "Happy to be alone with you. It's been a while."

"A good while," Eve whispered with a lilt in her voice. She grinned as she recalled how warm his hands were, how smooth his lips felt. But first, she needed to speak to him. "I ran into your friend Patrick today."

"Patrick McKenzie. I told him Juliette was doing better. Did he get to see her?"

"He did. She didn't remember him." Eve frowned. "But he said for you to call him about a trip south you're taking next month." She looked at Jesse and raised her eyebrow as if to question him.

"Oh, yes," Jesse said, realizing he was caught. "A trip back home to see my folks is all. Patrick is heading back early to finish his medical training before becoming a certified doc. I told him I could drop him off in Charleston. I'll give him a call next week."

"How long will you be gone?" Eve was relieved he was just visiting his parents. Maybe he would tell them all about her. Maybe the next time he visited, he would take her with him.

"I'm not too sure yet, Eve, but don't worry about that now." He smiled at her and moved next to her on the couch. He pulled Eve close, her head resting on his strong shoulder. "There now, this is better."

Eve smiled; being in Jesse's arms was her favorite place these days. She hoped it would last forever. "Jesse, I told Juliette."

She could hear the concern in his voice when he asked, "What did she say?"

With a sigh, Eve told him, "She was angry. She yelled at me and stormed off. I don't know if she was more upset at what we did or that I didn't tell her." Feeling tears begin to well up again, Eve sat up and hid her face in her hands.

Jesse put his hand under her chin and lifted her face so that she was looking at him. "It will be okay. Give her some time, and she'll be alright," he promised.

Overcome, Eve cried out, "She called me names, Jesse!" Fat tears rolled down her cheek as Jesse pulled her head back onto his chest. He smoothed her hair while she bawled and talked, her sister's words stinging all over again.

When she calmed, Jesse again looked her square in the eye. "Juliette knows you're not a harlot. I know, and you know. She's upset at you and me. Soon, she'll realize how we feel, and she'll be happy for you."

Eve only nodded, while Jesse used his thumb to brush her tears away. He kissed the wet spots off her cheek and stroked her arm. The stinging words of her sister faded, and Eve responded.

Without a word, Jesse lifted her into the air and carried her to his bedroom; Eve kicked her shoes off along the way.

Fuming, Juliette walked without direction or purpose. She argued both her side and her sister's in the confines of her head. Eve had hurt her, betrayed her. Eve had willingly done the one thing Juliette was never given the option of doing. *How could she sleep with Jesse so soon after finding me raped and alone? She knew my pain; she knew my hurt; and now, she's parading herself around with Jesse, letting him . . . touch her?* Juliette shuddered at the idea of any man touching her sister's delicate skin. She couldn't imagine Eve ever enjoying what had caused her so much horrifying pain.

But on Eve's side, Juliette found herself arguing in favor of love, of openness, and of willingness. *Eve loves Jesse and wanted to show him just how much she loves him. They made love; she wasn't forced. She enjoys Jesse's company and touch.*

All that aside, Juliette was still left with the fact that this had happened weeks before, and her sister neglected to tell her. Had Eve just been protecting her as she claimed? Or was Eve purposely hiding this from her? Just the idea of having such a secret between them made Juliette feel sick to her stomach. She ducked behind a bush where she was walking and felt her stomach heave, but nothing happened.

"I feel terrible," she said to herself. "I feel so lost, so alone. I have nobody to talk to, apparently, because my twin sister lied to me. To me! First, I'm . . . well . . . and now my own sister betrays me. I might as well walk into the ocean and end it all right now." Juliette stopped in her tracks and thought better of what she was muttering. Life was bad, yes, but it was better than not having a life. She shook her head as if to shake the troubling thoughts away.

Juliette had walked for nearly an hour before she felt her stomach grumble. Her anger subsided for the time being, her throat parched and dry. Glancing around, she noticed the Blue Rooster, the restaurant owned by Booker Winston. She had seen him in passing once or twice but had not had the chance to dine at his restaurant. Juliette knew that her family had plans with the church that evening; and she knew she had no interest in joining them, so she walked through the door and took a seat in the back, next to the kitchen.

The aroma of freshly made seafood and hot butter greeted her. She had intended on getting only a drink, but she ordered shrimp and grits, a southern staple. Ordering her iced tea was almost an afterthought. But her waiter, a slender young man who couldn't have been any older than she was, delivered a glass of champagne to her table.

Juliette shook her head. "I'm sorry; I didn't order this."

The young waiter smiled at her. "Compliments of Mr. Winston, Miss Nicholas." He turned and walked away.

Mr. Winston? He was giving her a glass of champagne? Juliette was not a regular drinker and had never tasted anything more than beer before the beach party where Buzz had drugged her and given her that fateful drink. But she had always been told that champagne was different from other alcohols—flavorful, sweet, and romantic. She looked around the restaurant. Most families were off celebrating the holiday; not many tables were occupied.

She spotted him at a table off to her right. She looked at him over her shoulder, and he nodded her direction. She lifted the champagne flute in silent thanks. She watched as Booker Winston held up one finger, a pause, and stood. He walked toward her, laid a quick hand on her shoulder, and disappeared into the kitchen. He emerged seconds later with two plates of food and set one in front of her, the other at the empty place across from her.

Juliette was not one taken to blushing like her sister. But when Booker smiled at her, she couldn't help herself. "Bon appetite," he said, his almond eyes creasing as he smiled.

"But I'm dining alone tonight. I don't need two plates of food," she explained. Now, she was embarrassed to have walked in alone—no date, no friend, and no family.

"You may not need two plates, but I will need one," he replied. Juliette was baffled. "That is, if I may join you for supper." Juliette nodded, her curly hair echoing the movement. Booker spoke again. "We're quite slow tonight. In fact, I just surprised my staff and told them to get lost. The restaurant is now closed to everyone except us. I'll be right back."

Panic filled Juliette's mind and took over her senses as Booker walked off to take care of a few things. *Did he say "alone?" I can't be alone with him, with anyone!* This was the first time she had been alone with a man since she had been with Buzz. She began to breathe heavy, and she saw spots before her. Juliette struggled to regain her composure before she passed out. She stood as slowly as possible and made her way to the bathroom before she began shaking violently. She splashed water on her face and sat on the lid of the toilet with her head between her knees.

What is wrong with me? I know what's wrong with me—Buzz Herbert is wrong with me. I'll never be able to trust another man as long as I live, thanks to him. I'll never be able to have another man flirt with me, kiss me, or want to be alone with me. Thanks a lot, Buzz! Not only did you rob me of my virginity, but also of my self-worth and my dignity. No loving or just God would let anything like this happen to anyone. We're all alone in this world, looking for someone to love us, and now I can't even have that.

After she had calmed, she felt ready to go back out into the dining room. She would just tell Booker that she had to go, nothing more. Then she would hightail it home and lock herself in her room for the next three years.

Slowly, she opened the door. As she came back out, two tables of patrons were still finishing their meals, one waitress left to re-fill their teas and sodas. Her own waiter pushed through the door into the kitchen, clearing salt and pepper shakers and gathering up loose ends. Juliette made her way back to her table, realizing they weren't completely alone and that she was safe. She sat back down and let out a huge sigh of relief. Juliette figured she could eat her meal and leave before the place was completely quiet and they were truly alone.

Booker came back over to her table and sat across from her. Apparently, he was none the wiser about her hasty run. "You look wonderful, Miss Nicholas," he said as he placed a napkin in his lap.

Juliette hadn't bothered to put on any make-up that day. She was wearing faded denim cutoffs and a black tank top. Her curls were loose and wild, spilling all over her face and neck. She thought she must look terrible. She smiled thanks weakly and took a huge gulp of tea, avoiding the champagne.

"Would you mind if I blessed the food first?" Booker raised an eyebrow to see if she would protest. Juliette was surprised that he would want to bless the food; but since she was used to it, she put her glass down and bowed her head. She peered at Booker from under her eyelashes as he said a quick prayer. "Lord, thank You for this food and the hands that prepared it. Please allow us to enjoy this wonderful holiday as we celebrate the nation You gave to all people—black, white, brown, and red. Amen."

After repeating the amen, Juliette lifted her head. "You don't have to join me, Mr. Winston," she offered. Maybe he had plans and was sitting with her only since he had the deal with her mother's bakery.

"I know that," he said as he tasted the freshly baked bread on his plate. "And please, call me Booker. And I'll call you Juliette. Shakespeare's own masterpiece."

"I'm hardly a masterpiece, Booker. More like a mess," she said with a small smile. She sampled her shrimp, and her eyes lit up. "Hey, this is wonderful!" And then she promptly took another bite.

"I'm glad you like it. Shakespeare's Juliet was a mess as well. If you recall, she pledged her undying love to Romeo after a brief meeting and, in the end, committed suicide. We're all imperfect, Juliette."

"Yes, we are." She sighed. "Some more than others."

Booker narrowed his gaze on her. "Should I be offended, or is something on your mind?"

Not wanting to give anything away to a man she hardly knew, she quickly spoke. "I'm sorry. My sister and I had a fight today. I'm a little preoccupied."

The smile returned and Booker reached his hand out to hers. "A fight with Eve? Or the younger sister? Alice, is it?"

Juliette now smiled. How did he know . . . ? Ah, her mom must have shared more with him than she thought. "Alisa. But you're right with the first one, Eve. Being a twin isn't always fun and games. I guess my mom told you about all of us?"

"A little. Actually, I knew your brother, Pete, first."

Surprise came over her at the mention of Pete. He was living on his own now and engaged. "Pete? Really?" When Booker nodded, she added, "Actually, Pete is our cousin, but he was raised with us, like a brother. But Pete doesn't live at home any more. How do you know him?"

"I was a year behind him in school, but we knew the same kids. I went straight to culinary school and managed to buy this restaurant from an old widow," he said, eyeing Juliette. "How much older than you is Pete?"

Sure he would back away when she revealed her age, she shyly answered, "I'm only eighteen."

Booker ran his hand over his long, braided hair and blinked several times. "Well, I thought you were a little older than that . . . " He chuckled a little. "That's okay. There are no rules on age when it comes to friends having dinner. Especially when they're alone on a holiday."

Juliette felt more comfortable and relaxed back into her chair. She took a drink of her tea and smiled a little. For the first time in a while, she felt at ease. Booker was a nice guy. Juliette knew she would never date him, but being friends was good.

By the time they finished their meals, they were both rolling with laughter. Juliette loved his sense of humor and how his braids moved when he laughed. She enjoyed watching his face as he broke out into a full laugh and laughed till he was nearly in tears. Juliette laughed until she felt tears in her eyes—the first non-pained tears she had since before she was violated—and she reveled in how wonderful they felt.

As she pushed her plate away, Booker stood and disappeared into the kitchen. Juliette glanced around and realized now they were alone. The other couples were long gone; the two employees had cleared out as well. Trying not to panic again, Juliette took several deep breaths as she waited for Booker to come back out of the kitchen. The longer he took, the more fear rose in her chest. She fought the urge to run for the door without looking back.

As the kitchen door burst open with Booker behind it, Juliette jumped and let out a little yelp. He came out with his back to her; and when he turned, he produced two slices of chocolate cake. Juliette felt silly for getting so scared, but was glad to be fully alert.

"Did I startle you?" Booker smiled. "I'm sorry. This is your mom's cake. She mentioned that you loved chocolate."

The jump forgotten at the mention of her mother's cake, Juliette cast Booker a sideways glance. "My mother told you I loved chocolate?"

This time, Booker blushed. His cinnamon-colored skin reddened as he admitted, "She did. I asked her a few weeks ago which dessert was your favorite. I ordered a chocolate cake the minute she told me. I've gotten one each week since. It's very popular."

Juliette blushed for the second time that day. Booker was on a roll. "Why did you ask which dessert was my favorite?"

He scooted his chair closer and leaned toward her. "Because it would have been a little too forward for me to ask your mom if I could take you out. So, I asked about your favorite sweet instead." He took her hand and kissed it lightly—nothing more and nothing less.

It was enough, though. Juliette felt a flutter in her heart. Not fear, but longing. Not pain, but joy. Before, she would have offered Booker more to kiss, but not now. Her hurt was still too raw, despite her feelings for him. And she knew that feelings could be deceiving. Without pushing Booker away, she cautiously removed her hand from his and picked up her fork. She smiled at him as she took a bite of her cake, putting it between them in case Booker decided to press closer to her.

Thankfully, he didn't. He took a bite of his own cake and closed his eyes as he savored the taste. With a swallow of his tea, he changed the subject. "Can I take you to see fireworks tonight?"

Juliette shook her head. "Thanks for the offer, Booker, but I shouldn't."

He smiled at her brush-off. "No pressure, I promise. My father's church is doing a show down on the beach."

"Your father's church?"

"Yeah, my dad is the preacher at Zion AME just about two miles from your dad's church," he said. "Our dads have lunch together on occasion."

Eve was again surprised. "I had no idea our families were so intertwined. You went to high school with Pete; our dads know each other; and now you and my mom are working out business deals."

He stood and stretched his arm out, his palm up, waiting. "What do you say we mix it up a little more? We can just walk down to the water, watch an awe-inspiring display, and enjoy getting to know a new friend."

Hesitant, Juliette wavered. Dare she trust again so soon? It wasn't a date by any means; it was a church function. Those were safe, weren't they? She closed her eyes, wishing for something to guide her. She felt her arm rise to meet Booker's and took his hand. If anything happened, she was prepared this time. He left the dirty plates on the table and led her outside as the sun was starting to set.

Five blocks away was the Atlantic Ocean—peaceful, serene. No white caps to be seen—not like there was that horrid night. This was a different section of beach, but beach all the same. Juliette hadn't been to the beach since then. Would Booker pick up on her tension? She hoped he wouldn't, but part of her hoped he would ask what was bothering her.

He led her over to a group of people, not quite twenty in all. He hugged an older man who looked much like him, and Juliette guessed he was his father. She hung back, not wanting to intrude and also not wanting to be introduced as his date. But her plan to blend into the background did not last long. After a few words, Booker was looking for her, pulling her forward with a huge grin across his face.

"Juliette, this is my father, Earl Winston, the pastor of Zion AME Church. Dad, this is Juliette; she's Pastor Harvey Nicholas' daughter."

Earl Winston stepped forward, his Hawaiian shirt flapping in the breeze. He held out both hands for Juliette, and she obligingly took them. "Harvey Nicholas can't have a daughter this old. Or this beautiful," he said with a full laugh much like his son's. "There's no way you came from Harvey—not with hair like that, girlie."

Juliette smiled. He was right; she looked nothing like her father. She was her mother's daughter through and through—from the curly hair to the full breasts and hips. Eve favored their father more with her straighter hair and slender figure.

"No, sir, I look like my mother. So does my little sister," she told him. "My twin sister Eve, however, does resemble our father. So does our brother Joseph."

"Well it's nice to meet you, Juliette. Sit down; join us!"

She nodded and smiled. Booker took her arm and led her to a thick blanket to sit on. Juliette again wanted to hesitate, but something told her that she would be safe in this crowd. She sat keeping her distance from Booker anyway, lest he try anything more daring than talking. While they waited for the show to start, several people passed by and said hello to Booker and nodded to her. They were obviously curious about the girl—a white girl, nonetheless—sitting on Booker's blanket.

Out of the corner of her eye, Juliette noticed a woman watching her. She tried to glance nonchalantly to double check. Sure enough, a beautiful Asian woman was staring her down. She had long, black hair braided over one shoulder, and her eyes were large and inviting. A beautiful woman indeed. Juliette could hardly keep from staring back at her and wondered why this woman was looking her way.

Unable to stand the gaze any longer, she nudged Booker. "There's a lovely woman over there watching us intently," she whispered to him.

Booker looked around her and laughed. "That's my mother!"

Shocked, Juliette blurted out, "But she's not black!"

"No, she's not. My dad is black, and my mom is Japanese." Booker chuckled, his eyes glistening in the moonlight. "They met while my dad was in the navy during World War Two."

Picking her jaw up off the ground, Juliette apologized. "I am so sorry. I didn't mean to be rude. I just never suspected that your mother was Japanese. But now that I look, I can see that you have her eyes." *And amazing eyes they are,* Juliette added in her head.

As if on cue, Booker's mother walked over to them and knelt in the soft sand. "Hello, my son." She then turned to Juliette and spoke. "I am Booker's mother, Lucille Winston." Her voice was melodic, like a bird's song wafting on the breeze and as beautiful as the one who spoke it. Though she must be over forty, she didn't look many more years older than her son.

Booker made the introduction. "Mother, this is Juliette Nicholas. Her father is the pastor at Respite Baptist Church. And her mother owns the bakery I get my cakes from." Lucille nodded, and Booker added, "Seeing as Juliette didn't have plans for this evening, I asked her to join me here amongst friends."

Juliette lowered her eyelashes and spoke softly. "It's a pleasure to meet you, Mrs. Winston."

The woman smiled, her expression sincere. "And for me as well. It is good you are here tonight, Juliette. God has big plans for you, and I think they will be set in motion soon." Lucille Winston smiled at Juliette, then at her son, and stood. Without brushing the sand off her knees, she glided away toward Booker's father.

Booker whispered into her ear, "Mother can be kind of deep at times. Some say she's prophetic. I can tell she's quite pleased that you're here, which means God is pleased you're here."

Juliette started to speak up to protest that God did not exist and if He did, He certainly wouldn't be using her for any of His plans. But before she could speak, the first firework soared up and exploded above their heads. Torch lights that had illuminated their surroundings were doused, and all talking ceased.

The first burst was yellow, then green. Light colors filled the sky. But then they turned darker. The next several were red and scarlet—the color of blood. As they shot overhead and burst into glorious color, Juliette began to weep. She tried to stop, and she tried to hide her tears, brushing them away before they could slip past her lashes. But each clap in the air, each explosion of color, brought forth fresh tears. As the display continued, she stopped trying to hide her cries, now just trying to keep herself from running away.

Booker was by her side the moment he noticed her tears. He didn't know what was going on with her or why. He didn't ask. He just clasped Juliette's hand as the tears fell; and as the sobs grew louder, he offered his arms as her sanctuary. Juliette didn't hesitate this time. She flung herself into his offered embrace and sobbed a fury of tears, washing his shoulder in a flood of anguish. She wept until there was nothing left. She wept until she felt as limp as a lifeless doll, a used rag. And it felt wonderful.

After the finale of fireworks ended, the torches remained unlit. Juliette didn't know if Booker's family was still around, and she didn't care. She felt safe, protected, and secure with his arms around her. Her grief felt settled and still, not fresh or gaping as it had been. Minutes ticked by, but Booker didn't urge her to move. He stayed in position, his arms wrapped fiercely around her, his head pressed to hers, his hair falling over her own. Juliette could feel him breathing as if he were breathing for the both of them. She could hear his breath as well—only it wasn't his breath. He was speaking, no, mumbling. Booker Winston was praying, quietly—not even audibly—but praying all the same.

Feeling selfish and self-conscious, Juliette moved her arm as a sign that she was ready to be released. As she lifted her head, she felt lighter. Her past—Buzz Herbert—was no longer weighing her down, and it felt wonderful. She no longer wanted to walk into the ocean and not stop until she drowned. She didn't know what had happened, but she was glad it did. And she was thankful that Booker had been there for her.

"I'm so sorry, Booker," she gushed. "I had no idea the fireworks would . . ."

"Shh, Juliette, it's okay," he murmured as he moved her hair out of her face. "Didn't my mother say that God had a plan, and it would be set in motion soon? I don't know what that was about, and I won't ask. But you were set free of something tonight. I could feel it."

Too happy and tired to argue about a fictitious God, Juliette smiled. A broad, genuine, fully happy smile. "I feel it too, Booker. Thank you for bringing me here. Thank you for holding me and letting me . . . well . . . Just thank you."

He reached out and cupped her cheek in his hand, strong but delicate. "You are most welcome. Juliette, would you think I was too bold to ask you out?"

Her heart sank. Yes, she felt free now after her rape, but she didn't feel ready to date yet either. "I really like you, Booker. I do. But I'm not in a position to date right now. I hope you understand."

Without moving his hand, he nodded. "I do. When you are ready, consider me first in line." Juliette looked down to avoid his gaze, sure he would see fresh tears spring up in her eyes. "Come on; let me take you home."

Buried in the Sand

JULY WAS ALWAYS THE HOTTEST month in Myrtle Beach. Add in little air circulation and a bakery full of tourists, and Juliette was ready to throw in the towel. She was supposed to be working with her mother and Eve, but once again, Eve was home sick. She really didn't know what her sister had come down with; at least everyone else was feeling all right. But once again, they were left short-staffed.

Glancing at the clock, Juliette was thankful that her mother closed the bakery at three o'clock every day. "Who needs a doughnut after three?" her mother had argued when setting the hours for her store. It was now nearing two—just over an hour of chaos left before they could clean up, prep for the next day, and go home.

It had been a full week since her fight with Eve. A full week since her embarrassing episode on the beach with Booker. Granted, Juliette was amazed at the difference in her attitude and demeanor since then, but she still felt like such a child breaking down like that in front of a man like Booker Winston. And all he did was pray. Perhaps he had prayed for her to leave quickly, as she had not heard from him or seen him since.

Foot traffic through the door slowed in that final hour. A few minutes before closing, Juliette began cleaning tables and counters and preparing things for the next day. Her mother was in the back getting ingredients together for the morning's baking. Everything needed for each batch of goodies was separated, and she prepared whatever she could beforehand for the morning rush.

Not even one minute before Juliette could lock the doors, the bell jingled. She let out a silent moan. She had just cleaned and put things away, and she was in no mood to pull it all back out. She turned with a plastered-on smile to greet the intruder when she saw Booker standing before her. The false smile faded into a genuine one as he smiled at her.

"Hello, Juliette," he said softly.

"Booker, how are you?" Juliette leaned on the counter and put her hand to her chin.

"I'm very good, thank you." He looked around the empty bakery for a moment before asking, "Is your mom around?"

She should have known. He was there to talk business, not see her. She felt foolish, and her smile fell a little. "She's in the back getting things together for tomorrow. Do you want me to get her?"

Booker shook his hands as he quickly said, "No, no, no. I wanted to see you. I was hoping she would have left already." He blushed, much like he had the week before over dinner. "I thought I could give you a ride home, if you needed one."

Juliette glanced around the bakery. It was clean; her work was done. "Actually, I'm all done here. I'll go tell Mom I'm catching a ride home with a friend." Booker smiled, and the corner of his eyes creased. Juliette thought it was adorable how they did that. Too bad she wasn't dating anymore.

She poked her head into the kitchen, where her mother was pulling eggs aside for various dishes. "Mom? I'm finished in the front. Would you mind if I took off?"

Her mother turned toward her, her apron covered in flour, stray curls flying loose from her bun. Juliette saw a picture of herself in twenty years' time and hoped she was as beautiful and passionate at forty as her mother was.

Abby smiled. "Is someone here to pick you up?"

Juliette had a feeling her mother knew who was waiting for her, but she didn't share. She responded only, "Yes. Is that okay?" Her mother nodded with a slight laugh and turned back to her eggs. "Love you, Mom," Juliette called as she came back to the dining room.

She put her apron on the hook and smiled at Booker as she extended her hand to him. They left the bakery and got into Booker's car.

They did nothing but ride. The radio played The Mamas and The Papas quietly, and Juliette sang the song in her head. She glanced over at Booker, who was mouthing the words himself. She stifled a giggle.

Booker noticed her smile and smiled back. "Sorry, I tend to move my lips to the radio sometimes," he confessed.

"I do, too," Juliette told him.

As he pulled his car into the driveway of Juliette's house, he paused, but made no motion to turn the engine off or get out of the car. Juliette was impressed with how slow Booker was taking things with her. He didn't seem to have intimate things on his mind like other young men. That, or he was truly just interested in being friends—maybe like business associates—since their fathers knew each other, and he collaborated with her mother.

But before the thoughts went too far in her head, Booker reached over and brushed a stray curl from Juliette's cheek. She felt an immediate rise in temperature, and she knew she was blushing.

"Can I call you later this week?" he asked with a small grin.

Juliette smiled wide. "I would like that, Booker," she said, her voice low. With that, she got out of the car and walked off. She risked a glance back, waved, and found Booker still watching her. She turned away before he could see the pink come up in her face.

Eve had been waiting for Juliette to get home all day. She was tired of not speaking to her sister, her best friend. An entire week had gone by since their argument, and Eve still wasn't sure if Juliette was more upset over what Eve had done or hadn't done. Was she upset because Eve had slept with Jesse? Or because she hadn't told her twin sister? Maybe it was both. But one thing was certain—Eve had felt terrible since that night. She had been sick in bed all morning—all week, really. And she needed her sister to talk to.

Peering out the window, Eve watched a light blue car pull up to the house. She could hear Juliette's laughter rise up to meet her. She was happy, Eve realized. Who was she with? Her own twin, and she didn't know who was with her. She watched as Juliette waved, and the car pulled away from the house. She waited as she heard the front door close, then listened to Juliette's soft steps ascend the stairs.

Eve grabbed a book and opened it to a random page as she heard the door knob turn. Juliette came in quietly. Eve glanced up and smiled at her sister, hoping she would speak. Juliette turned from her and sat facing the wall on her bed. She slipped her shoes off and kicked her feet up onto a pillow, letting out a sigh of relief.

Eve licked her lips and spoke softly. "Long day?"

With a flat tone, Juliette responded, "You would have known if you had been at work."

"I wish I was." Eve sighed. "My stomach has been in knots since last week, Juliette." She put the book down and turned toward her sister. "I promise I never meant to hurt your feelings either way, Jules. I love you and just wanted to protect you."

Her sister laughed. "Protect me? From what? From you falling in love? Eve, I want you to fall in love. I just don't want to see you do things and get hurt. Even with my talk of free love, Mom and Dad taught us not to give ourselves away. I had no intention of sleeping with someone until I was at least engaged, if not married. Free love is an idea of the mind, not a bodily offer like Buzz thought."

"I'm sorry," Eve said, tears in her eyes. "But I do love Jesse. And he loves me. Truthfully, I think he's *the one*. I think we could be engaged by the end of summer, Juliette."

"You do?" Now her sister sat up and faced her.

"I do. And, Jules? For what it's worth . . . You didn't give yourself to Buzz. You can still keep yourself until you're engaged or even married. Don't let him ruin you. He may have taken your body's virginity, but not your heart's. And that's more important, isn't it?" Eve took a deep breath and moved to Juliette's bed.

Juliette sat up, tears swimming in her eyes. "Yes, it is," she said. "Last week, on the fourth of July, I was watching the fireworks, and I cried and cried, Evie. I cried until I had nothing left; and when I looked up, my outlook on life was changed. Buzz Herbert wasn't ruling over my life anymore. I have felt like a different person since then."

Eve hugged her sister close. "I'm so glad to hear that! Oh, but to be alone in that time must have been terrible." She held her sister at arm's length and searched her face, but she found no sadness there.

"I wasn't alone, Eve. I was with Booker Winston. I went to his restaurant, and he invited me to watch the fireworks with him." Eve watched as her sister's skin flushed, and she could tell Juliette liked this man.

"And he . . . ?"

"And he sat with me and held me when I needed him to," Juliette said. Then she added, "And he never touched me otherwise." She sighed with relief, as did her sister. "He wants to take me out; I told him he could call me. Eve, he prayed for me."

"Prayed for you? What did he say?"

Eve watched her sister think a moment. "I don't know exactly. After I blubbered into his shoulder, I could hear him praying, but I don't know what he said. I didn't want to debate God with him that night, so I never mentioned it. How could someone so good-looking believe in such a silly idea as God?"

"It's not *silly*," Eve said. "I think God brought me Jesse. And look at Mom and Dad. Maybe some notions are a little far-fetched, but I feel better knowing that there's something bigger than us out there."

Before Juliette could respond, Eve held up a finger and ran from the room. She made it to the bathroom just in time to lose the little bit of lunch she had eaten. At least, she felt better afterward. She quickly brushed her teeth and went back into her room. Sheepishly, she apologized to her sister. "I'm sorry, Juliette. I don't know what's wrong with me. I'm not sick otherwise; no one else is sick . . . "

Eve sat on her bed, not wanting to get too close to Juliette in case she was contagious. But Juliette came to her side of the bed and looked closely at her. "Eve? When did you sleep with Jesse?"

She turned crimson at the question. Was her sister still upset? "I'm sorry, Juliette! First it was about six weeks ago, just once. But last week, after you stormed off, I was so upset, and . . . and . . . Jesse was there. Please don't be mad at me anymore."

Juliette shushed her. "Just stop. Six weeks ago? That was when I realized I wasn't pregnant after . . . well, after. And I had it again almost two weeks ago. Eve, when was your last cycle?"

Eve scrunched her eyebrows and thought. She and Juliette weren't always the same, but sometimes they were. When Juliette was relieved to find she wasn't pregnant, Eve never considered her own cycle. She hadn't thought about it since then. It had been two months since her last. She should have had a cycle the week before, she realized, but was too wrapped up in her fight with Juliette to realize she had missed it.

Suddenly realizing just what Juliette was asking, fear rose in her body. "Two, two months ago. I've missed two cycles." She clamored to her feet and began to pace. "Oh, Juliette. This can't mean . . . ? No, no, no." She shook her head, her red hair trailing behind.

Juliette was on her feet behind her and caught her by the shoulders. "Okay, calm down. Maybe there's another reason. How have you felt, aside from nauseous?"

"Bloated. Sore. My chest has been very tender," Eve admitted. "Last week, when Jesse and I . . ." she trailed off for a second but then picked back up. "Last week, when he would touch my chest, they were very tender, almost in pain."

"How about your clothes?" Juliette asked as she winced. She was preparing for the answer; Eve could tell.

"Remember last week? I thought those jeans had shrunk or something? I haven't been able to wear my tight jeans since then." Eve fell to her bed and buried her head in a pillow. Her sister was right behind her, running her hand over her hair. Eve rolled her head to the side and sobbed, "Oh, no, Juliette! I'm pregnant!"

Her sister jerked her up by the arm. "Come on, let's go," she said as she pulled Eve toward the door.

"Where are we going? We're not telling Mom and Dad, are we?" Eve's eyes grew wide, and fear gripped her. Her feet grounded and refused to move.

"No, we're going to a doctor, who can tell you for sure. If you are pregnant, you'll tell Jesse, and then you'll tell Mom and Dad."

"But you didn't tell Mom and Dad what happened to you!"

"What happened to me didn't result in a baby in the works!" Juliette spoke forcefully, but quietly, so other ears wouldn't hear. "Now, go get in the car, and I'll be out in a minute."

Eve did as she was told. She sat in the passenger side of the car, her head reeling. Could she really be pregnant? While the notion scared her, it also warmed her heart. She and Jesse had created life. And that would solidify their life together. They loved each other, didn't they? Maybe an end-of-summer engagement would turn into an end-of-summer wedding. And the idea of giving Jesse a son or daughter made Eve smile. So what if they weren't married yet? They would be soon enough; and this was modern times, wasn't it?

Juliette ran out of the house, keys in hand. She slid in the driver's seat and sped off toward the hospital, where Eve could be tested and they wouldn't have to tell their mother—yet.

Inside the hospital, they sat in the back corner of the waiting room. Juliette had taken charge, and Eve was thankful. She felt so scatterbrained. Her sister had marched up to the desk and said, "My friend, Susan, here needs a pregnancy test." How smart to use a false name, Eve thought. Susan Merit was a friend of theirs who had moved away; she could use the name without a second thought.

Eve hated the tension, even though her sister held her hand while they waited. She smiled at Juliette. "Thank you, Jules. I love you. I don't ever want to fight again."

Juliette looked at her and returned the smile. "I love you, too."

"Tell me about Booker Winston," Eve asked, wanting a distraction.

Now, her sister's face lit up. Juliette told her all about Booker's restaurant and how she had panicked when he said they would be alone. She told Eve about meeting his parents and how his mother had predicted a change in her life. How right she was! But more than anything else, Juliette told Eve what a gentleman Booker was. How he wanted to take her on a date, but was willing to be patient and wait. "I told him he could call." She paused. "But I don't think I'm going to date at all anymore, Evie."

Eve smiled and patted her sister's hand. "You will; I can guarantee it." And she laughed.

A booming voice came from the open door across the room. "Susan Merit?" Eve and Juliette stood and made their way to the grizzly looking nurse, who was nearly as wide as the doorway. She led them down a hall and into a stark white room. "Who's Susan?" she barked.

"I am," Eve said unconvincingly, but the nurse didn't care. She was used to teen girls coming in and using pseudonyms. At least one a week nowadays—most being false alarms.

"Sit here," she ordered, and Eve obeyed. Juliette held fast to her hand, while the nurse lowered the back of the chair so that Eve was lying prostrate. The woman, whose name tag read Nurse Nelson, began pulling out tubes and needles, making Eve nervous. "When was your last menstrual cycle?"

"Early May," Eve squeaked out.

"Hmm," was all the nurse said in return as she began tapping Eve's arm. She drew a vial of blood and left the room.

The girls looked at each other. Was that it? When would they know?

Strolling back into the room empty-handed, Nurse Nelson pulled out something that looked like a microphone. "Missing two months' courses and being sexually active is a good indicator of you being pregnant, Miss Merit. Let's give this a try. It's called a doppler, the latest technology."

The microphone hummed to life when the nurse switched it on. White noise filled the room while the nurse pulled Eve's shirt up and exposed her abdomen. As Eve peered down at her stomach, she didn't think she looked any different. When the nurse spread a gooey substance onto her belly, Eve winced at the cold and sticky feeling.

The nurse put the apparatus onto Eve's belly and moved it around. Suddenly, a faint thump could be heard coming from it. It was fast and strong. Eve looked to her sister, whose grip on her hand was as tight as ever. The stout woman smiled at Eve. "Congrats, Miss Merit. It seems you're going to be a mother. The blood test should confirm it."

Eve fought back tears but wasn't sure if they were from fear or joy or both. As the nurse wiped her stomach off, Eve looked to Juliette who already had a tear running down her face. Eve then allowed her own tears to fall freely, for whatever reason they chose to fall.

The nurse softened. "I'll give you a minute; then you two come across the hall to my station." She left them alone, shaking her head as she went.

Eve sat up and moved into Juliette's open arms. They both cried for a moment. Eve didn't know why Juliette was crying, but it didn't matter. She was there with her, and that was all she cared about. After a minute, they both wiped their faces and met the nurse at her desk.

"Now, Miss Merit, how old are you?"

"Eighteen," Eve replied. "I'll be nineteen in September."

The nurse frowned, and Eve was sure she was judging her. "Okay, then. You have a few options. First is to keep the baby. Unless you were married very young, I'm going to assume you're not married." Eve shook her head. "If the father's around, you might see to getting married rather quickly. Second, you can find a family to adopt your baby. There are several couples in the area whose names we keep on hand because they would like to find a healthy white baby to raise." Eve glanced sideways at her sister. That wouldn't do; this baby would be mixed race.

Sensing that wasn't an option, the nurse continued. "There is a third option. Though illegal, I can pass on the name of a doctor who will help you get rid of the baby. Now, I could get fired for telling you—"

"No!" Eve cried out. "No, I'm keeping my baby."

The nurse nodded and picked up a pamphlet and handed it to Eve. "This will tell you a little about pregnancy. Based on your past menstrual cycle and the heart rate I heard, I would guess you're close to eight weeks along."

"But I didn't have sex until six weeks ago," Eve protested.

"We go off your last cycle to determine how far along you are," the nurse reassured her. "In about four weeks, you'll enter your second trimester, and your risk of miscarriage lessens. If you do want an abortion, get it done now. If not, in about two more months, you should feel the baby move for the first time. I would guess that you'll be having this baby in February. Now, go to the front desk and make an appointment to come back and see Doctor Grierson in about a month. By then, the shock should have worn off. And please use your real name next time, sweetie." She stood, forcing Eve and Juliette to stand with her, and shooed them out of the room.

Eve and Juliette nearly stumbled out of the hospital doors. They rushed to the car, lest anybody they knew saw them. As they sat in their seats, Eve turned to Juliette and said, "I'm going to be a mother."

Juliette laughed nervously. "Yes, Evie, you are. What are you going to do now?"

Eve pulled her hair back behind her ears and stared at her sister. "Find the right time to tell Jesse, I suppose. The sooner, the better. Maybe we can be married before I have to go see this Doctor Grierson."

Juliette only nodded as she put the car into drive and headed toward home. Eve began to pray. *Lord, please hear me. I know I'm not the best Christian girl out there. But now, I need You. I'm pregnant. But I guess You knew that. I'm scared and happy and more scared. I don't know if I'm happy to be carrying Jesse's child or not. I don't know if Jesse will be happy or not. Surely, he'll be happy, won't he? But my parents, God. I'm the pastor's daughter! I'm not supposed to get pregnant out of wedlock! What will Dad say? Will they disown me? Will Jesse and I have to leave—our child never knowing my parents? No, my parents wouldn't do that. Would they? Help me, God! I'm scared—so, so scared.*

Salty Tears

EVE STOOD SIDEWAYS IN FRONT of her mirror. If she pulled her shirt very tight against her belly, she thought she could see the slightest bit of rounding already. Flowing dresses and shirts had become her uniform in the last two weeks since her appointment with the nurse. She wished she was curvier like her sister, so she could hide her condition a little longer.

She had tried to tell Jesse her good news. Every time she tried, she chickened out. But if they needed to get married quickly, she needed to tell him today. He had spent the last week traveling, visiting family back in his hometown of Orangeburg, South Carolina. She missed him like crazy and had cried when he left. She had wanted to tell him then; but Patrick McKenzie was there, and Eve didn't want anyone else with them when Jesse found out.

But Jesse had come back the night before. He called her and said he needed to see her right away, and Eve knew this was the night she needed to tell him. August was only a few days away, her appointment with the doctor only two weeks away. Somewhere in there they needed to get engaged—possibly married—and had to tell her parents. Only Juliette knew her secret.

As she turned from side to side, trying to determine if she *looked* pregnant, there was a knock on her door. She quickly grabbed a tube of lipstick and opened it, bidding the knocker to enter.

Her mother's face poked around the door. "Eve? Can I come in?"

"Yes, Mom, of course. Any time," she said, hoping her mother didn't detect the waver in her voice. She ran the lipstick over her mouth, then set the tube down. "What's up?"

Her mother sat on her bed and patted the space beside her. "Come sit down, Evie. I need to talk to you."

Eve's heart beat faster, and she thought it might burst. Could her mother have found out? She didn't want to tell them without Jesse by her side. Trying to be calm, she sat. "Sure, Mom."

Abby eyed her eldest daughter. Eve thought for sure she could tell a secret was being hidden. "Eve, do you remember your old friend, Susan Merit? She moved to North Carolina a few years ago."

Eve gulped and wished she had a glass of water. Fear filled her heart. "Um, yes. But I haven't seen her in a while. Why do you ask?" She could feel every thud of her heart against the wall of her chest. Surely, her mother could see the movement of it, giving her away. Eve blinked her eyes a few times, trying to keep them from filling with tears. *Do you know, Mom?*

"Well, Mrs. Nelson came into Sweet Treats yesterday and told me that Susan had come into the hospital a while back for a pregnancy test. Did you know she was back in town?" Her mother didn't seem to know that she was the Susan at the hospital. Not yet, at least. *Thank goodness!*

"Susan? Oh, my," Eve muttered. Where was Juliette when she needed her? "Who is Mrs. Nelson?"

"She comes into the bakery all the time," Abby explained. "She's a nurse. I'm sure you've seen her. Short lady with graying hair. She's a tad plump, though I promise she was that way when I first met her." Her mother laughed.

Eve tried to laugh with her. "Oh, right, Mrs. Nelson." So, the nurse had known all along she was using a false name. Eve was thankful the nurse hadn't given away her secret, but that made it all the more imperative that she tell Jesse and her parents as soon as possible.

"Well," Abby continued. Eve tried her best to look her mother in the eye without the guilt gnawing away at her. "If you do see Susan, please tell her to come see me. Maybe we can help her out."

"Okay, Mom." Abby smiled at her daughter and stood. She gazed at Eve for a second before letting herself out of the room and closing the door behind her. Eve's eyes filled with tears, and she cried about lying to her mother about her condition. "Tonight can't come soon enough," she said to herself.

When Jesse came to pick her up, he seemed impatient. He had told her to go ahead and eat dinner, that he wanted the evening free to talk. That suited Eve just fine, as she didn't have much of an appetite anyway. He suggested that they walk on the beach, and Eve agreed.

Outside, Eve started down the sidewalk, since the beach was only a few blocks away. But Jesse stopped her. "I thought I could drive us down there."

Eve laughed. "But it's so close."

"Please, Eve," he begged. She could see in his eyes that something was amiss. Was everything okay? Then she thought that perhaps Jesse planned to propose all on his own tonight. Maybe that was why he needed his car.

"Okay, Jesse." They got into the car, and he drove the few blocks to the nearest public access parking lot.

They got out and wandered down to the sand. The water was calm, the air quiet. They were the only two people on the beach that night, which was unusual for a balmy July evening. Jesse picked a white yard fence and leaned against it, Eve following suit. She looked at him—his beautiful eyes, his full mouth. Even with as worried as he appeared, he was still gorgeous. Eve's heart swelled with love. Surely this night, they would plan their wedding.

Jesse started first. "Eve, I need to talk to you."

Eve gushed in response, "And I need to talk to you, too, Jesse. It's very important."

He stopped her. "I'm sure it is, Eve. But I need to do this now." He took a deep breath. Eve held her own, wondering if he would get on one knee with a ring in his hand. But Jesse didn't lower himself or pull a box from his pocket. "Eve, I'm going back to Orangeburg. I'm moving back for good."

Her heart sank as the bubble she was building up burst. Confused, Eve searched his face. "What? I don't understand."

"I was down there last week conducting an interview for a program at school. I got in," he said. "I'll leave the beach in about ten days." Jesse didn't look at her and stuffed his hands into his pockets.

"Well, I'll go with you, Jesse. That's okay. I don't mind," Eve said with a smile. They could make it work. Sure, she would miss her family, but it was still South Carolina, wasn't it? How far away could it be?

"You can't come with me, Love," he said, closing his eyes. "I got into seminary, and I can't take you with me."

Eve took a step back. "Seminary? You're going to become a preacher? You never told me that." How could a man who wanted to become a preacher sleep with someone out of wedlock? And how could she not have known he wanted to be a preacher? They had never talked about it.

Jesse stepped toward her, but Eve stepped back, wary. "That's not all, Evie."

Full of uncertainty and anger, Eve spit out, "Not all? What else is there?"

Jesse took a deep breath before he spoke. "Now, Eve. You will always be special to me; just remember that."

"Then take me with you!" She felt her chin quiver, her face turn red, and burning tears spill over her cheeks.

"I'm getting married next month, Eve."

"What?" Eve could hardly believe her ears. She felt like someone had stabbed her in the heart. A wave of nausea passed over her, but she did not lose her constitution; she would not let it. Did Jesse really say he was getting married? He didn't mean to her, though. He was marrying someone else? Eve sucked her breath in and felt everything around her start to spin.

"Frances and I have been together for four years, Eve. I proposed to her before I came here this summer." Jesse's voice was soft, almost sweet.

The spinning stopped instantly, and Eve was overtaken with rage. Shocked and hurt, she instinctively slapped Jesse across his cheek. "How dare you," she seethed. "You slept with me, having no intention of staying with me. You said you loved me, while you have this other woman waiting to get married? Why, Jesse? Why did you tell me you loved me?"

Jesse again stepped forward, this time catching Eve by the arm. "I do love you, Eve. I love you in a way I could never love Frances. You're youth, and excitement, and fun. She's comfort and stability. And if I'm going to become a powerful black preacher like Doctor

Martin Luther King, Junior, I need a strong, supportive black wife. I'm sorry, Eve."

Eve didn't try to hide her tears. She wanted to be furious, but she just felt sick. "Doctor King wouldn't turn his back on the woman he said he loved for appearances. And he would never turn his back on his child." Her fiery hair was wet with tears, and it clung to her face, but Eve didn't care. All she cared about was hurting Jesse the way he had hurt her.

It took Jesse a second for her words to register. Even with dusk settling in around them, Eve could see the surprise come across Jesse's face. "Excuse me?" he asked.

"You heard me, Jesse. Your child. I'm pregnant." Eve stood strong, her head held high, her hands on her hips.

"You can't be." His dark eyes shone in defiance. But despite his words, Eve could see that he believed her.

"I had it confirmed two weeks ago. I'm nearly three months along," she admitted.

"No, Eve, please tell me you're lying." Jesse put his head in his hands and groaned. Eve watched Jesse grapple with the news, his face showing the fight going on within his head.

"Juliette went with me. We heard the heartbeat and everything," she said. "Your child will be here in February." Maybe now he would realize he couldn't marry this other woman. Speaking quieter now, Eve added, "I was hoping we could get married before the summer was over."

"I can't have a white wife and a mixed-race baby, Eve," he said blatantly. "I'll pay for an abortion."

His words cut Eve to the bone, and she felt her heart break in millions of pieces.

"All this time, we've talked about white people not accepting blacks into their communities and into their lives. Yet here you are not accepting me because I'm white!" She nearly screamed. "I'm not getting an abortion, either. I'm keeping this baby, Jesse. How could a man who wants to preach God's love refuse his child and try to destroy it?"

"That's not what I want," he said. As he turned toward the little sunlight left, Eve could see tears staining his face, but she felt no remorse. "But it's what needs to happen. If you won't get an abortion, you'll be raising this child alone. I won't claim him at all."

Eve was conflicted. Jesse was in pain over this; she could see that. But his decision had been made. Regardless, they would never be together. Should she take his offer and get rid of the baby? It would rid her of any reminders of Jesse; whereas, a baby would be a daily reminder for the rest of her life. But killing her baby, a life she had heard and would soon feel, was not only illegal but also immoral. Her parents had taught her that life began at conception and that each life was precious to God. So, this life was precious to her as well.

Eve clutched at her stomach and stood firm. "I will not kill our child, even if you would."

Jesse looked at her, studied her. His eyes rested for a moment on her middle as more tears fell down his face. "I'm sorry, Eve," he said. He leaned toward her as if to kiss her, but she backed away.

"Yes, you are," she replied coldly. "Goodbye, Jesse." Eve turned and marched back up the sandy embankment.

It was the day her sister would tell their parents about her condition. Juliette was scared to death and couldn't imagine how Eve was feeling. The night before, Eve had come home early and incredibly upset. Things had gone terribly wrong with Jesse—that much she knew. Eve had managed to croak out between sobs that Jesse was leaving and getting married to someone else in the next month. Her sister had told her that Jesse offered to pay for an abortion right after saying he was going to become a preacher.

Juliette had held her sister, consoled her as best she could. She tried to give her the same love and respect Eve had shown her earlier in the summer. But she wasn't as compassionate as her twin. Juliette was a little rougher around the edges. But she had convinced Eve that she had to tell her parents the truth and do it now. Eve had agreed. Without Jesse, Eve was all alone and would need all the support she could get from her family—as long as they did support her.

Not being the type to pray to any Deity, Juliette wasn't sure how to handle wishing the best for her sister on what had to be a very hard day. But she supposed that praying at all was better than not. Besides, Booker had prayed for her, and she felt better. Maybe there was something to it. Did she need to address God a certain way? Was there a special name she needed to use? Her father knew all kinds of names for God, but she knew only God. Juliette decided she would just talk to this supposed God and not actually pray.

Listen, God, she started as she looked out the window of her bedroom. *I don't know what You think You're doing with us. This has been a terrible summer. First, if You do exist, You let me get raped. What kind of God allows that? And now, Eve is pregnant, and Jesse left her! How could You tolerate that? But listen to me, God. Eve needs her family; so, You better not let Mom and Dad kick her out or disown her or anything, okay? Eve needs us, and I need her. Her baby needs a family; so, please don't let Dad kick her out. Please, God. Amen.*

Juliette glanced at her sister who was still sleeping after a long, rough night. Eve looked so angelic with her red waves rolling over her pillow, a few strands across her cheek. Her breathing was still ragged after all the crying she had done during the night. Juliette decided to let her sister sleep and tiptoed down the stairs.

The house was quiet. Her father was visiting shut-ins and sick parishioners around town, and her mother had taken Joey and Alisa to the bakery with her for the day. The twins had been given a blessed day free, and Juliette couldn't have been happier for that.

Normally, they would have bounded off for the beach in search of some sun and cute boys. But neither girl had been up for much beaching this summer. Juliette still struggled with the beach, not trusting it or the strangers who would wink in her direction. And Eve had been preoccupied with Jesse all summer. Now, it wasn't just her summer ruined; it was her life. Juliette didn't think Eve should get rid of the baby; it was innocent in all this, but maybe putting it up for adoption was something to consider now. Surely, someone wouldn't mind raising a mixed-race baby.

Sitting at the kitchen table, Juliette heard the door creak open. She grabbed an apple and bit into it, not wanting to look like she was obviously deep in thought. Her father walked in, patting his suit pockets as he looked around.

"Oh, Juliette. Hi there, sweetie," he said as he looked around the counter.

"Hi, Daddy," she said as she swallowed a bite of apple. "Lose something?"

"I had a card earlier with an address on it. Mrs. Timberland had moved in with her son a few weeks ago, and I was going to visit, but I can't find the address. Have you seen a small, yellow card with an address?"

Juliette looked near her on the counter and table for the paper. Spotting it under her father's placemat, she picked it up and waved it around. "Here you go, Dad."

Taking the paper from her hand, Harvey kissed his daughter on the forehead. "Thanks, Princess." He turned to head out the door again but stopped and turned back to Juliette. "Is everything okay, Juliette?"

Nerves filled her stomach. Had he heard Eve crying last night? Did he suspect anything with either of them? Harvey Nicholas was a good father, albeit a little absent tending to his "flock," as he called them, and not spending as much time with his daughters.

"I'm fine, Dad," she said with a smile and took another bite of the apple in her hand.

"Was Eve crying last night?" So, he had heard her. Still chewing, Juliette only nodded her head slowly. Her father spoke again. "Is she okay? Did she and Jesse have a fight? I know she had gone out with him."

Swallowing hard and slow, Juliette replied weakly, "Yes, they had an argument. But it's not really my place to tell you about it, Dad."

Harvey held a hand up and nodded. "Say no more. I understand; it's girl stuff. I remember when your mother was eighteen. I'm so thankful to God that you and Eve have each other to lean on. Just remember that Mom and I are here, too. Okay?"

"We will, Dad," she said and she took another bite of her apple to avoid saying more. Her father squeezed her arm before patting his pockets again and disappearing out the front door.

Everyone would be home around four o'clock, and Juliette didn't want to sit around all day waiting for a family meeting she dreaded.

As much as she distrusted the beach these days, it sounded like the perfect escape from what was to come. She rushed upstairs, woke Eve, and told her to get her bathing suit on.

"But I don't feel like the beach today, Jules," Eve protested.

"So, grab a book, and just come sit with me. This is going to be a long day once you tell Mom and Dad, so let's go enjoy the first part of it," Juliette begged. "Please, Evie."

Eve relented and got dressed. She didn't put on a bathing suit, opting instead for a loose-fitting blue dress that ended mid-thigh. Juliette put on her most modest bathing suit—an apple-red one-piece from the year before—along with a pale yellow cover-up.

They walked the few blocks to the beach, Eve dragging her feet the whole time. Juliette knew exactly how she felt. It was how she felt just a few short months ago. *How could so much have transpired in one short summer?* They both had lost so much, but at least they had each other. Juliette vowed to herself to never abandon Eve as long as she needed her.

An afternoon at the beach made Juliette feel better. The warm sun felt wonderful on her cheeks and shoulders, and she enjoyed watching families play in the sand. Eve was silent, preferring not to talk, and kept her nose in her book the entire time. But at least she looked relaxed, Juliette thought. Juliette studied her sister next to her. Eve's happy and carefree nature seemed altered. Her sister's shoulders were taut, even as she read. When Eve moved the book closer to her face, Juliette considered her abdomen. Eve had not been as slender as Twiggy, but she had rounded out already, her stomach slightly protruding, her face a little fuller already.

The girls had always been able to judge the time by the position of the sun; and when they guessed it was close to four, they packed their towels and headed home. They got home just as their mother pulled into the driveway. Their father was already home.

Abby greeted them as they walked up to the house. "Oh, girls, you haven't gone to the beach in a while. Did you enjoy your day off?" Their mother smiled as she unloaded unsold bread from the car. Unsold breads and cakes were a staple in their house.

Eve was silent, but nodded to her sister. An unspoken message. *You tell them we need to talk, please,* her sister said with a single nod. Juliette nodded back in understanding. She turned to her mom. "Yes, we did." She smiled but squinted as she looked into the sun. "Mom, can we talk to you in a few minutes?"

Abby smiled. "Of course, Juliette." She unlocked the door for her four children, Eve slipping past them all to get through the door first. Juliette glanced at her mother, concern for her oldest daughter showing plainly on her face.

There was no point in hiding anything anymore this day, so she simply added, "Dad, too," before running in the house after her twin. She left her mom, brother, and sister behind her wondering what was going on.

Back in regular clothes, Juliette took Eve by the shoulders. "You can do this, Evie. I'm with you, okay?"

"Okay," Eve whispered. "Jules, I'm scared."

"I know," Juliette said, hugging her sister close. "It will be okay. I promise." She looked Eve in the eye and pushed her hair behind her ears like a mother would do for a child. "I love you," she told Eve.

"I love you, too."

When the girls came down to the living room, they found their parents sitting on the couch. Their parents lived a modest life. While her father had been raised in a wealthy Charleston family, he had cho-sen the life of a minister over that of a shipping magnate—a position their uncle and cousins had happily taken over. Their house was large, but sparse. Older couches with worn cushions occupied the spaces; the walls were covered with family pictures of everyone and anyone who would give them a picture.

The house was quiet, and Juliette guessed that their parents had sent Joey and Alisa away. That meant they knew this was serious. But did they know why? Did they have any idea what she and Eve were about to tell them? And how would they respond once they found out?

Juliette gave Eve's hand a quick squeeze as they took position across from their parents. She could remember Pete taking the same posi-tion not long before when he had told their parents he was going to propose to his girlfriend. And Pete had also faced them when it came time for him to choose a college. This was the serious talk position, and Juliette was trying to be strong for her sister.

As they sat, their father cleared his throat. Juliette glanced at her mother, who looked nervously at her husband. Harvey spoke first when none of the women offered. "Girls, what's going on?" When neither spoke up, he continued, "You both have been behaving very secretive this summer. I understand you're growing up, but you both seem to be out of character."

"Your father's right, girls," Abby said. "Things just seem off with the two of you. And we don't mind you two sharing secrets, but we think it's time you clued us in as to what's going on with you."

Eve looked at Juliette. Would her sister out her secret to lessen the blow of her own? Eve slowly closed her eyes and opened them back up. *This is my assembly*, Eve seemed to be saying. *Don't worry.*

Juliette turned toward her parents and spoke despite the dryness in her mouth. "Well, of course we graduated this year, so we have been trying to find our own ways. We've both learned a lot about ourselves this summer. Some good and some bad, actually," she said as she licked her lips. "Unfortunately, it's the latter that brings us down here."

Her mother's face turned red, a trademark sign of tears to come. It didn't matter what was wrong, Abby cried at all news, bad and good. But Juliette knew that any bad news about any of her children would bring forth a wealth of tears from Abby Nicholas. She looked to her sister, who had inherited her mother's abundance of tears, and she was also turning pink in the face. Surely, her parents would know now whom the bad news was about.

"Have you two decided to move far away?" her father guessed. She knew he was using it as a decoy question to break the tension.

Eve shook her head. "No."

Harvey chuckled a little. "You're not joining the foreign legion, are you?"

His efforts did not work. "No, Dad," Eve said with a straight face.

Abby straightened her back. "Girls, whatever it is, we're here. We may not be the hippest parents in town, but we love you. If you need anything from us, we're always behind you."

Juliette looked at Eve, who returned her gaze for a moment. Juliette nodded lightly to her sister, a nod to go ahead. Eve, in turn, blinked her eyes quickly; she was scared. Eve looked away; she wanted Juliette to say something first.

"We know you love us, Mom," Juliette said. "And we know that will never change. But not all love lasts forever." She looked to her sister.

"Did something happen, Eve?" their mother guessed. Juliette saw her parents join hands under the folds of her mother's skirt. They were preparing themselves.

Eve took a deep breath. "Jesse's going back to Orangeburg in a few days and leaving the beach for good."

Harvey straightened his back. "Are you going with him?" They liked Jesse well enough, but had voiced their concerns over the adversity a mixed-race couple would face in life.

Eve shook her head no. Juliette answered, "She can't go with him."

Their parents turned back to Eve for an explanation. "He's marrying someone else next month," she cried, tears slipping down her cheeks. Eve turned her head away from them all, bringing her hand up to her face to hide as much as she could.

Abby sighed. "Oh, Eve, I'm so sorry he lied to you. That's terrible."

Juliette put her hand on Eve's arm. "He's also going to seminary."

Both their parents looked shocked. "Seminary?" her dad squeaked out. "I cannot imagine someone who would string you along, then marry someone else, going into seminary. That's certainly not a very good foundation for a preacher to start on." He shook his head in disappointment.

"That is so upsetting, girls," their mom continued. "And while I can see just how hurtful this is for you, Eve, I don't understand." Abby shifted uneasily in her seat. "I don't understand why this warranted such a serious family meeting."

"It's not that he's moving back, or that he's going into seminary as a liar and a cheater," Eve said heavily. "It's not even that he's marrying someone else." She paused and took a deep breath. Juliette closed her eyes and opened them again, preparing herself for her sister's words.

Hoping her parents wouldn't order Eve out of the house the minute she told them.

Eve continued, "It's not that he's leaving me. It's that he's leaving our baby."

She fell back deep into her seat, tears flowing freely down her face. Juliette also cried. She cried for her sister and for her parents. But mostly, she cried for her unborn niece or nephew. Abby put her face in her hands and wept, but Harvey stood to his feet and went to Eve. Juliette watched as her father cradled her sister the way he would a small child, and he began to pray softly under his breath. She couldn't hear him but knew what he was doing. He held her head to his chest and stroked her hair as she cried, his own tears falling as well.

Juliette looked away from the tender moment between father and daughter and instead turned to her mother. Abby had lifted her head and was watching the scene before her, tears still falling. Abby looked to Juliette and raised an eyebrow as if to ask, *You knew all along?*

With a nod of her head, she confirmed that she had known. Her voice feeble, their mother asked the next logical question, "When will the baby be here?"

Eve's sobs grew louder, so Juliette answered for her. "The middle of February, according to the nurse at the hospital."

"Mrs. Nelson," Abby guessed. "I thought her comment about Susan Merit was strange. But it wasn't Susan, was it, Eve?"

Finally able to speak, Eve bobbed her head. "You're right. I used Susan's name when I went in."

"When was this?" her father asked.

Again, Juliette spoke for her sister. "I took her about two weeks ago, once we figured it out."

The tears hadn't ceased for anybody in the room, but at least Eve hadn't been immediately turned away from the house; for that, Juliette was thankful. Harvey continued to hold Eve in his arms, and she allowed him to cradle her. Juliette could tell that their mother wanted to hold Eve as well but was giving their dad a chance; her turn would come soon enough.

"Did you tell Jesse about the baby?" their mother asked. "If you didn't, maybe knowing will change his mind. Surely, he would not abandon his child; he seemed like such an upstanding young man all summer."

"I told him; he said he would leave anyway," Eve answered with a sniff.

"Tell them, Eve," Juliette encouraged her. "Tell them what he said."

Eve sighed deeply, and she swiped tears from her red-rimmed eyes. "Jesse said he would pay for an abortion when I told him."

Harvey reddened, infuriated. "I can't believe that! Regardless of anything else, this is a life. You can't destroy it, Eve."

"And I told him as much. I told him I would keep our baby, even if he chose to kill it." Eve sat up straight, proud of how she had stood up to Jesse in that moment. Then she added, "I don't know what to do now, though. When I found out I was pregnant, I thought we would get married by the end of summer. Little did I know, he already had plans to marry someone else. I never would have . . . I promise. Mom, I thought he really loved me and wanted to marry me. I don't want to lose my baby, Dad."

Harvey paced the room as he thought. "Well, adoption was the first thing that came to my mind. There are many couples out there who long for their arms to be filled."

Juliette spoke up. "No, Daddy. Eve and I talked, and she doesn't want to give her baby up."

Abby spoke. "That's understandable, girls, but you're eighteen years old. You're still children yourselves. Eve, you're not married, and the father of this child has left you."

"I know, Mom," Eve said as tears rolled down her flushed cheeks. "But I just lost Jesse. I see now that he is a loser, but I loved him. I thought it was forever. I can't lose him and this baby. Please."

"What about when Aunt Emmeline had Pete? Even after Uncle Peter died, nobody took him away from her," Juliette piped up. *Please, Dad, Mom, understand Eve wants to keep her baby.*

"That's not the same," Harvey retorted, shaking his head. "Peter loved Pete. He wanted to be there but died fighting for his family. And there were two sets of grandparents—three, counting mine—and several aunts and uncles who helped him whenever needed."

"But Eve has you two," Juliette reminded them. "And me and Pete, Joey, and Alisa. She's not alone. I'll help her." She reached out next to her and took Eve's hand in hers. They were a strong, unified front. Their parents couldn't deny that.

"Well, let's just take this one day at a time," Harvey said, his shoulders drooped. "For now, we agree that this baby is a life and should be respected as such. Over the next few months, we can discuss what the best option is for both you and this baby."

"You're not going to kick her out?" Juliette held her breath, waiting for her parents' response. "Please don't kick her out."

Abby stood and went to Eve's side. With her hand on her daughter's shoulder, she said, "Of course we're not kicking her out. We love both you girls more than anything. And we will love you despite any poor choices or challenges that come your way. God has a plan for both of you and for this child."

Eve cried tears of relief. Juliette herself took a deep sigh and sunk down in her seat. She didn't know if there was a master plan for all their lives or if her parents' God was the One leading them. But for now, she was happy that her sister would remain at home where she belonged. They would make it work however they could, Juliette thought.

That night, with the shock finally wearing off of Eve's announcement, both Juliette and Eve could hear their parents talking well into the night. They weren't eavesdropping per se; but with their window open, every word their parents said from the back porch came up to their room loud and clear.

"Well, Abby, maybe we should send Eve up to your parents' house this fall until the baby comes," Harvey said. Eve looked at Juliette with worry over her face. Juliette shushed her and shook her head.

"I don't know that my parents could keep up with Eve, sweetheart," came the reply. "They wouldn't ridicule her, but they wouldn't make it easy either. Do we really need to send her away?"

Good job, Mom, Juliette thought.

"She's pregnant, for heaven's sake! She can't be gallivanting around town with a growing stomach and bare finger," Harvey said in a raised whisper. The girls still heard every word.

"And when she comes back with a baby, it won't matter if she was seen in town with a pregnant stomach," Abby reminded her husband.

"Maybe we can still talk her into giving the baby up. Surely, someone out there would love to have a baby—even a mixed-race one."

Eve sat up straight. "No," she whispered in response as if she were in on the conversation.

Juliette put her hands on her sister's shoulders and shook her head again. "They wouldn't, Evie. I promise," she reassured her sister. "Mom won't let Dad do that."

"Maybe you are right, Harvey. I know there are families out there who would love to take in a baby," Abby said. Juliette shook her head in disbelief. Surely, her mother would not agree to this. "But how far would we have to go to find someone who wants a mixed-race baby?"

Harvey sighed. "Maybe we can pass it off as a Hispanic or Asian child. I've read in the paper where couples from bigger cities are adopting Korean and Vietnamese children."

"We can't lie about the child's background, Harvey, and you know that," Abby said crossly. "Besides, nobody would love that baby as much as Evie and us. Even after what Jesse did to her. Why don't we contact the police and get them involved? They can track him down."

Harvey sighed. "To what avail? Our daughter will still be pregnant with a colored child. Putting that boy in jail won't save her any injustice." Juliette could hear her father sigh. "Let's send her to your parents; and when she comes back, we can say she got married, and the father died."

"What?" Abby nearly screeched. "She's already three months gone. How are we supposed to send her across the state, say she got married, her husband died, and she had a baby all within six months' time? That would not work," she told him. "And I don't think Juliette would let you touch Evie or that baby if she thought you were going to give it away."

Juliette raised an eyebrow to her sister. *See? Told you*, she conveyed to her sister.

"Speaking of Juliette," Harvey continued. "I have to admit, I'm surprised it's Eve who's turned up pregnant and not Juliette. She's always had a wilder streak than her sister."

Eve looked shocked and glanced at Juliette. Juliette could feel the heat rise up in her cheeks. Did her father really just say that? She thought she had hidden that side of herself from her parents better.

"Juliette may spout ideas of free love, but she's smart. She would never be intimate with someone without loving them very much. We can only hope that means marriage; and for her, that will be a long way off," Abby said. Juliette blushed again, but this time out of anger. She would have saved herself for someone she loved if she had been given the choice. Her mother continued. "Eve is different. She was looking for love. She wanted to be in love, and she thought Jesse was it. Unfortunately, that mistake will change the rest of her life."

Looking at her sister, Juliette could see the pain in Eve's face. It would change her life forever. Would Eve find the love she longed for with a child in tow? Would she be able to find a job if an employer knew she was an unmarried mother? There was such a stigma attached to the title "unwed mother." Could Eve shake that? Juliette hoped she could.

As quietly as she could, Juliette closed their window, returning their parents to the private conversation they thought they were having. Both girls got into their beds. Juliette turned toward Eve and watched as her sister smoothed the sheet over her body. A small roundness pushed against the thin cotton where it used to dip at Eve's stomach. Her niece or nephew rested there, not knowing the chaos it had caused in their otherwise peaceful family.

Seasons in the Sun

"NOTHING FITS ME ANYMORE," EVE grumbled as she threw down another shirt. "When will this be over? I'm tired of being fat!"

Her mother looked at her with a knowing smirk. "Not too much longer, Eve. After Christmas, the weeks following will fly by. Then you'll have a baby and all his or her gear to tote around. You'll miss everything being attached and bundled up."

"And at least now you don't have to change diapers." Alisa laughed.

Eve smiled at her younger sister. "I'll make you change the diapers," she warned with a giggle.

"Not me!" Alisa ducked behind a sales rack. Eve wished she was thirteen again and so carefree. Alisa didn't have a care in the world, and Eve's entire world was about to become one single care—her child.

She rubbed her stomach as she tried to find maternity clothes that didn't make her look like a beached whale. Only two more months until she could wear normal clothes again. She couldn't wait. But for now, she needed a Christmas outfit for church.

Her father's church had reacted much in the way they had expected when Eve's middle had started to expand. Lots of hushed talk and sideways glances. Her father had addressed several parishioners personally about their reactions to Eve's impending motherhood. The family was sticking by the story that Eve had been tricked, had been promised love and marriage, and then had been left by the man. It was mostly true, except she and Jesse had never talked marriage while they were together. Many people ignored her stomach; others simply ignored her. But lots of the church folks were sympathetic and still treated Eve like they would have anyway. Juliette, Alisa, and their mother had a baby shower planned for the first week of January. Eve hoped at least a few church ladies would show up.

Eve was brought out of her thoughts by her mother holding up yet another tent dress for her to consider. "What about this, Eve? This shade of green always looks so pretty against your skin."

Wrinkling her nose, Eve said, "I dig the color, but not the style. I'm sorry, Mom, but maternity clothes are just not hip." She was tired of the same old dress style, even if Twiggy did wear tents. She had the body for them.

"They're not supposed to be," Abby said. "You're about to be a mother; you're not supposed to be hip anymore."

"But I'm also only eighteen. I'm not old enough to be frumpy yet." Eve moaned. Her mother gave her a look that said she could have been living it up as a teenager. Eve shrugged. "I know, Mom. I know." She had seen that look before.

Despite everything, her parents had been wonderful. They hadn't sent her away to live out her pregnancy with her grandparents. They hadn't even mentioned giving the baby away to someone else. Everything had gone well. Juliette or her mother had gone with her to every doctor's appointment. Eve had worked odd hours at the bakery and the church to make some extra money. Her father and brother had even spent part of the fall turning the attic into a bedroom, so that Joey could move up there and Joey's room could become her and the baby's room. Everyone had pitched in to help.

Without finding any suitable clothes, Eve looked to her mother. "Do you still have the green tent?" Her mother held the dress up for her. "Let me try it on," she mumbled as she took the dress and waddled over toward the dressing room.

Looking in the mirror, Eve raised an eyebrow and stuck out her tongue. The color was nice, and the tent shape was not as hideous as expected. *Put some lights on me, and I'll look like a short, fat Christmas tree,* she thought with a giggle. It would certainly do for the Christmas Eve services at Respite Baptist Church. It would have to do—there was nothing else around.

After making their final selections, the trio headed home. In the car, Eve realized that she hadn't gotten many stares lately. Were people coming around to her specific circumstances? Or was it the fact that she was so ballooned up that people thought she could no longer wear a wedding ring? More than likely the latter, she scowled to herself. Maybe she should just buy herself a little silver ring and tell everybody that her husband was in the army. *Mom and Dad would not be happy if I lied about being married to cover my own mistakes,* she thought as she watched holiday shoppers rush by. But how could this sweet baby be a mistake? She wondered, *does God make mistakes?*

Footprints in the Sand

"DOES GOD MAKE MISTAKES, BOOKER?" Juliette felt like she had to ask him, even if they were playing pool at a local pub. Eve had come home earlier in the week sobbing and asking if her baby was a mistake.

"Could a baby—a human life—be a mistake, Jules?" Eve had cried into her shoulder. Juliette hadn't been able to answer. She didn't think her sister's baby was a mistake, but perhaps the actions that brought him or her into being were. Then Eve had asked if God was punishing her, but again, Juliette couldn't answer. But she knew who could.

Booker raised an eyebrow toward Juliette. "Are you asking me about God, Juliette Nicholas?"

She waved her hands in front of her face as if to shoo off an imaginary fly. "No, no, not for me," she quickly explained. "Eve was wondering if her baby was a mistake. If God made mistakes. I didn't have any answer for her."

Booker leaned in toward her, ignoring the clatter of pool balls making it into the corner pockets behind them. "God doesn't make mistakes, Juliette. You should know that, the daughter of a preacher and all."

Looking down, Juliette mumbled, "I don't even know if there is a God."

"What?" The noise in the pool hall wasn't terribly loud, but loud enough. She would have to speak up.

Juliette sighed. She knew it would have to come out sooner or later. A little louder, she repeated, "I don't know if there is a God." She kept her eyes down, averted from Booker. She knew he believed in God with every ounce of his being. She didn't know why, just that he did. She could not bear to look into his chocolate brown eyes when she told him she did not believe in the thing that he believed in most.

Booker placed a finger under her chin and lifted it. When she met his gaze, she could see the questions and the hurt in his eyes. They had been seeing each other more frequently over the last several months. Juliette was hesitant to call it dating, even though that was exactly what it was. They saw each other almost every day, even if it was just him stopping by the bakery or her getting lunch at the Blue Rooster. Booker had been completely open and honest with her without pushing her into a response. But Juliette was afraid to admit her feelings for Booker, regardless of how strong they were. She had secrets she wasn't ready to tell him.

But now her first one had come out. She did not believe in the God Who consumed his time as much as he consumed hers. And Juliette could see that it stung. It stung her back to see his reaction. He was obviously hurt that she did not believe in his Almighty God. And, of course, hurt that she had waited so long to tell him. How would he react to her other secret? she wondered. Juliette sighed. It seemed she would find out sooner or later.

Booker set some loose bills on the table and took her hand, leading them away from the chatter of friends and the sound of pool cues striking their targets. He opened the car door for her, and she slipped in silently. He got in the car without looking at her and put the car into drive. Juliette knew not to say anything. Minutes later, they pulled into the driveway of the Winston house. Booker had converted their unused garage into a small apartment for himself. It kept his expenses at a minimum, but he could still come and go as he pleased. His parents and two younger siblings were more than likely asleep, Juliette guessed. Despite being upset with her, Booker still rounded the front of the car and opened Juliette's door for her. He was such a gentleman, she thought.

Inside, Juliette stood in front of a small, green couch that sat at the foot of Booker's bed. To her right was a small refrigerator, sink, and hot plate that served as a makeshift kitchen. To her left was a closet and bathroom. It wasn't much, but it impressed Juliette nonetheless. She watched as Booker paced the floor for a minute.

"Juliette," he began, her name coming out as a sigh. "Juliette, I thought . . . I just assumed . . . " He stopped to collect his thoughts once more. He stood in front of her, shoulders square with her own. "I've never pushed you to talk about the things that bothered you. And I was fine with that. I always thought you were giving those burdens to God, though. But tonight, you lay on me that you don't know if you believe in God? After all these months?"

Anger burned inside him; Juliette could see that. But it wasn't just anger—there was more. She knew he would be upset when she did tell him, but she hadn't counted on the hurt and disappointment she now faced.

"I'm sorry, Booker," she said, her voice barely audible. "You were just so excited about religion, I didn't want to argue with you about it."

"Religion? Baby, religion has nothing to do with it. You lied to me."

Shaking her head, she countered, "No."

"You never told me this before. In the five months we've been to-gether, you've had ample opportunity to share this tidbit with me." Booker balled his hands into fists and raised them for a second before spreading his fingers out before her. He closed his eyes and was quiet for a moment. "Why?"

Juliette licked her lips much the same way her mother and sister did when they were nervous. "I don't see how there could be a God with all the hurt and pain in the world. All the war, all the destruction and hate," she explained. "How could there be a God Who claims to love all people when peaceful civil rights protesters are being jailed and even beaten in public? How could there be a God Who allows wars and death to happen to blameless people? If there was a God, how could He let such a terrible thing happen to . . . to Eve? And her baby? How can these things happen and there be a God, Booker?"

"Wow," he responded. "That's more questions than I was expect-ing." He rubbed his chin for a moment while he processed all of her questions. "God loves all people, but that doesn't mean that all people love God. People sin of their own free will, Juliette. People who beat peaceful protesters are not acting out of love and don't know how God's love can change them. And while God does not condone war, He realizes that at times, it's a necessary evil to restore peace in the end. And God, Juliette—God was there for Eve. When Jesse left, she had you and your family. God provided that. You said you were afraid your parents would make her give up the baby, and so far, that's not the case; and God worked in their hearts so that she could keep the baby."

Juliette shook her head and interrupted him. "So, this God takes credit only for the good things?"

"No, not at all," Booker continued. "Haven't you ever seen God at work?"

"No," came her simple reply. She hadn't. This God had allowed her to be raped, her sister to become pregnant, and countless other atrocities she couldn't think of at the moment. But the two she could think of were plenty.

"Look at my parents," Booker said. "My dad was stationed in Japan during the war. He met a beautiful, young girl, who called herself Lucille for American soldiers, and they fell in love. They got married in a Japanese ceremony after knowing each other only a few weeks. But when Dad was shipped out of Japan, he wasn't allowed to take my mom with him."

Her curiosity was piqued. "How did she get here, then? And what does this have to do with God?"

"God was testing them. The Japanese—and my mother—were the enemy of Americans. My dad's friends and family tried to convince him to forget about her and marry a nice American girl he had known from school. But my parents loved each other. After months of my father trying to either get my mother out or getting himself back in, something happened." When Juliette cocked her head to the side, he continued. "My dad was already a minister, and the opportunity came up to go back to Japan as a chaplain and not a soldier. He took it. He was back, but my mother was nowhere to be found. By the time he saw her again, more than six months had gone by. They lived together on an army base for a year before the war ended and my father could go home. Even though my mother was not supposed to be allowed to leave with the Americans, my father loaded her into the plane with authority and a prayer, and nobody questioned him. I was born nine months later."

"That is an amazing story, but that's just luck, isn't it?"

"Maybe luck plays a part; but without God, there is no luck. Juliette, you've told me a lot about your family. Including that your father was also in World War Two. Tell me your parents' story," Booker prompted her.

"Well, my dad grew up in Charleston, my mom up near the mountains," she started, still not sure how God worked into all this. "He went to school at Clemson College, and they fell in love. When the war broke out, my dad and uncle left. My uncle Peter died; and shortly after the war, my aunt Emmeline died, leaving my parents with Pete to raise. And during the war, my father was injured in the blast that killed my uncle. When he came home, he almost married someone else because that girl had told him that my mother had run off with another guy. My mother drove to Charleston and found him," she said with a smile. "Dad dumped the liar and married Mom. They took Pete and raised him. But it took them five years to have Eve and me. Mom said they were very rough years, but well worth the wait."

"So, God led your parents back to each other," Booker pointed out.

"They got back to each other after Dad was nearly killed and nearly married to someone else. My mom lost her brother and sister-in-law, and they were handed a baby to bring up within weeks of getting married. I don't see many miracles there. Just death and confusion and heartache."

"How about you and Eve? Are you not the miracles your mother waited five years for?"

Juliette softened and looked down. "Mom's always called us her miracles."

"Even with obstacles in their way, your parents fought and prayed their way back to each other. Even with heartache, they found joy in you and your siblings. God may have tested them, but they trusted the Lord to get them through it."

"God tested them?"

"God tests us. He tests us to see what we do. Do we turn to Him and trust in Him? Or do we lean only on ourselves and fail miserably in the process?" Booker raised an eyebrow to Juliette.

"I'm not failing miserably!"

Booker laid his hands on her shoulders. Despite the sweater she wore around her shoulders, she could feel the heat radiating from him. "Juliette, I love being with you. But you are failing. You've been depressed. And at times, it's like you're clawing your way out of a sandpit and can't get a foothold. Like on the beach on Independence Day. Something in you broke. I prayed over you, and something in you changed that night. A small change, but a noticeable one. I have prayed for that pain in you for all these months, but I always thought you were praying, too. Now I know why my prayers weren't as effective as I would have liked."

"Why?"

"Because if you don't want God to change you, He won't. He gives you free will."

"Do I need to be changed?" Juliette was curious. Wasn't she fine as she was? Booker sure liked her well enough, and everyone else seemed to like who she was. But he was right—she was stubborn, and she knew it. She had been forever changed that summer and had never even thought of changing back into the Juliette she was before Buzz Herbert darkened her doorstep.

Booker fixed his eyes on hers, and Juliette saw the flicker of light reflecting from her eyes to his. "Do you need to change?" he asked back to her. "Because if you let Him, God will take you in and change you."

She blinked several times. "God doesn't want a wreck like me, Booker," she said, her voice barely a whisper. She sat on the shabby, green couch and covered her eyes as the tears began to flow.

Booker sat beside her, stroking her curls. "God wants all of us, especially the wrecks. They are His prized children. As the song says, 'Amazing grace! How sweet the sound that saved a wretch like me.'" Booker sang the familiar tune in a smooth, baritone voice.

Juliette knew the song, of course. But she had never thought about the words before. She had never processed just what those stanzas meant. Her blank stare drove Booker to continue the song. Juliette closed her eyes and allowed the soft, deep voice to convey the meaning straight to her heart.

"Amazing grace! How sweet the sound

"That saved a wretch like me. I once was lost, but now am found

"Was blind, but now I see."

He laid his hands over hers as he continued.

"T'was grace that taught my heart to fear,

"And grace my fears relieved.

"How precious did that grace appear

"The hour I first believed."

"Booker?" She wanted to ask him a question, but he placed a finger over her lips and sang on.

"The Lord has promised good to me.

"His word my hope secures;

"He will my shield and portion be,

"As long as life endures.

"Amazing grace!

"How sweet the sound

"That saved a wretch like me.

"I once was lost, but now am found,

"Was blind, but now I see."

Suddenly it all became clear to her. God had brought her through that summery night and allowed Eve to find her. God had protected her from many things and provided her with so much more. She saw that now. She saw how God had worked all around her in the lives of others—her parents, her siblings, Booker. He had brought Booker in to her life at a time when she needed him most—a fireworks-filled night when she wasn't sure if she should live or die.

Juliette felt renewed and awakened, but also confused. How would this fit into her life? Would she suddenly be changed? Would she be able to forgive Buzz? More importantly, would she be able to forgive herself? She felt as though she saw the light, but was still fumbling around.

"I don't—I don't know what to do," she whispered. Tears still slipped down her cheek, even while her eyes remained closed.

She felt Booker's hand on her cheek, wiping a tear away with his thumb. "Do you want to change, Juliette? Do you want God to change you and fill your heart?"

With a deep breath and fresh tears, she nodded. "I think I do, Booker. I need something in me to change. But I don't know God. I don't know how to begin."

"Lucky for you, I do," he said. Juliette could practically hear the smile in his voice. Booker's hands cupped over hers gently. "We pray."

Her voice warbled, "Our Father, which art in heaven—"

"No, just talk to Him, Juliette."

"I don't . . . I don't know how."

"Just like you're talking to me right now. Like you're on the phone. Talk to Him, Juliette. He's been waiting."

"Waiting for what?" But she knew the answer.

"Waiting for you to call." But it wasn't Booker's voice she heard. It was Someone Else. Could it be?

"God?" she asked aloud. "Can I really just talk to you?"

Of course, you can.

"God, I don't know what to say really. But I need help. I guess I need Your help, please. I have been so mixed up and messed up for months now, and You know why. How could You let that happen, God? What purpose did that serve?" she cried out, not caring who heard her.

I'm sorry, My child, came the reply. *As you've been told, when someone doesn't love Me, they often don't act in the manner they should. But I love you always. Did I not send your sister to find you? Did I not protect you from conceiving? Did I not send Booker to help you? And most importantly, if that hadn't happened, would you be seeking Me out right now?*

"Surely, there was a better way, Lord," she pleaded.

This is the way it worked out, Juliette. I am so sorry for how you were hurt. But please believe I never want harm to come to you. Buzz meant much more harm to come your way, but I protected you. You just didn't know it.

"How can I change my heart? I don't understand what I do now."

It's faith, Juliette. And faith doesn't always just appear like magic. I'm God, not a magician. Just as I'm speaking to you now, I will always guide you. All you have to do is listen.

"I will listen for You, God. I will do my best to stop and listen for You. Thank You, Lord, for helping me. For bringing Booker into my life at such as time as this and helping me to find You." When she paused and heard nothing in response, she peeked out from under her lashes. "Booker, how do I hang up?"

He chuckled and whispered, "Amen."

"Amen," she said, feeling foolish for forgetting such a simple word that had been among the first she had ever spoken. She opened her eyes and gave them time to adjust to the light. "Ah, I can see now." And she smiled when she realized the double meaning behind that phrase.

Booker smiled as well. "I didn't realize your sister's condition was so heavy on your heart."

"My sister?" Had she mentioned Eve in her talk with God? No, she was sure she hadn't.

"You asked God how He could let that happen, remember?"

Oh. Juliette hadn't meant Eve, of course. She had selfishly meant herself. She struggled over telling him what had happened to her. Did he need to know? What should she do? Pray.

Quickly she shot up a call to her Heavenly Father. *God, what do I do? Do I tell him and risk scaring him away? Or not tell him and risk him being angry for not telling him?* The answer came quickly and just how it had been promised. *Okay, God. I'll tell him. Here goes nothing. Remember, this was Your idea.*

"I didn't mean Eve when I said that, Booker." She winced as she spoke.

Understanding filled Booker's face, however. As if he knew she was now speaking about herself. "Does this have to do with what happened on the Fourth?"

Juliette sighed. "Yes, it does." The memories flooded her head as if her wounds were fresh. She could practically smell the salt air around her.

Booker inched closer to her and put his arm around her. "I've known since then that something was bothering you. You don't have to share tonight if you don't want to."

"God told me to."

"Ah, well, then. Can't argue with that one."

"It happened this past June. My parents had invited some new parishioners over for dinner—a widow and her son. He was a nice guy, about your age, and my parents had prompted Eve and me to be nice and show him around. He had invited me to a party at the Sea Horse; and always open to a party and a date, I agreed. Eve had wandered off to talk to friends, leaving me alone with Buzz . . ." She trailed off.

Juliette's breathing became labored; and hot, angry tears stung her face. It wasn't Eve's fault that she had left Juliette with him or that Buzz had drugged her. It wasn't her own fault either; she realized that now.

Her arms covered in goosebumps, Juliette was thankful when Booker slowly rubbed his hand over her chilled skin. "It's okay. Take your time." Juliette could see from the look on Booker's face that he was pouring over the possibilities in his head. Would he be able to guess before she had to say it?

"I was alone with him, but in plain sight of everybody, so not really alone. He got us drinks, and he brought me back some terrible cocktail of something. But I didn't want to seem ungrateful, so I drank it anyway. It turns out, he had drugged me. He led me away from the party, and he . . . he . . . " Tears spilled down her cheeks, splashing onto her light blue blouse, staining it dark. She could barely speak, her sobs caught in her breath.

Booker shook his head. "Juliette . . . Juliette, please tell me it's not what I'm thinking."

Quiet as a mouse, Juliette whispered, "He forced himself on me that night. And then, he ran away, and nobody's seen him since."

Booker pulled her close and held her head against his chest. Juliette could hear and feel the steady but torrid breaths fill his lungs. She could smell the mixture of cologne and heated anger on his clothes. As she breathed him in, she felt her own heart rate slow back to normal. She was safe with Booker; she knew that. It was a safe feeling she hadn't felt in a long time. And now that she had told him her secret, she felt like she could finally relax.

When his own breaths had calmed, Booker spoke. "When you say he was never seen again . . . that means you never reported it?" Juliette shook her head. "Your parents?"

Lifting her head, Juliette shook her head again. "They don't know. The only people who know are Eve and you. Well, and Jesse. For what a louse he wound up being, he was a lifesaver that night. He carried me to his car and took care of me and Eve."

"What about seeing a doctor, Juliette? What if you had been seriously hurt?" Booker looked concerned. Even though the event had been six months ago, he was reacting like it had just happened. Juliette could hardly blame him.

"Jesse called in a friend who was in medical school. He came and looked me over, treated a few scrapes and cuts," she explained. Booker stood and paced in front of her several times. She could see the anger and the pain in his eyes. Didn't he know just how much it pained her to tell him? She cared for him. And she suddenly realized she cared more than she had recognized before.

"I knew something was wrong, Juliette," he said, finally holding still. "But I had no idea it was this. I didn't know someone had violated you."

"I'm so sorry I didn't tell you before, Booker. It was so fresh when we first met, I couldn't talk about it. And then, as time went on, I was trying to heal on my own. And I didn't want anybody to know that I was ruined like that. I'm so ashamed. I understand if you want me to go." She stood to show that she was serious about her offer to leave. Obviously, he was upset about her news; Juliette figured he wouldn't want to see her anymore.

"No, please!" Booker jumped in front of her. "Juliette, you have no reason to be ashamed. You did nothing wrong."

"I drank his concoction. I walked away with him. I was stupid, and now I'm damaged, Booker." Juliette tried to look away as fresh tears sprang forth. Juliette wondered if her eyes would ever dry up.

"Stop that right now. He hurt you, but you are not damaged. God has healed you," he said, trying to meet her averted stare.

"He can't give that night back."

"No, but He can make you whole again." He finally got Juliette to meet his gaze. She softened under his touch. "Just pray for God to make you whole again, and He will. That night cannot be erased, but God can make you white as snow again."

"White as snow?"

"Pure."

Juliette's eyes lit up. God could make her pure again? Why didn't she know that before? How could she achieve this wonderful state of being? She closed her eyes and prayed for God to make her clean and pure again—as white as snow. Immediately, Juliette could feel a warmth start in the pit of her stomach and grow. It spread from her middle, to her shoulders, and down her arms. It shot down her legs and up to her head. She felt radiant. She felt beautiful for the first time since that dreadful night.

She threw her arms up and around Booker's shoulders. "Thank you, Booker! Thank you!"

"Don't thank me, Juliette. I didn't do anything. It was all God," he said with a great big smile. "See? God can make an instant change in you."

"I can't believe it. I actually feel different." Juliette beamed. She felt almost as if she were glowing. "I feel like I need to tell everybody I know about God's love. It's amazing!"

"Yes, it is, Juliette. Yes, it is."

They talked a little more; then Booker took Juliette home. She was exhausted from sharing the secrets she had been keeping from him, yet exhilarated from coming to know God. It was all she could do to keep from falling asleep in his car.

Eve noticed a big change in her twin sister in the week leading up to Christmas. Was Juliette simply feeling festive? Or was something else going on? Maybe, Eve thought, Juliette and Booker were more serious than she knew. She hated not knowing. And it wasn't that they were hiding things from each other—just that Eve was always tired, and Juliette was always on the go. They had hardly seen each other since Thanksgiving.

Christmas Eve was always a busy day in the Nicholas house. Harvey spent the morning at Respite Baptist Church preparing for the candle-light service that evening. Abby was in the kitchen making loaf after loaf of fresh breads. Eve's favorite was her great-grandmother's recipe for Irish soda bread. It was a Nicholas family tradition to have Irish soda bread with Christmas dinner. Joey and Alisa were busy with cleaning upstairs, while Eve and Juliette were sprucing up the downstairs.

"I'm so glad we got the tree up last night. Isn't it beautiful?" Juliette smiled at her.

Eve watched as her sister danced around the tree. Juliette seemed to have a special light around her. Eve was jealous. Sure, she was happy her sister was happy, but she wanted that feeling, too. Since Jesse had left, Eve had felt depressed. Depressed and fat. Her baby kicked in protest. She smiled, loving the feeling, but also lamenting in the what could have been with the baby's father.

When she didn't respond, Juliette stopped dancing. "Eve? Are you okay?"

"Tired is all," Eve said. It wasn't a lie. She was exhausted all the time. "The baby is kicking; come feel."

Juliette rested her hands across Eve's belly. In response, the baby punched back. Too big now to roll, the child had resorted to kicking and punching to let people know he—or she—was still there. As if Eve could forget. The twins smiled as one felt the movement from the inside, the other from the outside.

"I love feeling that, Evie. It's groovy." Juliette sighed.

Eve sighed in response. "I know. But as cool as it is to feel the baby move, I'm ready for it to vacate my body. I want to see who this tiny person is, and I want to have my body back to normal."

The girls laughed for a second and rested on the couch. "Eve, do you think we could steal away for a few minutes and talk?" Juliette looked serious, like she had something she really needed to get off her chest.

Eve looked around. The living and dining rooms were impeccable. The tree dazzling. All the places at the table set for a feast. And they couldn't clean the kitchen until their mother was done. "Let's go," she said. When Juliette bounded to her feet, Eve could lift only her hands. "Let's go—if you can help me up, that is."

"Right," Juliette said and laughed. "I can't believe you can't get off the couch." She hoisted her sister up from her seat with an umph.

"Oh, believe it, Jules. One day, it will be your turn." Eve laughed. Not being able to get up was another reason she was ready for this baby to come. Six weeks and counting down. At the door, the girls put their jackets on, even though Eve's no longer closed. She had refused a new jacket, saying it was silly to get a jacket when she would be back to normal in a few months and she was always so hot all the time anyways. "Where are we going?"

"It's not terribly cold out; can you walk to the beach?"

Eve shot her sister a menacing look and laughed. "I can try, I suppose." Once outside, Eve was pleased with the temperature. Not too chilly, but she was glad she had her jacket on to keep the breeze off her skin. "What's up, Juliette?"

"We've barely had time to talk lately. I seem to always be going from here to there, and you're always sleeping," Juliette told her. "I've missed you."

"I've missed you, too. And you would sleep all day, too, if your stomach kept you awake all night. I think this baby has day and night confused." Eve stopped at the end of the driveway and leaned against the car. "Um, the beach may have to wait. I'm winded already."

"That's okay. I don't care where we are; I just needed to talk," Juliette said, leaning next to Eve. Their shoulders touched, and they instinctively moved closer to each other. It was something they had done their entire lives—nuzzled together for warmth and comfort.

"Needed to talk? Is everything okay? With Booker? Or maybe . . . " Eve trailed off. Juliette was happy, so surely nothing bad had happened with Booker or otherwise. What could she need to talk about?

"Everything's great, Evie." Juliette beamed. "Better than great. I just feel so blessed. Especially this season."

Eve blinked. Did her sister just say *blessed*? Her sister, who didn't believe in God? Eve's own wavering faith had been pushed to the side of non-believing since Jesse had left her pregnant and alone. But Juliette hadn't really believed in God since she was a little girl. And now she was blessed?

"I just . . . I don't know. I've always loved Christmas, but this year is different," Juliette went on. She looked at Eve. Eve got worried because this was so uncharacteristic of her sister. "Eve, I have to confess something to you."

A Splash in the Ocean

AH, THIS WAS IT. JULIETTE had done something wrong and was trying to cover. *A poor cover,* Eve thought. "Go on, then."

"Last week, Booker and I were at the Surfside Pool and Pub, and I had asked him about when you asked if God had made a mistake with the baby."

Eve's heart thumped. She had been so upset that night, wondering if God had been mistaken to give her a baby. Or if God were punishing her for her poor choices. "What, um, what did he say?" She squinted, partially from the sun and partially because she was afraid of the answer.

"Of course, he said that God doesn't make mistakes ever," Juliette reassured her. Eve sighed a breath of relief. Regardless of God's actuality, Eve was glad to know that no mistakes were made. "But then, I confessed that I didn't believe in God."

Her own concerns pushed aside, Eve immediately thought that Booker had broken up with Juliette. "Oh, Jules, how did he react?"

"He took me back to his house because the bar was noisy. He was angry that I hadn't told him this before. But then we talked. A lot. I can't even tell you everything. But in the end, he said that I had a choice and that God could change me if I wanted Him to. But I had to want it to happen."

Eve could hardly believe this was her twin sister talking. "Then what?"

"I had felt like I was sinking ever since . . . since that night," she said. Juliette took a breath and kept talking. "I knew I needed help. I knew I needed to get out of the pit I was falling into. Booker even said he noticed it. So, I told him I wanted to change. And he helped me pray. And Evie, God talked to me. I heard Him!"

"You heard God? Are you sure?"

"Of course, I'm sure. He told me that He was sorry how things had happened for me, but that it was all to draw me to Him."

Eve snorted, and her belly shook. "He could have found a better way to do that than Buzz Herbert, Juliette."

"I know. I still struggle with that as well. I really think—no, I know—God was with me. Then and now. But God said He led you to me to find me. And He protected me from being hurt more because apparently Buzz had planned to hurt me even more than he did."

Tears swam in Eve's eyes. Did her sister really believe all this? And if she did believe it, was it true? "Are you sure about this, Juliette?"

"Absolutely. Then I prayed for God to change me, and He did. It was amazing. It happened in an instant. I felt like I was glowing Jesus or something." Juliette laughed. "I know it sounds corny, but I promise, Eve. It was like I was able to see after being blind for so long. God loves me, and I can actually say I love Him, as well." Juliette took a deep breath and was smiling bigger than Eve had ever seen. "And I told Booker all about Buzz."

"Oh, Juliette, that must have been terrible for you," Eve said, laying a hand on Juliette's arm. "What did Booker say about that?"

"He was upset, of course," Juliette said, her face turning more somber. "But I'm glad I told him. We've known each other for months now. I know he's been ready for our relationship to go farther, and I wasn't ready. Not that I'm ready to jump into anything serious still, but I do feel like we can make baby steps forward."

Tears stung Eve's own eyes. Grief and happiness and confusion washed over her. She was so distressed that her sister even had a tragedy to share. She was confused about her sister's complete change and sudden faith in a God she had claimed to be false. Regardless, Eve felt thrilled that Juliette was so happy and joyful now.

"I'm so glad that you're happy with Booker," she said with a smile.

"Listen, though, Eve. It's not about Booker. Not at all," Juliette exclaimed. Her smile and excitement were infectious. "It's all about God, Evie. Seriously. I know it sounds hokey, but since last week, I have felt like I was floating on a cloud. Things are clearer now, and I'm praying all the time. All the time! And God is answering my prayers."

Eve looked down at her fingernails and picked at a jagged one. Her sister's newfound faith was wonderful news—for her sister. Eve hated that she felt jealous and bitter. Why wasn't God talking to her? Did she not pray when she needed something? She went to church every Sunday. Sure, she had made mistakes, but she wanted the bliss that Juliette was currently high on. Where was this God Who had suddenly revealed Himself?

"Eve? Are you okay?"

"Oh, yeah, Jules," Eve said, looking up, hoping her face didn't betray her feelings. "I'm sorry; I'm just feeling very uncomfortable right now." She rubbed her expanding stomach for effect. "I am happy for you. You sound happy, and you deserve it."

"But I don't deserve it," Juliette practically yelled. "I am a huge sinner and fall completely short of God's expectations. But that's okay. I accept that Christ died to save me. I am so relieved to know that Jesus paid the price for my sins and I can live eternally in spite of my past sins." Juliette grasped Eve's hands and squeezed them tight. "And the best thing, Evie, is that He has washed me clean. I am made pure again with God. You can be, too!"

"I can be what?" Eve scrunched her forehead and studied her sister. Was Juliette mad? Sure, maybe Juliette could be made pure again by some spiritual process—losing her virginity was forced on her. Eve had lost hers willingly to a man she thought loved her. And now she bore the marks and belly of a tramp, where the rest of the world was concerned. She would never be pure again—not with a child in her body or her arms.

"You can be pure again," Juliette repeated. "God can make you white as snow. I'm not an expert yet, but I can let you know what to pray if you'd like."

Eve winced. Who was this Juliette, and where was the skeptical sister she had always loved? Her hippie sister had been replaced with a Jesus cheerleader, it seemed. Was she for real about everything? A week after her conversion, did she really know what she was talking about?

"Look, Juliette, I don't think—"

A voice came from behind them and saved Eve from having to turn her sister down. "Girls! There you are! Come on. Pete will be here any minute, and we need to get dinner rolling," their father called. Eve let out a sigh of relief that she could get away from Juliette's offer to make her pure again. *As if that could happen.*

Right on cue, a car pulled up in the driveway. Pete and his fiancée, Linda, had arrived for the Christmas Eve service and dinner after. Eve's cousin, Pete, had been raised more like an older brother to her and her siblings. He was as tall as her father, close to six feet, and had the same curls Juliette had, except his were sandy blond like his father's had been. At twenty-five years old, Pete was just as athletic as he was in high school. And he was still in high school—as the boy's basketball coach and gym teacher. He loved working with kids, and the kids loved him—or at least the girls did. Rumor had it that all the girls at his school were in mourning over Mr. Walker's impending marriage to the eclectic art teacher, Linda Mint.

As they got out of the car, Eve studied the woman Pete would marry come summer. Linda was nice; Eve had met her several times before. She was a stunning woman of about twenty-two and was in her first year of teaching. Her bleached blonde hair was piled high on her head, and her sky-blue eyes were lined thick. Eve thought her skirt was about three inches too short. But Harvey and Abby Nicholas loved her because she made Pete happy, and she could recite Scripture like it was nobody's business. Even with her outrageous appearance, Linda seemed to be a wonderful girl; and Eve knew Pete wouldn't marry anyone who didn't share the faith in God that he had. Eve figured that now Juliette and Linda would get along just fine.

"Evie!" Pete cried out. "Look at you. You're a whale!" He trotted up to her and threw his arms around her. He had seen her at Thanksgiving, and she didn't think she had grown that much since then.

"Thanks a lot, Petey," she said with a scowl. Her cousin's presence was not improving her mood.

"Aw, Evie, you know I love you. You look wonderful—huge, but wonderful. How's our little football player?" he teased. He crouched down to her middle and spoke, "Hey there, Buddy! I'm your uncle Pete. I'm gonna teach you to play ball!"

"What if it's a girl?" Eve protested.

"Girls can play ball. I taught you, didn't I?" Eve had to laugh at that. She loved Pete tremendously.

"Let's go in," Juliette said, waving them toward the door. "We've been waiting for you."

The entire family enjoyed an afternoon together, just the way Eve remembered from her childhood. Her parents had gone to Respite Baptist Church before the rest of the family to get set up, so the kids piled into Pete's old Chevrolet and headed to the church for the services. Eve, who was squished in the back with Joey and Juliette, was thankful it was a short drive. Any longer, and she would have been sweating despite the cool December air.

Inside the church, Eve waddled to the family's pew—second row on the left—and immediately sat down. Joey immediately sat next to her, a protective vigil he had kept for months now.

When Eve's condition became apparent to the church parishioners, her family had tried their best to be positive. They had all agreed not to lie about what had happened to Eve. But still the stares and whispers came. Some people even pointed at Eve as they talked behind their backs. Harvey had done his best to discourage the gossip. While he and Abby had gone so far as to speak with several people personally about their behavior, Joey had taken it upon himself to sit beside Eve and stand guard over her, so nobody would dare to say anything to her personally.

The service began with one of Eve's favorite Christmas songs, "Silent Night." She stood with the rest of them to sing. The song had newfound meaning for her with motherhood knocking on her door. Except, she was no round virgin like Mary was. She was used and cast aside. *Oh, Eve,* she thought to herself as she sang from memory, *why must every little thing be a reminder? Why does everything remind you of*

Jesse? Of what he did and what you did willingly? Stop tormenting yourself, *and enjoy the music!* Oh, how she wanted to enjoy herself again, like she did as a child. Singing Christmas carols and hymns was one of her favorite memories from years past.

As she settled into her seat and tried to get comfortable, her father launched into his sermon. Her father was an excellent speaker and always held his congregation's attention during his hour on the pulpit. Harvey Nicholas was always relaxed, always ready, and always willing. Eve loved that about her father. She just wished she could share in his faith.

Eve didn't understand how God could have turned on her. Here she was—just nineteen years old, and she was about to become an unmarried mother. Most of polite society had turned their backs on her or ignored her. Some people who didn't ignore her were downright rude to her, and she would have preferred being ignored. And the man she had loved had left her and their child to marry someone else without second thought. Where was God and His love in all that?

She believed that there was a God; she just didn't believe that He was kind and powerful. Eve didn't believe that God loved her and cared for her. She didn't think God did what was best for her. The God she had been experiencing was One of anger and vengeance, like when He killed everyone in the Great Flood and destroyed Sodom. This was just a new and modern vengeance, and Eve didn't appreciate it at all. She loved her baby—she could never deny that—but she certainly did not love the God Who had allowed her situation to take place.

Juliette watched as her sister lumbered up to their shared bedroom. Soon, she would move into Joey's old room with a newborn crying out for his mother. Juliette was not jealous of Eve's predicament, but she also warmed with the idea that one day she would also have someone depend on her the way Eve's child would depend on Eve.

She sat on the couch and stretched out her feet. Tomorrow would be Christmas, and it was tradition for the family to stay up and play board games and eat cookies until nearly midnight and one by one they would make their way to their own beds. Joey pulled down several game options and swiped Juliette's feet from the couch to make room for himself. Soon, the rest of the family gathered around them.

They started with Monopoly; and when Alisa lost out, she wearily made her way up the stairs. A round of Scrabble sent Joey to the den he and Pete would be sharing that night, since Linda would be in Joey's room.

But before beginning another game, Harvey asked to have a word with Pete and Linda. "It's about Eve," he said, sternly.

Juliette, who had been feeling drowsy, was suddenly alert. What about Eve?

"What's wrong, Pop?" Pete used his pet name for Harvey; Uncle had never seemed to fit for the man who sacrificed and raised him from an infant.

Juliette watched her father sit close to her mother and put her arm around her. "This is something Abby and I have debated on for a while now, but we feel we need to ask," he began. "As you know, Eve will have her baby in a few short weeks, and we're still unsure what will happen with the two of them."

Juliette sat up, alarmed. "But, Dad, you said you wouldn't let anything happen to them, that you wouldn't send Eve away."

"And we didn't, Juliette," he responded calmly but firmly. His forehead wrinkled, and Juliette could see the lines of age beginning to show around his mouth. "But that does not mean we are set in what to do once the baby arrives."

Pete interjected, "What do you mean?"

Abby cleared her throat and spoke. "Eve is still a girl. She's not married, and she can't raise this child on her own. Sure, we can help her, but we would rather see her go to college, maybe find a career and a stable young man. She can't do those things with a baby on her hip."

Juliette's blood boiled, and her hands felt clammy. What were her parents suggesting? Would they force Eve to hand over her baby once he was born? Juliette could not speak, however, so she prayed for clarity. She prayed for Eve to keep her child no matter what; she vowed to help them however she could. Juliette knew from the instant they found out about the pregnancy that she would give up her own freedom to help her sister raise the child.

"We don't want the baby being raised elsewhere; we know that," Harvey picked back up. "And with your impending marriage, we thought perhaps you two might consider adopting the child yourselves. We know it will be born a little before the wedding, but we know a nice family who would keep him or her until you can bring the baby home."

Juliette blinked. They wanted Pete and Linda to raise the baby? Right under Eve's nose? She looked to her cousin and slightly shook her head; he could not accept.

"Wait, wait, wait," Pete said, sitting forward. He pulled his arm from around his fiancée and put his elbows on his knees. "You want my future bride and myself to raise what will essentially be my niece or nephew?"

"Yes," Abby said softly. "We just thought—"

"You just thought that since you did it for my parents, I would do it for Eve? That since you raised me, we would just step in and raise Eve's child?" Pete was angry, and he ran his hands through his sandy-colored curls.

"No, sweetie," Abby reasoned. "That's not why. We thought that since you were getting married, you would be the most logical choice. And this way, Eve could see the baby and know it was okay."

Finally, Linda spoke up. "But we're not married yet. Not until the baby will be . . . what? Almost five months old? And it's not fair for Eve to watch her child be raised and not be a part of his or her life." She shook her head, her blonde locks swaying. "I'm saying no. Absolutely not. It's not fair to us; it's not fair to Eve; and it's not fair to that innocent baby. I respect you, Mr. and Mrs. Nicholas, and the hardship you're under, but this is not the answer."

Juliette could have thrown her arms around Linda in gratitude had she been able to move. She was still shocked and frozen in place from her parent's suggestion.

Abby nodded, still calm and collected. "We thought you would say that, and you have every right to say no; we just want what's best for both our daughter and our grandchild. We don't want to see either one suffer." She sniffled quietly and quickly wiped her eyes with the tips of her fingers.

Linda smiled and took Abby's hand in hers. "They won't suffer. I promise you that. We will help Eve and the baby as much as we can. We will help all of you, won't we, Pete?"

"Of course. We would love for the rug rat to spend the night, so we can spoil him or her the way an aunt and uncle should. We will help as much as possible. But Eve would never forgive any of us if we did this. And from the look on Jules' face, neither would she." He glanced at Juliette, who still sat rigid in her seat.

The foursome looked to Juliette. She took a deep breath and stared them down. After meeting each gaze, she stood and said, "Let's never talk about this again. Do not let Eve know this idea was even brought up. She loves that baby and would protect it with her life if someone tried to take it—even you, Petey." She looked to him. "But thank you, both of you, for defending her."

She went to the kitchen for a glass of water and a chance to cool down when her mother trailed in after her. "I'm sorry, Juliette," she said, tears still in her eyes. "We don't want Eve to have to give her child up. We just want her to live life to its fullest, to go to college. We want her to reach the full potential God has for her."

Juliette, still new in her faith, challenged her mother, "Maybe being a mother is what God intends her to be, Mom. Give her a chance."

With that, she gulped down the water in her glass, set it down, and marched upstairs to her bed. She sat a moment and stared at her twin, her hair braided out of her face, her body contorted to find a comfortable position. Juliette offered a quick prayer for sleep and peace over her sister and lay down in her own bed, wishing sleep to come quickly.

Swept Away

IT WAS THE DAY BEFORE Valentine's. Just days before her due date, Eve sat at the end of her bed and studied her new room. A small, wooden crib had been painted white and set opposite her bed next to the closet door. A little dresser waiting to be filled with baby clothes was next to it. Eve was thankful that her parents had allowed Joey to move into the attic and her to have his room. She missed sleeping in a room with Juliette, but supposed it had to happen at some point. Soon, she would be a mother and have all the responsibilities that came with that title.

Eve thought about Jesse. Before he left, she thought they would be married by now and living on their own. Perhaps in a little apartment near the beach. Now, here it was Valentine's Day, and she had no man in her life except her father and brothers. Eve wondered if she would ever have a valentine again. But regardless, Eve knew that her child would be her valentine for life, even if a man never entered that picture.

Her mother slipped in quietly and sat beside her. Without speaking, Abby slid her arm around her eldest daughter's shoulder. Eve leaned back against her mother, knowing it would soon be she who cradled her child. She wanted this last chance to be the child before she became a mother. Abby reached her hand up and smoothed Eve's flaming locks against her head. Eve felt tears begin to fall down her cheeks at the comforting gesture of her mother.

"I'm so sorry, Mom," she said, her voice barely above a whisper.

"Well, you are making me a grandmother before my days, but I'm looking forward to it. I can't wait to spoil my grandson or granddaughter," Abby said with a smile. She always knew just what to say to ease Eve's unsettled mind.

"I wish I knew if it were a he or a she." Eve sighed.

"Many mothers have a sort of intuition about it. When I was having you and Juliette, you two let me know that you were girls."

"We did? How?" Eve sat up and turned to her mother.

"Your father and I were talking about what to name you. I said maybe you were both boys, and one of you kicked in protest. Then when I suggested one boy and one girl, I got more kicking. So, when I said two girls and got calm in response, I knew you would both be girls. But a lot of mothers-to-be seem to just sense it," Abby explained.

"How would I do that?"

Eve turned more toward her mother, her stomach protruding out before her. Abby laughed and smiled. "When you think of the baby, do you usually call it a her or a him in your head?"

"I usually think her or she, actually," Eve said. She perked up as she thought about it. "I almost always think feminine, girl. Does that mean it's a girl?" She could hardly contain her delight. A girl! How fun that would be!

"Well, we can't be sure until she—or he—arrives. But if your mother's intuition is right, we'll be adding more pink to the Nicholas household," Abby said and laughed.

As Eve contemplated frilly dresses and pigtails, the doorbell rang downstairs. Eve could hear her brother Joey open the door.

"Evie? Mom?" he called up the stairs. "You have a guest." *His voice is higher pitched than usual*, Eve thought. Something wasn't right.

Abby looked to her daughter. She also sensed that Joey's voice wasn't normal. "Expecting anyone?"

"No, I'm not." Eve shook her head.

They stood and quickly exited Eve's room and headed down the stairs. Eve never expected who greeted her in the living room.

"Dee?" Jesse's sister stood in front of them, just inside the door. A curvy girl, she was about Eve's height with the same dark complexion as her brother. It was a wintery Tuesday morning, but Dee was dressed for spring in a bright, flowery skirt. Her face was anything but bright and flowery, though. Eve could see pain in Dee's eyes; it was obvious coming to her house was upsetting for Jesse's sister.

Eve was immediately mindful of her condition and tried to cover her stomach with her arms. It was a useless effort, she knew, but she tried all the same.

Dee didn't hesitate. "I'm sorry to just come unannounced. But I knew I needed to come right away."

Always the hostess, Abby immediately motioned to the couch. "Dee, is it? Please have a seat. How can we help you?"

Dee took a seat on the couch, but stayed perched on the edge as if she were ready to flee at any moment. Abby whispered to Joey to get a pitcher of water and some glasses before sitting across from Dee in her favorite reading chair. Eve was unsure if she should sit in the other chair or on the couch next to Dee. Finally, she opted for the chair to be nearer her mother.

"Again, Mrs. Nicholas, I'm sorry to barge in like this. We haven't met. I'm Dee, Jesse Washington's sister."

Abby's face showed her surprise at who she was. "Oh," was all she managed to say.

Joey set a pitcher of water and three glasses on the coffee table. Abby muttered thanks before he nervously fled the room. Eve wished she could do the same. She still tried to position her arms so that her bulging middle wasn't so obvious. She had no idea if Jesse had told his family about getting her pregnant.

Dee shook her head. "I'm sorry I haven't come before, Eve. I knew all along about what Jesse had done to you and your baby. I wasn't sure, but I see it's not come yet."

A sigh escaped Eve's lips. "Not yet," was all she managed, while she felt a mad blush overtake her cheeks. "Wha—what are you doing here?"

"I just come from Orangeburg back home. There ain't an easy way to tell you this, so I'll just come out with it," Dee said. She took a deep breath and exhaled. "Jesse was in a protest last week that went wrong. He got shot."

A sudden wave of emotions washed over Eve, and she gasped. Her eyes filled with tears as the struggle between pain and relief tore into her. "No!" Even if she hated Jesse, a part of her would always love him. Her mother's hand found hers and held on tight.

Dee wiped tears from her eyes. "His funeral was just yesterday. I came home and right here this morning," she said. "They was fighting peaceably for integration at a local bowling alley. One of Jesse's people thought peaceful wasn't working, so he threw something at the police." Dee's chin quivered as she spoke, and her voice choked. "The police thought they were being shot at and opened fire. Almost thirty people were injured, and a handful were killed. Jesse was one of them."

Eve clutched her own stomach. "No," she murmured. "No, no, no." Tears fell down her face, and she shook her head. Despite everything, she had always hoped that Jesse would at least want to know his child one day. Now, that chance would never come. She was overcome with pain and grief.

Her mother cleared her throat. "Thank you for telling us, Dee. I know this is not an easy time for you. We're so sorry for your loss."

Dee attempted a half-hearted smile. "Thank you, Mrs. Nicholas. Thankfully, out of about two hundred protesters, only those thirty or so were hurt. It could have been worse, I suppose." She paused a second and took a heavy breath. "Now, I need to tell you that apparently Jesse's wife, Frances, knew about you, Eve."

Drying her tears, Eve stopped and looked at Dee. "What? She did?"

"No matter how brave he was where civil rights was concerned, Jesse was a coward with you and a coward with Frances," Dee said matter-of-factly and with anger apparent in her voice. "About a month after the wedding, he sat Fran down one day and said that he'd had a girl up here that he'd got in a family way. They was already married, and Jesse knew Fran was a God-fearing woman and would never divorce him."

Eve let out a long breath, not realizing she'd been holding it in.

Dee pulled an envelope out of her small purse and held it tight. "Fran is a real nice girl, Eve. She said she don't hold nothing against you, that it was Jesse's fault for lying to the both of you. She comes from people who want to see equality for all people and who don't mind the races mixing. And she comes from money, I tell you. She doesn't want to see you and a half-black baby left with nothing because of a bad decision and a gunshot. She wanted me to give this to you."

With that, Dee reached her hand out, and Abby took the small, white envelope from Dee's hand and passed it to Eve. She turned it over in her hands, unsure if she should open it right away or wait.

Her mother seemed to be reading her mind. "Go on, Evie; open it."

Slowly, Eve tore open the flap. She pulled out a small note and read it aloud. "Miss Nicholas, please accept this for you and your child. I'm very sorry for what Jesse has put you both through. If he were still with us, I would have asked him to give this to you himself. Don't worry. I want nothing in return, and I will not contact you again. Sincerely, Frances Washington." She pulled out another slip of paper and unfolded it. "This is a check for five thousand dollars!"

Eve was shocked. "Fran said you was to use it for the child's education and whatever else you two need," Dee explained. "She said it was donations from people and some of her own money."

"I can't take this, Dee," Eve said. She put the check back into the envelope and thrust it back out toward the other woman. "I can't take this from Frances."

"She said she has plenty more money, trust me. She comes from a family with money, and she won't miss this. I promise you, Eve." Dee's hands stayed firmly folded in her lap. "She insisted that Jesse's child deserved more in life than Jesse gave it."

"I don't know what to say," Eve said, her hand retreating back to her own lap, the check clutched tightly inside her fist.

Abby shifted and finally spoke. "You say thank you, Eve." She turned toward Dee. "Please tell your sister-in-law thank you on behalf of my grandchild. Her generosity shows what a wonderful Christian lady she is. And we are very sorry for the loss you all have experienced."

"Thank you, Mrs. Nicholas. And I'm sorry again, Eve, for the way my brother did you wrong," Dee said. "I know I have no right to ask, but when the baby comes, can I bring a few trinkets by? I would like to meet my niece or nephew."

Eve smiled. "Of course, Dee. I'm due any day now, so feel free to come by in a few weeks. I would like for you to meet the baby."

Dee stood; Abby followed suit; and Eve struggled to stand. When she was upright, Abby showed Dee to the door. Many thanks were murmured among the women, and Dee disappeared.

With the door firmly shut, Eve stared at the check. Five thousand dollars—she couldn't believe it. She was happy to have the money, but wondered if it was worth the life of her child's father, Dee's brother, and the husband of a kind woman she would never meet.

"Why don't you go upstairs and rest for a while, Evie?" Abby suggested. "We can talk about this entire thing later, okay?"

Eve nodded and went upstairs. She slipped into bed and cried until her entire bed shook. Sleep did not come. The child in her womb fought with the rest of her body, making Eve's body feel as beat up as her mind.

After two hours of lying awake and in pain, Eve went back down the stairs to her find her mother. She found her absentmindedly wiping down the kitchen counter with a rag. Eve knew her mother's mind was reeling almost as much as her own.

When her mother looked at her, Eve asked, "What do I do with this money?"

"Let's go to the bank and start a savings account for the baby. You can use some when the baby is born for clothes and other small things, but be sure to save most of it for her education and future," Abby said sternly. "But first, let's sit down and talk about Jesse."

Eve nodded. She sat and sighed, rubbing her belly the whole time. The baby must have sensed her mixed emotions because it was none too happy. The baby stretched and strained Eve's back while its feet battled with her rib cage. Eve winced in pain as she fought to find a comfortable position.

"Are you okay?"

She nodded, then sighed. "I don't know. I'm so uncomfortable. But if you mean about Jesse . . . I still don't know, Mom." A tear slipped down her cheek, and she tried to hold more back. "Regardless, we were through. He said he would never claim my child as his own. But the fact that he told his . . . his wife means he did care. I'm very sad he died. I hurt for Dee and Jesse's family. And I hurt that this baby will never know the kinder side of her father. But at least she or he won't know the unkind side."

Abby just nodded, while Eve spoke everything that went through her mind. When she stopped, Eve looked to her mother. "Well, Mom?"

"It's a lot of emotions, I'm sure," Abby said. "I can't pretend to know how you feel, Evie. I know you won't miss the Jesse who left you, but I know you will miss the Jesse who loved you. And I know you will mourn for your child's loss. I imagine that's much the way I felt being left with Pete. Anything else you want to say about this?"

Eve felt searing pain rip through her body, and her stomach tightened up like it was constricting around her child. "One thing," she panted. "I think I'm about to have this baby," and she cried out in pain as her body doubled over.

"Oh! Eve!" Abby was kneeling at her side immediately. "Tell me what you're feeling."

"Pain, Mom! My back is in pain." Eve gasped for breath. "And my stomach feels like it's squeezing tight."

Another jolt of pain went through Eve's body. "Mom, help me!" She struggled to get air into her lungs. The tightness in her stomach pushed the baby's feet up into her ribs and left no room for her lungs to fill.

"Joey! Joey, call your father to get Juliette and Alisa! We're having a baby!" Abby ran her hand over Eve's forehead. "It's okay, sweetie. It's okay. Women have babies every day. You sit here, and I'll run upstairs and get your hospital bag, okay?"

"Hurry, Mom," Eve cried. She felt sweat spring up all over her body. She was scared to death. Where was Juliette? She was supposed to be by her side for this. The pamphlet she read said her water was supposed to break before she had a baby. Had it broken yet? She had no idea. She just knew that every few minutes, her entire body contorted and spasmed, and Eve was sure she would die. Where was her mother with that bag?

Eve felt another contraction begin. "Mom!"

Juliette rushed into the hospital, her father and sister on her heels. Her father had called the bakery in an absolute fit. "Eve's having the baby! Close the shop; I'll be right there."

Juliette was in the middle of lunch at the bakery. She had four customers eating in the dining room and several more in line to order their fresh sandwiches and cookies. When she had gotten off the phone with her father, she quickly announced that everyone had to leave— they were about to have a baby. Almost everyone in the shop was a regular and knew the family. The crowd erupted in applause and quickly vacated the premises, while Juliette and Alisa closed up. Fred, Abby's assistant, would have to take over for a few days, while the rest of the family was concentrating on Eve and the baby.

At the nurse's station, Juliette breathlessly called out, "Eve Nicholas, please. She's having a baby!"

The nurse nodded her head, the white cap snugly fit over her graying hair. "Room 315. Down the hall to the left, fifth door on your right," she said.

Juliette, Harvey, and Alisa fled down the hall and found Joey pacing outside the door. "Mom's in there with Eve and the doctor right now," he said. "I'm going to go call Pete now that you're all here." Joey fished a dime out of his jeans pocket and ran a lanky hand through his dark hair while he retreated toward the pay-phones. Juliette watched her brother for a moment and was so proud of him. Even though he was very quiet, he loved his family fiercely, and Juliette could tell that seeing Eve in pain caused Joey pain of his own.

When the door opened, Juliette turned back around. A doctor in a white lab coat and thick glasses came out with Abby on his heels. He nodded to the family and walked down the hallway. Abby closed the door behind her.

"Eve is resting, but she is in labor," she said. "Her water broke right as we got out of the car in the parking lot. Poor Joey—I've never seen him turn so red. Eve was none too pleased either. But we're going to have a baby!"

Juliette was impatient. "Let me in to see Eve. I need to be with her."

"And she's asking for you, sweetie," Abby reassured her. "But I do need to speak with you first. Alisa, sweetheart, will you take this money and go find Joey and get some drinks? We'll be here awhile."

"Aw, I never get to hear the good stuff," Alisa complained as she took the money from her mother. She stalked off in the direction her brother had gone a few moments before.

"What's going on?" Harvey asked. "Is everything okay?"

"Jesse's sister came by today to see Eve," Abby started.

"Is that why she went into labor? Is Jesse causing trouble?" Anger stirred in Juliette, and she was ready to come to her sister's aid in any way needed.

"No, no, just listen," her mother calmed her. "Apparently, Jesse was shot last week, accidentally. It was a fatal shot. Dee came to tell Eve and let her know that Jesse's wife knew about her and the baby."

"Oh, no." Juliette sighed. She knew Eve would have been shocked and upset about Jesse's death. No wonder she had gone into labor. She began praying for Jesse's family.

"She also brought Eve a check. Mrs. Washington—Jesse's wife— wrote Eve a check for her and the baby. Five thousand dollars."

Harvey gasped. "What?" Juliette watched her father's jaw drop much like her own. "Are you sure?"

Abby drew the check out of her back pocket and showed her husband. Juliette peeked over his arm. Sure enough, a check was made to Eve Nicholas from the account of Mrs. Frances Washington in the amount of five thousand dollars. When Harvey nodded, Abby tucked the check back into her pocket.

"Is Eve okay? I mean aside from having a baby," Harvey asked.

"She's confused. She said she's not sad for herself but for Jesse's family and for the baby," Abby said quietly. "She said earlier that she was glad that Jesse had told his wife about her and the baby, that it meant he did care."

"I need to see her," Juliette said as she pushed past her mother. She opened the door as slowly as she could and pulled a chair next to Eve. Her twin was resting, her eyes closed and her breathing light. Juliette cautiously watched her stomach rise and fall.

Eve's eyes fluttered open when Juliette sat beside her. "Jules, it's about time," she said, her voice heavy and tired. "Dee came to the house, Jules. Jesse—"

"Shh, I know," Juliette said as she rubbed her hand over her sister's arm. "I know; Mom told me. I'm so sorry, Eve."

Another contraction came, and Eve grimaced at the pain, but did not cry out. When it was over, Eve struggled to sit up more. "Frances, his wife, wrote me a check for five thousand dollars. For the baby and me."

"Did she? What will you do with it?" Juliette acted nonchalant, not wanting to cause her sister distress. She picked a damp washcloth off the nightstand and wiped Eve's face.

"Ah, Mom told you that, too?" Eve guessed. Juliette nodded. "I don't know what to do with it. What do you think?"

"Let's talk about that after this child makes his entrance, okay?"

Eve nodded in agreement. She flinched again from her body preparing to deliver her child. When the pain subsided, she spoke. "Jules, please get the nurse. I feel like I need to push."

"Oh, my goodness," Juliette said as she rose into a panic. "Okay. It's okay, Evie. I love you. I'll be right back." She rushed for the door and burst through. She grabbed her mother's arm. "Mom! Eve wants to push! Help!"

Abby raised an eyebrow and glanced at Harvey. He quickly stepped down the hallway to the nurse's station. Abby and Juliette rushed back inside to Eve.

"Okay, sweetie. You feel like you need to push?" Abby sat next to her daughter and held her hand. Eve nodded. "Don't push just yet, sweetheart. Just hang tight a minute for the nurse to come in."

Tears swam in Eve's eyes as another contraction tore through her body. Juliette cried for her sister. She wanted to help, but this was one thing she could do nothing about, so she prayed. *Lord, please help Eve. Please help her in this time. Ease her pain; help bring this baby through safely. I don't know what else to ask for. Just help her. I can't do it; only You can. I know she's not receptive to You right now, but she's hurting. I understand all too well that pain. Use it to draw her to You.*

Juliette had to conclude her prayer when Eve yelled out, "Juliette! Help me!" She was by her sister's side in an instant, holding her hand, crying with her. "Jules, please help me. Momma, help me," Eve implored.

"There's nothing we can do, sweetheart," Abby said in a soothing voice. "We're praying for you, Eve; but otherwise, this is your show."

A nurse burst through the door and quickly pushed Juliette and her mother out of the room. Eve called out after them; Juliette pressed her ear to the door, tears flowing down her face.

Abby wrapped her matronly arms around her. "She'll be okay, Juliette. I promise. Women give birth every day. I managed to birth both you girls at the same time and then your brother and sister after. Eve will be okay."

Wiping tears from her cheeks, Juliette nodded. "I know, Mom. But it's not every day my sister gives birth. I feel every ounce of pain she's feeling."

With a sigh, Abby softly said, "Oh, my twins. I never understood how you two felt what the other experienced. I always thought your aunt Reba and I were close, but it's nothing like you two."

The nurse came back out. "She's ready. I'm going to go get Doctor Brown." She swished her way past the family. "Shouldn't be too much longer now."

Juliette snuck back into her sister's room for a brief moment. "Evie? The nurse said it would not be too much longer now. Are you okay?"

Eve was crying, and her face was red as she struggled through another contraction. "No, I'm not okay, Juliette. I'm about to have a baby, and it hurts. And when this baby is born, I have no husband to go home to. As much as I hate Jesse right now for leaving and even for dying, I wish he was here. This is his child, and he should be standing outside that door."

Juliette held her sister's hand and leaned in close. "I know. I'm so sorry. But you're not alone. I'm here. Mom and Dad are here. And this baby is about to be here."

"Stay in the room with me, Jules," Eve said as she breathed heavily.

"I don't think they'll let me, Evie."

The door swung open again, and a team of people in white coats descended on the room. A stern-looking man Juliette guessed was Doctor Brown came to the bed. "Sorry, Miss. You will have to wait outside."

"Please, let my sister stay," Eve begged.

"I'm sorry, Miss Nicholas," a nurse with a sympathetic look said as she ushered Juliette from her seat.

"I love you, Eve; I'll be right outside," Juliette said with a smile. "I can't wait to see the baby!"

"I love you," Eve called after her as the door shut.

A tense hour passed, Juliette pacing the entire time right outside the door. At every sound, she stilled and held her breath, waiting. Finally, she heard what she had been waiting for—the first cries of a new baby. They were small but piercing.

Quietly, she called for her parents. "Dad! Mom!" She waved them over to her. They all listened to the soft cries that came from the room and took a collective sigh.

It was another thirty minutes before the door finally opened and a nurse emerged with a tiny isolette on wheels. She paused for a moment, so the family could see the new baby. Juliette peered at the fresh bundle and saw a tiny nose and mouth peeking out at her. It was the most beautiful sight she had ever seen.

"Is it a boy or a girl?" Alisa asked, breaking the silence.

"The new mom asked that she be the one to tell you," the nurse said with a smile. "Go on in and see her. We'll bring the baby back in after we get . . . uh . . . the baby cleaned up."

The rest of the family filed into the room where Eve recovered, while Juliette watched the nurse wheel the baby down the hall. She couldn't help but feel like a piece of her heart went with them. When they were out of sight, Juliette entered her sister's room.

Eve looked worn. She seemed to have aged five years in the ninety minutes since they had last seen her. Her hair looked matted, and she had dark circles under her eyes. But she also looked happy—immensely happy.

"There you are, Jules. Now I can tell you all. The baby is a girl!" She beamed, despite her fatigue.

Cheers erupted from the family, and everyone gave Eve a light hug. Juliette waited until everyone else had hugged Eve, then approached her bed. She got close to her twin sister, and she stroked her sister's damp, auburn hair and smiled.

"I'm going to name her Willow," Eve said quietly. Everyone heard her, but she was talking only to Juliette.

Juliette smiled at Eve. "I love it," she said. "Willow is a beautiful name." Juliette heard murmurs of approval from the rest of her family.

Rolling Waves

TWO MONTHS LATER, AND LIFE was completely different for the entire household. Eve and Willow had settled into a routine with the rest of the household coming and going. They always seemed to be in a rush to Eve, who was taking her life one day at a time.

She peered down at her tiny daughter and studied her. Her hair was already curly and black, but Eve could have sworn a few strands looked red like her own. Willow's eyes were dark, the bridge of her nose wide, and her mouth adorable and pouty. Her arms and legs had the appropriate amount of rolls and dimples. Eve thought her daughter's feet were the best part, and she loved to kiss them. Overall, Eve thought Willow looked like Juliette, except with a wider nose and already tanned skin. She was beautiful.

A knock on her door brought Eve out of her reverie. "Come in," she answered.

"Want to come to the store today, Evie?" Her mother padded softly into her room and gently rubbed the skin of her granddaughter's arm. "Now that Easter's over, we shouldn't be too busy today."

Eve smiled at her mother. "Sure, Mom, why not? I could use some time out of the house."

They got into the car, Eve cradling Willow in her arms, and went to Abby's Sweet Treats, where Juliette and Fred were already hard at work. Juliette had been doing more and more at the bakery over the past two months. She had even signed up for a baking class at the college and was enjoying mixing batters and creating new recipes. Eve was happy her sister had found something she enjoyed so much, but she still felt a little jealous that her sister enjoyed such freedom, while she did not. But Eve knew she wouldn't trade her child for anything in the world.

At the store, Abby pulled a tiny Moses basket from the back seat, so the baby would have a spot of her own while Eve worked. Not that they would be busy enough for four people working, but Eve knew she would not be doing too much. Baking was not her calling as it was her mother's and, apparently, her sister's. But she could clean the dining area and crack eggs with the best of them.

Inside, Willow was laid in her basket, where she wouldn't get stepped on or forgotten, and left to doze while Eve started washing windows for her mother. The April morning was bright and warm— perfect, in Eve's opinion. She sat her small bucket of soapy water on the ground, plunged her washrag into it, and began scrubbing the fingerprints and dirt from the glass.

Just as she began reaching up to the top of the windows, she was startled by a man's voice. "Eve? Is that you?"

She whirled around to see a tall man with blond hair standing before her. It took her a few moments to register who he was. Medical student and Jesse's old friend, Patrick McKenzie stood a few feet from Eve. Immediately, Eve put a soapy hand to her hair. She was disheveled with her hair in a sloppy ponytail, her clothes mismatched, and her mid-section still much thicker than she would have liked.

Patrick, for his part, looked impeccable. His nearly white-blond hair was parted and combed; he wore a basic, brown suit with oxford shoes; and even his fingernails looked well-groomed. Eve had never felt so frumpy in her life.

"Do you remember me? Patrick McKenzie?"

Eve nodded and tried to turn back to the window. "Oh, I remember you alright. You were Jesse's friend. I appreciate your help with my sister last year, but I would rather forget all about Jesse Washington," she told him.

Patrick cocked his head to the side. "Why is that? Did you two break things off?"

"Jesse was killed in a protest earlier this year, Patrick," she told him, trying to keep her emotions flat. "But we were over long before that."

Patrick shifted uncomfortably. "I'm so sorry to hear that, Eve."

"Yes, and his wife was sorry, too," she said with a quiver in her voice.

"Wife?"

Eve threw her rag into the water, and soap sloshed over her tennis shoes, saturating them. "Yes, his wife. Or did he not tell you when he took you to Charleston last year that he was heading back to Orangeburg to get married? And he left me alone—he left our child without a father!"

Fighting the tears that threatened to come, Eve grabbed the wet rag again and began wiping at the window half-heartedly.

"I'm so confused," Patrick said, taking a step toward her. "Jesse got married? And you had a baby? When was this?"

"He got married last year, just a few weeks after I last saw you. Apparently, I was just for fun," Eve said bitterly. She turned toward Patrick and sat on the wet window ledge, not caring about soaking her clothes. "Willow, my daughter, was born on Valentine's Day—just a week after Jesse was killed at that bowling alley protest."

"Jesse was killed in that protest? I heard about that," Patrick said with surprise. "Did Jesse know you were pregnant?"

Anger boiling, Eve looked up at the man she barely knew. "Of course, he knew. And he left us anyway."

"And you kept the baby anyway? Even though you're now an unmarried girl with a baby?" Eve's stare was answer enough. How dare this man speak to her in such a manner?

Eve moved to stand and go back into the store, but Patrick stopped her. "I'm sorry. I didn't mean for that to sound so bad. I promise I don't judge you at all. I was just curious. Listen," he said as he pulled a business card from a little case, "I'm now a full-fledged doctor. I graduated in December and joined a practice here in Myrtle Beach. I'm a pediatrician, a child doctor. If you ever need anything for your baby, come see me."

"Why should I?" Eve asked coldly.

"I just want to help children. I love children," Patrick said softly.

The door rattled behind them, and Juliette poked her head out the door. "Eve, you are needed inside," she said with a smile. When she spotted Patrick, she narrowed her gaze and ignored him, turning toward to her sister.

"Thanks, Jules," Eve said, picking up her bucket and moving past Patrick. She held the door open. "Are you coming in?"

Patrick came in after her with barely audible thanks, while Eve scurried away toward the sound of her fussy child. She washed the soap off her hands and took her child from her mother's arms. "Thanks, Mom. I got her."

She bounced Willow up and down for a moment while she grabbed a burp cloth. From the corner of her eye, she watched Patrick order scones and coffee. He turned down the bag Abby offered him and instead sat at one of the round tables in the dining area. His gaze kept coming back to Eve in quick glances, while she hesitated going to the back to feed Willow.

Juliette came behind Eve and whispered, "What's he doing back here?" Eve knew her twin did not trust Patrick McKenzie to keep her secret.

"Eating breakfast, I suppose," Eve offered as she turned to face her sister. "He said he's come back to the beach to work as a pediatrician. He didn't know about Jesse," she added.

Juliette looked over Eve's shoulder nervously. "I don't like him here."

"Neither do I," Eve agreed.

Once the baby was fed, Eve put Willow up on her shoulder and began to move about the bakery with newfound ease. She avoided Patrick as he finished his coffee and stood to leave. But he sought her out anyway.

"Listen, Eve, I'm sorry to disturb you further," he began, running his hands through his hair. "I heard that your father is a pastor, and I've been looking for a good church in town. I haven't found one yet."

Eve stopped and switched Willow to a cradled position. "Why would you want to find a church? Don't you have faith in science?"

Patrick cautiously reached his hand out and stroked the baby's soft curls. "She looks like your sister," he commented. "I think God created science. I place my faith in Him."

"Talk to Juliette then," Eve retorted. "I don't have faith in things that aren't in front of me anymore. She can tell you about church."

Just then, Eve's mother approached the pair. "Are you talking about church, Eve? Invite your friend to our church, then." She beamed. "Harvey, my husband, is pastor at Respite Baptist Church. You would love it there . . . " She trailed off. Eve could tell she was fishing for a name.

"Thank you," he said, extending his hand to Abby, who took it eagerly. "I'm Doctor Patrick McKenzie. I met Eve last year. We shared a common, um, friend."

Abby nodded, and her smile faded. "Oh, so you knew Jesse, then? Well, we're just happy to have a healthy little girl, aren't we?" She cooed at her granddaughter. "It's a pleasure to meet you, Doctor McKenzie. I'm Abby Nicholas, Eve's mother. I'll assume you also met Juliette over there?"

Patrick glanced at Juliette, who quickly looked away. He only nodded his head in confirmation.

"Well, come on out Sunday, Doctor," Abby offered. "We would love for you to join us. The Lord delights in those who delight in Him."

Patrick smiled at her, and then shifted his attention back to Eve. "I would love to. Thanks for the invitation. I better get going now."

With that, Patrick wove through the tables and out the door.

"What a nice young man, Evie," her mother said coyly. "And a doctor!"

Eve rolled her eyes. "Mom, I'm nineteen. I have a baby. I do not need a matchmaker. Let me and Willow have some peace. We don't need a man; do we, little one?"

Abby patted her daughter on the arm. "No, but one day you will want one," she told Eve. "Now, give me the baby, and get back to the windows."

Juliette was impressed. Patrick McKenzie had come to the bakery every day since he first saw Eve there and ordered breakfast. On the days Eve was there, he stayed and ate at the table in the back of the dining room. And if she wasn't there, he got his food to go and took it with him. After a week, Juliette was certain the man had a crush on her sister.

But Eve would have no part of it. Patrick reminded her of Jesse, and that brought her pain. Juliette hated to see her sister hurting, but she thought Patrick McKenzie might be just the thing to help her heal. Him and the Good Lord, of course.

She sat in her room a few moments before dinner and looked at the empty side of the room her sister used to occupy. How things had changed in one short year. Their entire lives had been turned upside down. Juliette was grateful for her salvation and for the fussing she heard from elsewhere in the house, but the methods of how God got Eve and herself to these points she had to disagree with.

She made her way down the stairs and began to set the table for the evening's dinner. It was a rare night everybody was home to eat, and Juliette knew her mother liked to take advantage of the opportunities as they arose.

An unexpected knock came to the door right as Abby was calling everyone from their separate corners of the house to the table. "I'll get it," Abby called out, while the rest of the family made their way to the dining room.

Juliette heard her mother greet someone, who began crying hysterically right away. She looked at Joey, who merely shrugged. Their father quickly rose from the table to aid their mother.

Alisa carried Willow into the dining room and said in a hushed whisper, "Boy, is she upset. Just blubbering away!"

"Who is it?" Joey asked.

"Mrs. Herbert," Alisa said with her eyebrows raised.

Juliette froze. Mrs. Herbert? Buzz Herbert's mother? She had continued attending church after Buzz had hightailed it out of South Carolina, and Juliette had done everything in her power to avoid the matronly woman and had so far been successful. Juliette didn't know if she should find out what was going on or run from the entire situation, but either way, she was glued to her seat and not moving.

Eve quickly slipped into the room. "Jules!" She looked alarmed, her emerald eyes wide and scared. She stood with her back against the wall, trying to eavesdrop and not be seen. "Something has happened."

All four of them knew not to go into the living room, where their parents now comforted and talked to Mrs. Herbert in hushed tones. Juliette still felt the need to flee; but instead, she began to pray.

Lord, please, get Mrs. Herbert out of the house. Let Mom and Dad tell her they will visit with her tomorrow or something—anything. I don't know what's going on to upset her so much, and I pray it's not her health because she does seem like a nice enough lady. Too bad she didn't raise her son that way. I can't handle this reminder right now, God. I don't want the truth to come out.

All Juliette heard in response was a tiny Voice in her head murmuring, "The truth will set you free."

Suddenly, she rose from her chair and slowly crept into the living room and faced the mother of the man who had raped her. She said nothing, but watched her own mother pat the woman's back and whisper that they would help her however they could.

Her father looked up at her and Eve standing right behind her. "Girls, this is none of your business; please excuse yourselves."

Juliette felt Eve take her hand and hold on tight. She knew what was about to happen, sensed it, and let her sister know she was just a step away.

"I need to know what's going on," Juliette said calmly, but firmly.

Harvey turned to her. "Really, girls, this is a private matter for Mrs. Herbert."

The plump woman looked at Juliette with a quizzical expression on her face, her red-rimmed eyes narrowed. "You two knew Buzz briefly while he was still here in town; maybe you can vouch for him!"

Juliette felt a shudder go through her body at the mention of Buzz's name. And the idea of vouching for him made her want to vomit. Eve squeezed her hand in reassurance.

Mrs. Herbert continued, "I just received a call. My sweet little boy has been wrongfully arrested. Accused of . . . of . . . hurting girls," she wailed. "Can you imagine? My son? He would never hurt anything, let alone be forceful with a young lady."

A wave of guilt washed over Juliette. Other girls? She had never before considered that Buzz would do this repeatedly and hurt other girls. A sick feeling rose in her stomach as she realized that in the almost year since that night, Buzz had the opportunity to force himself on a different girl each night. There could be hundreds of girls who were attacked because she didn't speak up in the first place.

As she tried to maintain her balance, Juliette took a deep breath. "Yes, he would," she whispered. She didn't think anyone had heard her except Eve.

"What was that, Juliette?" her mother asked as she stood.

"Yes, he would," she said a little louder. "He would hurt people. He . . . he did hurt someone." She stammered out that last sentence.

Now her father rose, his face turning red with anger. "Who?" he demanded. But the answer was already forming in his mind.

Juliette looked her father in the eyes, while tears welled up and spilled over down her cheeks. "Me." The word stuck in her throat. No sound actually came from her mouth, but everybody heard it. It was deafening to Juliette, who immediately crumbled into a heap with Eve standing protectively by her.

When she came to, Juliette could hear crying that was not her own. She shifted her eyes and saw both her mother and Mrs. Herbert crying openly. Juliette felt she had smashed a stained glass window, and the shards had cut deep into everybody in the room. She felt Eve's arms wrapped around her, holding her up. Her sister was whispering that everything would be okay now.

Her father appeared before her and helped her to her feet. His eyes were also red, and he wore an expression of guilt himself. Harvey sat his daughter in a chair and knelt beside her. "Honey, why didn't you tell us? When was this?"

Juliette looked up at her sister, who nodded to her. She looked back at her father. "Um, last year, when he took Evie and me to that party," she said softly. "I was so ashamed. Eve wanted me to tell you; but I just wanted him to disappear, and he did, so I never did anything."

Abby spoke next. She looked from her daughter to Mrs. Herbert. "We would all like to know what happened, Juliette. Please," she said, coming closer to Juliette and sitting on the edge of the coffee table. She took her daughter's hands into her own.

"We went to the party. Eve was talking to some friends," Juliette began. "Buzz—he offered me a drink. I didn't know what it was, but I drank it anyway. It tasted funny, but I still drank it anyway. Then he suggested a walk on the beach, even told Eve that we were going. By the time we got to the pier, everything was fuzzy. I couldn't walk, and . . ." she trailed off, the hot tears rolling down her cheeks and landing on the pink lace of the shirt she wore.

Words eluded her, so Eve finished the story. "I thought something was amiss when Buzz told me they were heading one way and I saw them go the other," she recalled. "After a little while, I began to worry, and Jesse . . . Jesse was at that party, and he went with me. We found her under the pier, bloody and dirty and unable to stand up. Jesse ran for his car and took us to Dee's house to clean up."

"I don't understand why you didn't come home and tell us," Abby said.

"He was the son of a parishioner, a nice boy," Juliette replied, looking at Mrs. Herbert. "I figured you would think I had been loose and maybe deserved it."

Harvey slammed his fist on the mantel. "Nobody, least of all my daughter, deserves to be raped and found under a pier." He turned to Eve. "Why did you not tell us?"

Eve cried over her own memory of that night; Juliette knew that the memory was so much harder for her with Jesse gone. "I made a promise," she said, reaching out to her twin sister. "And I don't break promises to my sister."

Mrs. Herbert cleared her throat, and all eyes turned to her. "I can see that my son duped me as well. I cannot begin to apologize for the harm he has caused your family, Pastor Nicholas," she said. "I thought the accusations from college girls in Tennessee were just for publicity or because they were . . . less than virtuous and needed someone to blame. But I can see now that the pain is real, and my son caused it. I am so very sorry." And with that, Mrs. Herbert walked out the door without saying goodbye.

Juliette felt exhausted. And relieved. It was as if a massive weight had been lifted off her chest. She felt a peace that only God could provide. "What now?" she asked aloud, sniffles still affecting her breathing.

Harvey raked his hands through his graying hair. "We should call the police here and have them get in touch with the police in Tennessee. It's better for you and the other ladies if you're united in your accusations." He shook his head and turned away.

"Do we have to?" Eve asked. "Isn't there a time limit on these things? What about Juliette's well-being? Jules, do you want the whole world to know what happened?"

Juliette's head spun with all the possibilities of what could happen. If she didn't come forward, she could keep her quiet, little life and forget about the whole thing; but Buzz Herbert might get off easier than if she did join in the case. But if she did report it, she would be thrust into the center of what could become a big court case. And Buzz would be held responsible for all the crimes he committed and not get away with a single one.

"I don't want to, but I have to," she said finally. "I have to come forward. I see that now. I'm so sorry, Daddy, that I didn't before. I can see that I was wrong in keeping it a secret."

"We'll go tomorrow morning to the police department and file an official report," Harvey told them. "If you're okay now, let's sit down and eat our supper."

Juliette nodded, and they all made their way into the dining room, where Joey and Alisa quickly sat down.

Alisa eyed Juliette as she rearranged the cold beans on her plate. "I'm sorry, Juliette," she whispered to her sister next to her.

"I am too, Alisa. Thanks," Juliette replied. And she smiled, knowing her family loved her.

The next morning, Juliette and her father went to the police station to see what could be done almost a year after Juliette's innocence was stolen from her.

Churning Waters

EVE WAITED ALL MORNING, REPLAYING the previous night in her head over and over again. Buzz has been arrested for raping other girls, well after her own sister was raped. Why had she not forced Juliette to come forward? Why didn't she tell her parents anyway? So many innocent girls would still be innocent.

She cradled her daughter close to her and whispered, "Promise me you'll tell me if anyone ever hurts you, Willow." The baby gurgled in response.

The car rolled up into the driveway, and Eve watched as her sister and father made their way up the stairs to the front door. Harvey looked angry. Juliette looked defeated.

Eve threw the door open and immediately asked, "What happened? What did they say?"

Juliette sighed. "Not much. They don't take you too seriously when the crime is almost a year old. And I was interrogated about whether or not I was actually raped or I just regretted sleeping with him." Juliette's face turned red, and Eve's heart broke for her.

"I can't believe they actually said that," she commented. Her heart broke for her sister, who hated recalling the events from that night.

Her father added, "They said without a witness, there wasn't much they could do; but they would be in touch with the authorities in Tennessee and see if Juliette could be added to their case."

Eve thought a moment. "What about me? I found her!"

"You're her sister, and you didn't see it happen," her father argued.

"Darn that Jesse Washington. If he had lived, he could testify. Why did he go and die?" Eve said, stamping her foot. The thought of Jesse added to her frustrations.

"Wait," Juliette cried. "Wait. What about Patrick McKenzie?" Her face lit up. "He saw me afterward. He can attest to the state I was in. He's my witness."

Harvey turned toward his daughters. "You mean Doctor McKenzie? I thought he was a friend of Jesse's."

"He was," Eve answered. "And Jesse called him when Juliette refused to go to the hospital. He treated her for some scrapes and bruises. She would not allow him to . . . examine her . . . though."

"Can you call him, Eve, and see if he'd be willing to write out an affidavit about what he saw? That would be a start," their father asked. Eve nodded as he exited the room looking weary.

"This has been a rough year for us all, hasn't it?" Eve said to her twin. "You're accosted; I have a baby. I never thought about the ramifications on Mom and Dad. Or Joe and Alisa either. I know Joey has been teased at school for having a half-black niece." Tears came quickly. "I was so naïve."

"We both were, Evie," Juliette said, comforting her sister. "Listen. We need to do something about this. The cops told us that last year, there were over twenty-seven thousand rapes in the United States and that the number was expected to rise this year. I couldn't believe it. I thought I was alone out there, but I'm not."

"Aside from testifying, what can you do?"

Eve watched her sister pace the living room, her bell bottom blue jeans swishing as she walked. She pulled on a strand of hair as she thought. "I know," she announced. "I'll start a group. A support group for women who have been raped or molested. We can meet at the church and help each other through it."

Eve smiled at her sister. "That's totally awesome, Juliette. What a great idea."

"I need to write these ideas down," Juliette said as she ran up the stairs to her room.

Eve sat with Willow nestled in her arms. She was proud of Juliette. She was overcoming her hurdles—first admitting the rape and now planning to start a support group. Juliette seemed to have an answer for it all.

But it made Eve feel more than inadequate. She had no plans. No careers calling to her. No groups to organize or even join. She supposed she could start a group for unwed mothers, but it would seem like she was riding on Juliette's coattails. She was simply Willow's mother. Nothing more, nothing less. That was her identity now.

With a sigh, she stood and went to the phone and called Patrick's office number. When the nurse picked up, she asked, "Can I leave a message for Doctor McKenzie, please? Will you have him call Eve Nicholas? Tell him it's urgent. Thanks." She hung up and decided to lay Willow down for a nap. Maybe she would join her.

No sooner had she put Willow in her bassinet, the phone rang. She hurried down the stairs to answer it and heard a frantic Patrick on the line.

"Eve? What's wrong? What's so urgent? Is Willow alright?"

She was surprised at his concern. "Um, no. Well, yes," she stammered. "Willow is fine. It's Juliette."

"Juliette? What's wrong with her?"

"She needs your help. Apparently, Buzz Herbert was arrested in Tennessee for rape. Other girls, Patrick. College students, we were told. Juliette told our parents everything, but the police don't believe her. They said they need a witness, but I don't count as one since I'm her sister." She took a breath. "We were hoping you would be willing to help."

"I'm about to get off work. I'll head to your house as soon as I leave," he said, and then he hung up.

Eve would have told him that the visit was unnecessary, but she never had the chance. Instead, she went up to her sister's room and knocked softly.

"Who is it?"

"Don't you know?"

"Come in, Evie," Juliette said as Eve opened the door. Juliette was laying on her back, pen in one hand, paper in the other. Her bell bottom jeans and peasant blouse fanned out around her.

"There was a time we would have known who was on the other side of the door," Eve said. "And there was a time when knocking was completely unnecessary."

Juliette rolled over on her bed to face Eve. "You're right. Everything changed last summer, didn't it?" Eve nodded. "You don't have to knock to come in our—my room," Juliette added. "I miss you."

"I miss you, too," Eve said with a sad smile. Her sister was right. Everything had changed in the last year. They had been preparing to graduate, talking about college and boys. Now they were talking about horrendous crimes and diapers. When had they grown up? Even at nineteen years old, Eve felt ten years older.

"Are you okay?" Juliette asked.

"Yes, just realizing what a year it has been," she admitted. "I called Patrick. He said he would help; but before I could tell him we just need a letter of what he saw, he said he would come right over after work." She fiddled with the hem of her shirt, still a size larger than she would have liked after having Willow.

"He likes you a lot, Eve," Juliette told her. "He comes into the bakery every day. If you're there, his eyes follow you like a lost puppy."

"No," Eve said with a cross look on her face. "It's two things. One, he's a pediatrician, and I'm a potential client since I have a baby. And two, he knew Jesse. I think he feels guilty for not knowing what was going on."

Juliette smiled and shook her head. Her curls bounced all over the place as she did. Eve wished she had gotten some of Juliette's curls. "Nope, Evie, I'm telling you. He has a spectacular crush on you. Don't tell me you can't see it. I think he's in love."

Eve glared at her sister and turned the tables with a laugh. "And how about Mr. Booker Winston? Talk about love!"

Turning on her stomach, Juliette laughed in return. "Booker. He's amazing. And patient. He's barely kissed me all this time. If you count the Fourth of July last year as our first date, we're almost to a year together," she said. "Best of all, he's a God-fearing man who loves me for me. I think he may be the one."

Eve felt a pang in her heart. She attempted a feeble smile for her sister's sake. She was happy for Juliette, of course, but she could not help the feeling of abandonment that washed over her. Jesse, the man she thought was the one for her, was gone. Not just gone, but dead. Married to someone else and dead. Leaving Eve to raise Willow alone.

Eve was not prone to jealousy, but she could feel it creeping up inside her. She was jealous of Juliette. Jealous of how she was getting attention and help for the trauma she had faced last year. What about her own trauma? Was having a baby and losing the man she loved not bad enough? And Juliette was starting a support group, while Eve knew no other young mothers. And Juliette had a man who loved her and honored her. Eve had been used and cast aside.

She went back to the doorway slowly, trying not to let the hurt show on her face. "I'm going to go make some coffee for when Patrick gets here."

"Eve? Are you okay?"

She nodded. "I'm fine, Jules. I just have a lot on my mind is all." She slipped out the door before Juliette could ask anything else.

The doorbell rang just as the percolator huffed its last bit of water. Eve opened the door for Patrick, and he strode in, worry strewn across his face. Eve studied him. Why hadn't she met him first last summer? He was quite tall—at least six feet, Eve estimated. His white-blond hair hung just to his eyes, and his blue eyes were nearly clear. Several light freckles adorned his nose. He looked more like a surfer than a doctor. Eve guessed that all the young ladies who still saw pediatricians were drooling over Doctor McKenzie.

Suddenly aware of her staring, she quickly spoke up. "Thank you for coming, Patrick. Let me pour you a cup of coffee; then I'll get Juliette."

He sat at the dining room table, cup in hand, and Eve called out for Juliette. She poured herself a cup of coffee as well. Willow was still not sleeping through the night, and coffee had become a necessity for her.

"Are you doing okay?" Patrick asked. He sat back and rolled up the sleeves of his oxford shirt, revealing muscular forearms.

"We're all on edge right now, unsure what will happen now that Juliette has come forward like the other girls," she said, sitting in the chair furthest from Patrick.

"I understand," he said, "but I was asking about you specifically. Are you okay?" He leaned forward and put his elbows on the table and folded his hands. He studied her, and it made Eve turn red.

"I'm just tired, is all. A new baby will do that. She's still not sleeping all night," she confessed.

"Does she spit up a lot?"

What an odd question, she thought. But he was right. "Yes, she does. Is that a problem?"

"Bring her in tomorrow morning to my office, and I'll take a look," he offered.

"That's alright. She's fine. I'm fine." Eve looked down and fiddled with her shirt hem.

"It could help her sleep all night," Patrick tempted her. "Just a quick look. I won't hurt her, Eve."

The comment was sincere, and he meant nothing; but it made Eve want to cry. Shouldn't Willow's father be promising not to hurt her? And would everything in life remind her of the hole Jesse had left in both her and her daughter's lives?

Juliette entered the room, and Eve stood. She looked at Patrick. "Fine, I'll come in tomorrow morning. Now, you see if you can help my sister." She strode from the dining room and went outside, sitting in a chair weathered by the sun and salt air, tears staining her cheeks. She sat and quietly wept, exhaustion washing over her.

It was there he found her about ten minutes later. Eve was embarrassed. Her face was red; the wind had whipped through her hair.

Patrick knelt in front of her. "What's wrong, Eve?"

With a deep breath, she let it all spill out. "Everything reminds me of Jesse and that he's gone. And I hate him! I hate him, but he's dead. He left me and Willow the day I told him I was pregnant. He married another woman, and then he died. And everything around me reminds me of that fact. He should be the one promising to never hurt Willow, and he has! He hurt both of us," she sobbed.

"And on top of that, now everything with Juliette has surfaced. It brings back memories of Jesse when I thought he was a decent human being. It hurts my sister to relive this all the time, and I hate that. But more than anything else, I hate how I feel toward my own twin sister," she cried. "I'm jealous of her, and I've never been jealous before."

She fell into Patrick's shoulder and wept. He wrapped his arms around her and held her for a moment. He whispered into her hair, but Eve could not tell what he said. Finally, he pushed back up to sitting straight.

"Eve, why are you jealous of Juliette? Surely you're not jealous of what happened to her?" His eyes bore into hers as he asked.

"No, of course not. I hate that most of all. I wish I could have that night back, so I could protect her. But I'm jealous of the attention she's getting. I'm jealous that she's starting a support group for rape victims, but there is no group for teenage mothers. I'm jealous that she knows what she wants to do with her life, and I don't. And I'm jealous that she's found a guy who loves her and respects her and won't hurt her the way we've both been hurt this past year."

Eve took a deep breath. She felt better getting it all off her chest like that. It felt like a tight knot in her stomach finally unraveled itself, even just the tiniest bit, and she had some relief.

"I'm so sorry, Eve. I had no idea so much was weighing on you like this," Patrick said after a moment. "You're right. The jealousy is wrong, but sometimes we can't help those feelings. Have you prayed about it? Have you talked to God—and your sister—about how you feel?"

Eve snorted. "No, of course not. Juliette would be crushed if she knew how I felt. And God? Well, I used to have room in my life for God, but that door closed this past year. How could a God so wonderful and perfect allow such harm to come?"

Patrick shifted his weight and considered the question. "Eve, you need to have faith. Ephesians two says, 'For by grace are ye saved through faith; and that not of yourselves: it is the gift of God: Not of works, lest any man should boast. For we are his workmanship, created in Christ Jesus unto good works, which God hath before ordained that we should walk in them.'"

Eve looked at him. She had heard that Scripture before, but it meant nothing to her. Patrick, sensing her uncertainty, tried again. "Hebrews 11:1 says, "Now faith is the substance of things hoped for, the evidence of things not seen.' You can't see faith. You can't touch faith. You have to live faith. You have to believe that God has a plan, an ultimate and good plan that somehow all this fits into. We can't see it now; we wonder where God disappeared to, and we think we were forgotten. But it is all a part of a much grander master plan.

"Think about it. What happened between you and Jesse was a major blow. But would you go back in time, never meet him, and lose Willow?"

Patrick leaned in close as he asked and brushed a stray strand of auburn hair from her face.

"No," Eve said, furrowing her brow. "I would never give up Willow for anything in the world."

"There you go," he said with a smile. "Yes, Jesse hurt you. Yes, Jesse left your daughter without a father. But without him, she would not exist. 'And we know that all things work together for good to them that love God, to them who are the called according to his purpose.'"

Eve sniffled. "Thank you, Patrick. I will think about what you've said. I'm sorry to have blurted all this out to you. I just need time," she said. He stood, and Eve stood with him. "Thank you for your concern. You always seem to come to the rescue." She eyed him, very aware of how close he was to her. The breath caught in her throat worried her.

Laying a hand on her shoulder, he nodded. "I'm a friend if you'll let me be, Eve. Bring Willow tomorrow?" When she nodded, he took a step back. "I better go. Tell Juliette I will have her affidavit for you to take with you tomorrow."

The next day, Eve woke and trudged with Willow to Patrick's office. She thought the entire trip was a waste of time; but for some reason, she felt compelled to go. But it was most definitely not to see Patrick, she told herself. If they could stop Willow from spitting up so much, it would be wonderful, she argued with herself. It might be helpful. And since Patrick was easy on the eyes, it wasn't too much of a hardship.

"Eve, I am so glad you came," he said as he saw her in the hallway.

"I said I would come, didn't I?" she said angrily. She had not meant to snap at him.

She looked him over. Patrick did not wear the white jacket she expected all doctors to wear. No nerdy glasses, no stethoscope. He wore khaki pants with a flare at the bottom—not quite bell bottoms, but close. He wore his plaid oxford shirt with the top button undone and the sleeves rolled up. He didn't look like a doctor. He just looked like Patrick. If Eve had not known he was a doctor, she would have never guessed it.

He ignored her rudeness and motioned her into an exam room. "Now, tell me about what Willow eats. Do you breastfeed?"

Flustered by his direct question, it took Eve a few moments to answer. "Yes, I do. Not that it's any of your business," she finally said.

He did not look at her, but wrote some notes down on his tablet. "And how many times a day does she eat?"

"Five during the daytime. She usually wakes once during the night as well," she said. Willow began to fuss, and Eve put her over her shoulder and bounced her up and down.

"How many spit-ups a day, then?" He finally looked up. His face was all business. *Now, he looked like a doctor,* Eve thought.

"Every time," Eve said. "Usually about ten minutes after she's finished."

"And you burp her?"

"Yes."

"She's fussy a lot?"

"Yes." Her eyes narrowed, and she furrowed her brow. Eve felt challenged now. Was he mocking her parenting? Was he checking to see if she was qualified to parent her own child?

"Okay," he said, scribbling more on his papers. "Well, I think she has acid reflux, Eve."

Alarm filled her. Acid? Wasn't that dangerous? "What is that? Will she be okay?"

Patrick tried to hide a smile. "Yes, she will be fine. Acid reflux is when she digests her food, and it comes back up and burns her esophagus. It's mild and fairly common in infants."

Eve breathed a sigh of relief. She brought Willow close to her, kissed her forehead, and breathed her in. "What can I do?"

"Well, first, put her bed up at an incline. Roll up a towel, and put it under her mattress so her head is propped up just a little. It will help things stay down. I'm also going to suggest a new formula for her and give you some drops to give her if she gets really fussy," Patrick said.

"Oh, that's all?" That sounded too easy to Eve.

Now, Patrick did laugh. "That is all." He capped his pen and flipped the cover up on his tablet of paper. "I'll walk you out and give you some of that formula. I have samples. If that helps, let me know."

He opened the door, and Eve carried Willow out and waited for Patrick to lead the way. He reached behind a counter and gave Eve a canister of formula. She tucked it in her bag and murmured thanks. Patrick led her to a counter with a dour-looking nurse behind it.

"Jolene, don't worry about this one," Patrick told her, tapping the counter before them.

Jolene, for her part, raised an eyebrow to the doctor, then shifted her gaze to Eve. When she eyed Willow's dark skin, her eyes grew small and beady; and Eve thought she heard the woman tsk-tsking her. "Of course, Doctor McKenzie," was all she said.

Eve turned to Patrick. "That was unnecessary."

He looked into her eyes and stroked Willow's soft curls. "I know," was all he said. Then he turned and retreated into an office.

Eve shook her head as she exited the office and tucked Willow into her little seat. As she shut the door and moved to the driver side of the car, Eve saw Patrick chasing after her.

"Eve! I'm glad I caught you. I almost forgot about the affidavit for Juliette," he said, extending an envelope to her.

"Oh, thank you," she said, taking the envelope. "I know she appreciates your willingness to help."

"I'm glad I was the one to help," Patrick admitted. "I mean, I detest what happened to her and to you. But I am glad I was the one called. Not only that I was able to provide some assistance then and now, but also that I was able to meet you."

Eve blushed. She couldn't believe she was blushing, but she was. She quickly smoothed her skirt, realizing just how unsightly she was looking. She was wearing a green and yellow print shirt that barely fit because of the weight her body refused to give up and a green skirt. Her shirt wasn't even tucked in. Eve's red hair was tossed up into a ponytail.

"Patrick, I don't—"

He put a hand up to stop her. "No. I'm sorry. I just had to say something," he admitted. "From the first time I saw you, I felt drawn to you. I ignored it because of Jesse. But in these last few weeks, I just want to be near you. I know you're not ready. I just wanted to let you know."

Patrick shifted back and forth. Eve was unsure what to do. She, too, felt the attraction. But she was still confused from the pain Jesse had caused. And she had Willow to worry about now. She couldn't just go out with boys—men—the way she used to. She had to be cautious. She had to protect her daughter above all else.

"I just . . . I just don't know," Eve said. "I have to think about Willow." It was the truth without admitting or denying that she had been thinking about Patrick's piercing blue eyes for over a week.

She quickly got into the car and shut the door. Patrick took a step back as Eve started the car. She looked out the window at him. She did feel something; she just was not ready to admit it. For his part, Patrick was giving her space and time. He stood still, his hands tucked into his front pockets, the breeze tousling his whitish hair. Eve fought the urge to get back out of the car. Arguing with herself, she left Patrick standing in the parking lot looking after her.

Juliette had a hard time concentrating. She knew her mind was not on the class assignment before her—a chocolate raspberry torte—and instead on what might have been prevented if she had just gone to the police after Buzz raped her. So many other girls would have never known the pain she had endured. But no more, she vowed to herself; nobody else would suffer at the hands of Buzz Herbert. Nor would women have to feel such shame if they had been raped.

She had spoken with her father the night before about starting a group for women who had been sexually abused. He had thought it was a wonderful idea and said she could use the church's facilities any time. She was trying to spread the word about her group and had even drawn up a flier inviting women to the church the following Saturday morning.

"Miss Nicholas? Did you hear what I said?" A stout woman in a flowery dress approached her. Her instructor, Mrs. Victor, was a wonderful baker, and an even more wonderful taster.

Mrs. Victor's graying hair was pulled back into a severe bun. She insisted that everybody in the class keep their hair as far away from the food as possible. She began picking up Juliette's ingredients with her chubby fingers, checking that she had everything.

"I'm sorry, Mrs. Victor," Juliette said. "I'm afraid I did not hear you."

The woman tsk-tsked Juliette and repeated, "I said to be sure you carefully measure each ingredient. Especially the baking soda and baking powder. We do not want the wrong ratio in our cake. Baking is a precise art, Miss Nicholas. We must be fully devoted to our craft in order for it to come out properly."

Juliette nodded her head. "Yes, ma'am. I am sorry. Everything is carefully measured," she assured her instructor.

Mrs. Victor's beady eyes looked over Juliette carefully. "Just what do you plan to do when you have completed these courses, Miss Nicholas?"

Juliette thought a moment. What did she plan to do? She just knew she loved to bake, much like her own mother. She could help her mother at the bakery, but she really didn't need another baker. Perhaps her mother would want to retire soon. and she could take over the business, Juliette thought.

Finally, she said, "I'm not sure, Mrs. Victor. My mother owns Abby's Sweet Treats. I just know I want to bake like her."

The woman said nothing but nodded. She walked away to examine another student's work.

Juliette tried to push everything from her mind except her torte. When she finally pulled it from the oven and finished preparing it, she was pleased with it. Perhaps Booker would be willing to sell her desserts in his restaurant. She could make a living doing that, she thought.

As she exited the building, she hefted what was left of her cake under her arm and searched for Booker's car. Eve had asked to use their shared car that day.

Eve always seemed to have their car. Taking the baby to appointments, or to get new clothes because that child seemed to outgrow things way too quickly. They were always off doing fun things, it seemed. Not that Juliette was jealous, but she missed having so much free time to have fun. Between school, working for her mother, and dating Booker, she felt stretched thin. And the prospect of her new abuse survivor's group added to the list of demands.

But she was happy. Finally, after so long, she was content in her life. She knew what she wanted to do with her life. She had an objective, a focus. And she had a brilliant, young man who adored her. Juliette may have been missing the free time she once enjoyed, but she was excited about where God was leading her. And she fully credited God with taking her the direction she was going.

When Booker's car pulled up, Juliette hopped in and set her cake on her lap. "Wait just a second before you go, Booker," she said as she opened the box. "Taste this, and tell me honestly what you think."

She broke off a small piece and offered it to him. Booker ate it right out of her fingers, and it sent a tingle down Juliette's spine. He savored the bite and closed his eyes. When he opened them back up, Juliette stared into their almond shape with bated breath. When Booker smiled, she sighed relief.

"This is fabulous, Jules," he said. "One of the best chocolate raspberry tortes I've had in a long time."

She watched as the spring sunshine reflected off Booker's caramel-colored skin and felt overjoyed at both her accomplishment and the man in her life. "Thanks," she said with a shy smile. "My instructor lectured me on the sins of not focusing completely on my recipe. I was afraid it was a disaster. She doesn't provide a lot of positive feedback, you know."

"Always strive for your best, Juliette," Booker reminded her as he put the car into drive. "Never settle for anything less."

Juliette laughed. "That's a much nicer way of putting it than my instructor did. She's a big killjoy. But she did ask me something that got me thinking."

"What's that?"

"What I plan to do with all this training once I'm done with all this training." Juliette undid the ties that held her curls still, and they bounded out around her face. "I had always thought I would just work with my mother—that would be groovy—but I don't know if it's what's in God's plan for me."

"Well, you're thinking in the right direction. Following God's path is always the best answer," he replied. "Why not just keep working hard and see where the Lord leads you?"

Juliette reached out and squeezed Booker's hand. "That's the best answer I've ever heard."

"Speaking of where the Lord leads, Juliette, I have been thinking," Booker said, turning serious. Juliette eyed him cautiously. She did not like the tone of his voice. "I need to speak to you about something important."

"What is it, Booker? Is something wrong?" Worry filled her. Booker was a serious man, but he always had a fun and lighthearted side. The expression he was wearing did not look like the lighthearted man Juliette had grown to know.

He was silent for a few minutes as he drove. He pulled into the parking lot of the Blue Rooster and turned to face Juliette. "Business is down. It has been for a while. And with King's death earlier this month, I feel the need to take action."

"I don't understand," Juliette said, confused.

Booker licked his lips and rubbed his temple. "Tension for colored people is mounting. And with the civil rights movement, things are hard for me. I've been considering selling out and moving north. I think things will be better for me up there."

Shock did not cover what Juliette felt in that moment. Sell the restaurant? Move north? What was Booker thinking? What about his family? What about her? Would he just uproot and leave everything that meant something to him?

When she did not respond, Booker spoke again. "I know this is coming from left field, Juliette. But I had been considering moving north for a while now, well before I met you. In fact, I think you are the reason I've stayed here so long," he admitted.

"I had no idea," Juliette stammered. "Why didn't you say anything before this? Why didn't you tell me what you were thinking?"

"I wasn't sure. About the move or about you at the time. Then you told me about what happened, and the timing wasn't right. But with business going down, things need to change. And I think God is speaking to me." Booker ran his hand through his closely braided hair.

"And leaving your family, your business, me? That's the solution?" Juliette swiped at a few tears that spilled over onto her cheek.

"I've spoken to my parents about it. I'm almost twenty-five years old, Juliette. I can't live in their garage forever," Booker said. "The real estate agent said the restaurant should sell quickly. I want to go to

Washington, D.C., and get involved in the movement and try my hand at business there."

Juliette shook her head. She had just been thinking about how much she loved Booker. About how they might have a future together. And now he was leaving her and moving five hundred miles away? "I can't believe you," she said with disgust. "I can't believe you would just decide to leave your restaurant the minute things get tough. And leave me the minute I decide to join the court case against Buzz."

She fumbled with the car door for a moment but managed to get it open, and she flew from the car. She ran down the road away from Booker as fast as she could, fury flushing her face. As she turned a corner, she stopped to see if Booker was chasing after her. He wasn't. That upset her just as much as his decision to relocate. Did he not care at all?

After several blocks, Juliette took off the wedge shoes she was wearing. It was much easier to walk on flat feet. It was about two miles from Booker's restaurant to her mother's bakery, where Juliette planned to drown herself in chocolate confections. And when she realized her raspberry torte was still in Booker's car, she began to cry.

Tired from the walking and exhausted from crying, Juliette finally got to the bakery and pulled the back door open, slamming it behind her.

Her mother was there, her face and hands covered in flour and sugar, and she looked up at her daughter. "Juliette? What's wrong, honey?" Abby grabbed a towel and dusted off as much of the white as she could and rushed to her daughter.

Juliette broke down again, dropping her shoes on the floor, and sobbing into her mother's shoulder. "Booker is moving to Washington! Can you believe him, Mom?"

Abby pulled Juliette to arms' length. "Washington? D.C.? Why? What about the restaurant?"

"He's selling it. He wants to be more involved with this civil rights thing and thinks cooking in D.C. will do that," Juliette said with anger in her voice. "Doesn't he realize he's leaving me behind? I thought he loved me!"

Abby sat Juliette down on a stool. Juliette wanted to melt into the floor. "Maybe this is a big opportunity for him, Juliette. He can be a part of something bigger than himself."

Juliette didn't care about Booker being a part of something else. She wanted him to be a part of her. A part of them. She told her mother as much. "What about me?"

"Juliette, think of it this way. You want to help other women who were hurt by men, right?"

"Right." Juliette shifted her weight and sniffed as her tears dried.

"You would do anything to help them and make sure none of them were hurt again, right?" Abby stared her daughter in the eye. Juliette could see where her mother was going with the questions.

"That's right," she said followed with a sigh.

"For hundreds of years, Booker's people have been abused. They've been hurt. They've been treated like the scum of the Earth—not even human—and he wants to help them," Abby said with compassion. "He wants to do his part to help other blacks move forward in this world, just like you want to do your part for those who have been violated."

With a sigh, Juliette said, "Oh, Mom. I hadn't thought of that. All I heard was that he was leaving me."

Abby smiled at her headstrong daughter. "Did he say that, Jules?"

"No, no, he didn't say he was leaving me," Juliette said quietly.

"And did he say exactly when he was leaving? Tomorrow? Next week? Next month?"

Again, Juliette replied, "No."

Lifting her chin, Abby calmly said, "I think you need to speak to Booker some more about this before you decide your world is coming down around you. It will be a change, for sure, but don't make it out to be that the sky is falling when it might not be."

Juliette sighed deep. Her mother was right. She was always right. "Thank you, Mom. I love you." She reached her arms out, and her mother eagerly embraced her.

"I love you, too. Now, go find Booker."

A knock sounded on the back door as Juliette released her mother. She knew instinctively who it was. Making her way to the door, she smiled as she opened it and saw Booker standing there with a few freshly picked dandelions for her.

"There were no flower shops between there and here," he said, offering her his small bouquet.

"I'm so sorry I reacted that way, Booker," Juliette said. "I guess I'm just a little on edge."

Shaking his head, Booker stopped her. "No, no, I should apologize. I did not think about how you would react. And telling you in the car was probably not smart, either. Let's take a walk, huh?"

He held the door open for her; and when Abby gave the pair an emphatic nod, Juliette went with Booker. They walked in silence for several minutes as dusk settled in around them.

Finally, Juliette spoke. "When do you plan to leave?" She felt like her heart had leapt into her throat, but she knew they needed to talk.

"Not right away," he said. "The restaurant will still operate while it's for sale. And if the new owner wants to keep things going, I imagine we will work in tandem for a little while until he fully takes over. Then I hope to take about a week to go to Washington and look for an apartment there. I also want to take a small vacation, too. So, all things considered, I imagine it will be at least three months, possibly more if the Blue Rooster doesn't sell right away."

Eyes closed, Juliette felt relief. "So, you're not leaving tomorrow? Or next week?"

Booker took her by the shoulders. "Juliette, look at me." She opened her eyes and willed the tears not to come. "Do you really think I would leave so soon without talking to you first? Don't you know how much I love you?"

"I just—I, I don't know," she stammered. She knew she loved him, and she was pretty sure he loved her, but how far was that love willing to go?

"Let's keep walking," Booker suggested. He pulled her forward a little, and they resumed their pace.

Within minutes, they were approaching a pier. Even though it was not the one Buzz had taken her to, all piers were now associated with that night for Juliette. She stood motionless and resisted when Booker led her closer.

"Juliette?"

"I just—I haven't been this close to a pier since last summer," she said, feeling her body tense.

Booker released her hand and let her take a step backward. "It's just a pier, Juliette. Nothing here can hurt you," he promised. He looked into her eyes and smiled at her. Juliette could see just how much Booker wanted her to overcome her fear.

"You can hurt me," she whispered. "Leaving will hurt me. If you want me to know that you love me, then you have to know just how much I love you."

One hand stretched out to her, inviting her to join him. "Juliette, do you trust me?"

Strong arms waited to hold her. A loving smile and dazzling eyes longed to take her in. Booker stood facing her, looking both dashing and unfussy at the same time.

"Do you trust me?"

Tentatively, she reached her hand to his and smiled. "Yes, I do. I trust you."

He grasped her hand and pulled her close. She closed her eyes and breathed him in. He was heavenly, perfect. She felt his hands in her hair, and his thumb wiped away a lingering tear.

"I love you, Juliette," he said softly in her ear. "I want to marry you."

Shock filled her as Juliette pulled back and stared at Booker. "What? Booker?"

He broke into a wide smile and got down on one knee before her. "Juliette, I love you. I cannot imagine my life without you in it. I am so thankful to God for bringing you in my life. Please say you will travel this crazy journey with me as my soulmate, my wife."

Juliette clapped a hand to her mouth in disbelief. Was he really proposing to her? Before she could ask if he was sure, he produced a small box and popped open the lid. He was serious.

"Of course, Booker! Of course!" She beamed as Booker stood and put the ring on her finger. She glanced down at the simple but beautiful diamond solitaire, then back up at the man before her. Her fiancé. He swept her up and kissed her deep. "I can't believe it!"

"Believe it," he said. "I even spoke with your parents a few weeks ago to ask their blessing. They know all about my plan to move, and they're even okay with us going up there."

The elation wore off in that moment as quickly as it had come on. "Oh, I don't know if I can leave my family, Booker. I can't leave Eve and Willow; they need me."

"Don't cancel the plans yet, sweetheart," he said, cupping her chin in his hand. "Eve and the baby have your parents, your siblings. And it seems that Patrick McKenzie has taken a shine to her. I don't think they'll be alone." Before she could speak again, he added, "Why not talk to Eve about it tonight?"

Juliette nodded and decided the thought of leaving would not ruin the fact that she would soon marry the man she adored.

"When do you want to get married?" she asked him.

"Soon," was his only reply.

"I know," she said with a smile. "How about the Fourth of July?" It was one year from their first unofficial date. *It was perfect*, she thought.

Booker nodded in agreement and kissed her again. Slowly, they made their way back to the bakery, so he could drive her home.

Waves of Change

THE WEATHER WAS WARMER. WILLOW was a month older and sleeping better, and Eve could no longer deny that Patrick McKenzie had feelings for her. The past month has assured her of that. Not only was he in the bakery daily regardless of her own presence, but he had also taken to attending Respite Baptist Church and joining the family for Sunday dinners. He cooed over Willow and held her as much as the rest of the family when he was around.

For her part, Eve's resolute exterior was wearing down. Each time she saw Patrick hold Willow, she felt something tug in her heart. And when Willow giggled at Patrick and reached her little arm up to his face, Eve thought she would cry. He was being the father Eve had longed for her daughter to have. That notion was both heartwarming and dangerous at the same time. She didn't want her daughter to get attached to the man if he wasn't going to be around.

So when Patrick asked to be her escort for Juliette's wedding, Eve hesitantly accepted. She hesitated because she wasn't sure where her relationship with Patrick was heading—or where she wanted it to go. Nor was she sure about Juliette getting married. Oh, she knew Juliette and Booker were in love; that much was plain to see. But it meant yet another life change for the twins. Not only would her sister and closest friend move out, but she would also move hundreds of miles away when they left for Washington, D.C.

Juliette had thrown herself into wedding planning to get her mind off the upcoming trial in Tennessee for the case against Buzz Herbert. Eve had been pulled along into wedding planning, but she certainly did not have the passion for floral arrangements her sister suddenly possessed. While she was thrilled for her sister's happiness, the nagging feeling of jealousy crept up more often now. Maybe Juliette moving several states away was what Eve needed to feel like she was free from her sister's shadow.

The duo, along with their mother, Alisa, and Linda were at Mary's Bridal Shoppe in Myrtle Beach trying on bridal gowns.

Eve sat quietly, trying to keep Willow quiet as well, as Juliette paraded out of a dressing room time after time. Each dress was completely different from the last, and none were right for Juliette.

On the fifth dress, Eve huffed and said, "Jules, hang on a minute." She stood and got close to her sister. "Now, close your eyes. Go on." She waited. "Now, picture your wedding. Picture being at the end of the aisle, Booker at the opposite end. You're the happiest you've ever been. The music starts; everyone is waiting. What are you wearing?"

Eve looked at her sister. Juliette broke into a wide smile with her eyes still closed. "It doesn't much matter what I wear, does it? But I see something simple. Long, sweet, but not too over-the-top. Not too frilly, but feminine. I can see it."

"Okay," Eve said quietly. "Now find that dress."

Both of them went in pursuit of the dress. Despite the distance Eve had been feeling from her sister of late, they still had a deep connection. After a minute of searching, Eve finally called out, "Juliette! Here!"

She pulled a dress from the rack and held it up. "Oh, Evie, that's it!" Juliette rushed to her and hugged her close. "This is it!"

The dress was just as Juliette had described. It had thick straps and a long hem and was lightly ornamented but not fancy. A simple lace overlay covered the entire thing. Juliette rushed to try it on. When Alisa picked out a thick headband with a matching lace veil, Juliette was sold. Eve thought she was gorgeous.

With the bridal gown chosen, Juliette set to having Eve and Alisa trying on bridesmaids' dresses and even handed her mother a few dresses to try on as well. Eve smiled as her sister sat upon the settee and directed her family as she held a sleeping Willow in her arms.

"Something longer. Maybe in green," Juliette said as Eve emerged from a dressing room in a yellow frock. She didn't like the dress at all and was thankful when Juliette suggested something else.

But the next one was a winner. A great tea-length dress with just enough flair to cover Eve's still recovering mid-section in a beautiful shade of mint green. It went great with her red hair and fair skin and complemented Alisa's dark hair as well. And when the sales clerk said the dress came in a matching infant dress, Juliette said to wrap them up.

Back at home, Juliette went straight to the phone to call Booker's mother, to whom she had grown close in the past month, to relay the day's findings. As Juliette chattered away telling her future mother-in-law what dress to get for Booker's younger sister Billie, Eve opened the mail.

A letter addressed to Juliette caught Eve's eye. It was from Tennessee and looked official. She glanced up at Juliette and got her attention. She held the envelope up for Juliette to see. "Open it for me," Juliette whispered to her between sentences to Lucille Winston.

Eve tore the flap open and pulled the papers out. It was a summons to appear in court to testify against Buzz Herbert. The court trial was set for June twenty-fourth—only ten days before the wedding.

"Jules, you need to read this," Eve said quickly. She knew this would upset her sister on many levels. Not only would Juliette have to get to Tennessee and stay for the trial, but also, it was right before her wedding. And this wasn't even mentioning that she would have to face Buzz Herbert and sit on the witness stand and testify what happened to her.

"In a minute," Juliette said. She waved Eve off and turned around, leaning against the kitchen counter.

Eve huffed loudly. Juliette was choosing to ignore anything that had to do with the trial in favor of wedding planning. Eve knew thinking about the trial was painful for her sister, but it was a necessary evil.

She spoke up. "Juliette, they set a trial date. It's in June."

Whirling around, Eve could see surprise on her sister's face. "What? When?"

Paper extended, Eve told her. "June twenty-fourth."

Juliette's eyes widened. "Okay. I'm sorry, Lucille. Please forgive me. I need to get off the phone. My mother and I will speak with you soon. Yes. Okay. Goodbye." She got herself out of the tangle of phone cord and hung up. "Let me see this."

Eve watched her sister scan the summons. "No! No! This is only ten days before the wedding. I can't—I can't do this, Eve." Juliette's eyes met Eve's, tears swimming in them.

"You have to, Juliette. It should not be a long trial. You and a few others testify; he gets convicted; you come home. It won't take long at all," Eve tried to reassure her sister.

"What about all the wedding preparations?"

Eve narrowed her eyes. "Really? Juliette? You would rather worry about taffeta and place settings than make sure that a repeat rapist gets the punishment he deserves?" Sometimes, her sister's flippant attitude really got under Eve's skin.

With a sigh, Juliette replied, "I'm sorry, Evie. It's just so hard to think about. The trial will be so tough. I haven't seen him since that night. I don't know if I can face him again. I don't know if I can tell the world what happened to me. It's embarrassing." Tears slipped over her lashes and down her cheeks. "I would rather concentrate on my future with Booker than my past."

Filled with compassion, Eve knew how her sister felt. It was easier for her to think about her future with Willow than the events that led up to this point in her life. She took her sister's hand in hers. "I'm sorry, Jules," she said, "but this is something you need to do. You can't move forward without facing what's behind you. And you need to make sure other girls are safe from the evils of rape and abuse. You are a huge part of this case. They need you."

They were interrupted when Abby came in the kitchen with Willow fussing in her arms. "I think someone is ready for dinner, Mommy," Abby said to her eldest daughter. Eve reached her arms out for her growing child without taking her eyes off Juliette.

"Talk to Mom about it, Jules. She will agree with me." Eve looked from her sister to her mother. Her mother looked confused, but Juliette sighed again and nodded. She took the paper off the counter and handed it to her mother. Eve smiled and left the room, taking Willow upstairs to feed her.

Eve sat on her bed with her pillows propped up behind her. She preferred nursing on her bed, where she could stretch out and relax more than she could on the straight-backed chair her father had brought to her room. With Willow happily nursing, Eve closed her eyes and leaned her head back on her pillow.

So much was going on now. Wedding planning, a trial she apparently needed to help her sister with, a demanding infant, and the attentions of a good-looking doctor were enough to make Eve's head spin. She also felt like she needed to find a job soon to help cover the expenses her parents and Frances Washington's check were covering. But then, what would she do with Willow if she had a job? And with Juliette soon leaving, she did not want to sacrifice any of the time she had left with her best friend.

If only Jesse had lived. If only Jesse had lived and had done the honorable thing by her and married her when he found out she was pregnant. Eve felt like her entire life had turned into a giant "if only." But none of the things she had thought of could ever happen. She was not a married mother who had her child's father to provide for them. She was not a proud wife who kept the house and made the meals for a man who came home just in time for supper.

She didn't even feel like she had her father's church behind her. Eve knew they whispered about her behind her family's back. And they called themselves Christians. She had read parts of the Bible; she knew gossip was wrong, and she didn't even consider herself a Christian anymore.

A stray tear trickled down the side of her cheek. Eve was tired of crying over her situation. She was tired in general. What could she do? Was there a solution that would solve her problems?

Patrick.

His name just jumped into her head. The next day was Sunday, and she would see him both at church and for the family meal afterward. That had to be why his name came to her. Patrick was not her answer. Even if Patrick was interested in her romantically, surely he would not be interested in raising another man's half-black child. If her situation had been different, Eve would have welcomed his advances; but for now, she was left skeptical, and her heart was still healing.

But she could not get him off her mind. While Willow fed happily, Eve daydreamed about dating Patrick, about possibly marrying him. *Imagine*, she thought, *marrying a doctor*. Every woman wanted to marry a doctor, didn't they? And if only Willow was his child, there would be no issue at all. She could just see him coming home at the end of a long day, her having a hot meal on the table for him, and Willow running to greet her father home.

"It's just too much to hope for, isn't it?" she asked Willow, whose eyes were slowly closing as she drifted to sleep. "What do I do? Is Doctor McKenzie the solution? What a position to place him in—as a sort of savior for us. But he's not, is he? He's just a man. He can't save us, and I'm not sure that he wants to. He's interested, sure, but just how interested is he?"

With no response from her now-sleeping daughter, Eve carefully unlatched Willow from her body and laid her in her crib. She would wake in three hours' time for one more feeding before sleeping until morning. Eve was happy with their routine. It was comfortable now, familiar. She felt a certain amount of contentment from providing nourishment for her child. Nobody else could do that, and it gave Eve pride.

She went back downstairs to help her mother set up for supper and heard the voice she had just been imagining resonating through the house. Patrick McKenzie. Eve could feel a tingle run up her spine, and she stopped still at the base of the stairs.

"Evie? Is that you?" Her mother called out.

Clearing her voice, Eve responded, "Yes, it's me," but her feet still did not move. Why was Patrick at their house on a Saturday night?

Her mother and Patrick both made their way to her, since she was not moving forward herself. "We have a guest," Abby said, motioning to Patrick, as if Eve could not see him.

"Patrick," she said, trying not to allow her voice to waver. "What brings you here on a Saturday?"

He smiled at her. His blue eyes sparkled, and Eve felt like her knees went weak for a split second. "You did," he answered.

"Me?" Confusion filled her. Why was he there for her?

"I thought you could use a night out, so I stopped by on a whim," he said. "I thought I might take you to dinner."

Dinner? On this night? Eve shook her head. "Um, I'm not sure, Patrick," she said. "I'm very flattered, but I can't leave Willow—"

"Sure, you can," Abby said with a smile. "She'll be fine here. She's sleeping, right? I raised five children; I can keep my granddaughter for a few hours."

"But she'll get up in a few hours to nurse again," Eve protested. She was immediately embarrassed that she had mentioned nursing in front of Patrick. She could feel the redness creep up into her cheeks.

"I'll have you back before then," Patrick interjected. "I promise. Just dinner."

Should she accept? Eve wasn't sure. But dinner out sounded wonderful. Conversation that did not revolve around what a baby does sounded heavenly to her. And perhaps this would be a good time to feel Patrick out one-on-one to see what he really intended with her. They had never been truly alone before.

"Give me five minutes to change and get ready," she said with a flash of smile. With that, she turned on her heel and ran back up the stairs to change her clothes.

Rifling through her closet, Eve tossed aside several items from the previous summers that were still too snug on her. Juliette came in and silently helped her look through her clothes while the baby slept. Eve held up a pink peasant blouse, but Juliette shook her head. And when Juliette produced a yellow sundress, Eve quickly dismissed it. It was the navy blue mini that Juliette grabbed next that they both nodded to. Hopefully, it still fit.

Eve giggled as her sister zipped the dress up her back. "This reminds me of old times, Jules," she said quietly. A lump formed in her throat. How much time would they have left with Juliette planning to move? Would they ever stay up all night laughing and talking again?

Sensing her melancholy, Juliette shook her head. "No, Evie, not now. Don't start." She wiped a finger under her sister's moist eye. "You're just going to dinner. How about we sit down and have some ice cream when you get home? Me, you, and Willow."

Eve nodded and took a deep breath. "I can't believe we're growing up."

"We are grown, Eve," Juliette replied with a smile. "I'm getting married. You have a baby. We grew up. And you have a very far-out doctor waiting for you downstairs. Put on some lip gloss and get moving."

Lip gloss applied, Eve opened her bedroom door softly but then turned to face her twin. She hugged her close and held onto her. "I love you," she whispered.

"I know. I love you, too. See you when you get back."

Downstairs, Patrick smiled when Eve joined him. Nobody else was around. "Are you ready?"

"Um, maybe I should leave my mom some instructions for Willow real quick," she said, feeling like her palms were clammy.

"Your mother said it before—she raised five children, including you. She knows what to do, Eve," Patrick reminded her.

"Yes, I'm sorry," Eve said, feeling embarrassed. "I've just never left her before is all. Let's go."

Patrick opened the door for her and led the way to his car. He drove a beautiful black mustang. It looked new. Eve was amazed. It was far superior to the almost ten-year-old sedan she and her sister shared. He opened the door for her, and she slid into the passenger seat. When he got behind the wheel, she smiled at him, feeling a little nervous.

"Where are we going?" She hadn't thought to ask that before. Not that it mattered; Eve would eat just about anything.

"Have you been to Chappy's before? It's down on the inlet." When Eve shook her head, Patrick said, "Perfect. You will love it."

A few minutes later, with a glass of sweet tea in her hand, Eve was overlooking the marshes of the Grand Strand watching egrets and cranes wade through the murky waters.

"I never tire of the view, do you?" Patrick scooted his chair closer to the table and put his hand on the table next to hers. He did not hold her hand, but Eve felt his skin gently touching her own.

"I don't think much of it. I guess I take it for granted," she said gently. "I do like the beach, though. It's home."

"I grew up in Charleston, but never really noticed the beach until I came here last year. I just love seeing where the waves meet the earth.

I really feel God's hand in the land here. And I feel like God has placed me here. Myrtle Beach is where He wants me." Patrick smiled at Eve, and she smiled back.

She hadn't realized he was so religious. Maybe a year ago, before she had met Jesse, she would have found that appealing, but now it soured her mood. She knew Patrick went to church, but Eve had not realized he lived for God the way her father did, the way her sister now did. The way that she did not live her life. Their God had abandoned her, right along with Jesse Washington.

The expression on her face must have changed because Patrick changed the subject quickly. "I understand your father is from Charleston also?"

"He sure is. His family were the founders of the Nicholas Shipping Company. It's now run by my aunt and uncle. My father wasn't too interested in shipping after he met my mother," she said with a smile.

They discussed their families throughout their meal, and Eve found herself relaxing and enjoying the time with Patrick. He was an incredibly genuine man, honest and open. He was apparently quite the jokester in his family and used to spend his summers in Ireland, where his parents were from. Eve laughed a lot and found that she truly enjoyed Patrick's company.

But the fading sun and ache in her breast told Eve it was time to end their evening. Patrick also noted the time and stood, getting Eve's chair for her. Silently, they made their way back to the car where Patrick was ever the gentleman, holding Eve's door open for her. In the car, Patrick turned to Eve and stared at her for a moment.

"Is something wrong?" she asked.

Shaking his head, Patrick said, "No. Nothing. I just want to re-member this night and how you look." Eve felt a heated blush rise on her skin. Patrick continued, "I don't know how you feel about me, Eve. And I don't know if anything will come of this relationship. But I have to let you know that I do care for you a great deal. There's something about you that is so special, and I can't ignore it."

Eve thought a moment before speaking. "Patrick, I don't know what to say. It will take time for me to trust anyone again. And I have to put my daughter first." She looked down as she spoke and fiddled with the hem of her skirt.

"I know that. And please know that Willow is also very special to me. I adore her and love to be around her. But I don't like you because of her, nor would I back away because of her either."

"Even though she's half-black?" It was something Eve knew would make any potential suitor back away. She learned quickly that people treated her differently because of her daughter's skin color, and Eve knew she would have to be protective and cautious about it.

Patrick took her hand in his and spoke firmly. "Eve, look at me." When she raised her eyes, he continued. "I don't care if she's half-black or half-purple. I am completely over the moon for that child, and I'm getting that way about her mother, too."

Eve swallowed hard. "Patrick, I . . . "

"I know. I hope I'm not pushing you, Eve. I don't want to. But I needed you to know how I feel. My intentions are good, I promise. I want—no, I need—to see where this can go between us. I feel like you and Willow are to be a part of my life."

"I like spending time with you, Patrick," Eve confessed. "And if I tell the truth, you occupy my mind a lot these days. I don't know what will happen; but if you can be patient with me, we can see what happens."

He lifted her hand and kissed it gently. Eve felt a small fire light in her heart, and she knew this was the beginning of something. Patrick drove her home and dropped her off with a wave and a wink. Eve smiled all the way into the house.

Sun on My Skin

JULIETTE WATCHED HER SISTER THROUGH the window. Even in the fading light, she could see that Eve was grinning like a Cheshire cat. Juliette quietly clapped her hands together in excitement. Her sister's happiness meant her happiness, and Juliette had realized while Eve had been gone that she had not shown it lately.

Before the front door opened, a small cry erupted from Eve's bedroom. Willow was awake. Juliette snuck into the room, picked the infant up, and cradled her for a moment. She quickly changed her diaper and then propped Willow up on her shoulder before Eve came into the room.

Suddenly, she realized that once she and Booker were wed, they would have children. At least, she hoped they would have children eventually. And they would look very much like Willow. She laid the baby on Eve's bed and sat beside her. The crying began again, and Juliette studied the little person before her, imagining if Willow were her daughter. She realized she needed to learn a lot more about babies. How would she do that so far from her family?

Eve came into the room and immediately swooped down and picked up Willow. Juliette watched as the baby immediately calmed and Eve's body immediately began to sway and soften to the baby.

"How long has she been crying?"

Juliette sighed. One day, she would be a mother, too. "Just a minute. She woke up as soon as you were dropped off. It's like she knew you were home. I changed her for you." Juliette was proud of that fact.

Eve smiled. "Thank you, Jules." Her attention turned to her daughter. "I missed you, sweetheart. I did. I thought about you the entire time I was away. Are you ready for your dinner? I bet you are. And I'm ready for Aunt Juliette to get us some of that ice cream she promised." She smiled at Juliette, who quickly hopped up and headed out of the room.

"I'll be right back."

Downstairs, she grabbed two bowls and two spoons. She pulled the ice cream out of the freezer box and filled their bowls to heaping. Juliette thought they both deserved a little indulgence tonight.

Back in her sister's room, Juliette set one bowl next to her sister and the other bowl on the nightstand. She pulled the chair over close to the bed and propped her feet up on the downy mattress. She picked up her bowl and took a bite of ice cream while she watched her sister switch Willow from one breast to the other.

"Does that hurt?"

"Does what hurt?"

"Willow. I mean, not her, but um . . . " Juliette found herself at a loss for words when it came to discussing what her sister was doing.

For her part, Eve laughed. "Nursing? No. We are designed to breastfeed our children. I know giving them a bottle of formula is recommended these days, but women have been breastfeeding their children since the dawn of time. Nothing else is more natural."

Juliette quickly took another bite of her ice cream to cover her discomfort.

"Does it bother you?"

"No. Of course not. I guess I'm just curious."

Eve nodded. "Because you're getting married soon and want to know all about motherhood." *At least, her sister understood her,* Juliette thought. "I guess I won't be there to help you out when you have children."

With that, Juliette watched her sister's eyes well with tears. "No, no crying, Evie," she said, sitting up. "We can talk on the phone every day. And we'll see each other as often as we can."

"It's not the same, and you know it, Jules," Eve cried. "We have had a tough year, and it's only pushed us apart. We used to be so close. You were my best friend. Then everything exploded. Now I have a child, and you're getting married and moving across the country."

"It's not across the country. It's three states away. I'll still see you for holidays, and we can do family vacations." Juliette could see that trying to console her sister was not working. "I know it won't be the same. But it is what it is. Remember what I said before—we've already grown up."

Eve laid Willow down on the bed and covered herself back up. When she lifted Willow to burp her, she looked from her daughter to her sister and said, "How come nobody told me we had grown up? I would have paid more attention."

Juliette laughed. Her twin always made her laugh. "I don't know. I would have paid attention, too."

"Are you ready to get married?"

Smiling, Juliette sighed. "Yes. A year ago, I was recovering from the rape and completely swore off anything male. But through the grace of God, all that changed. And Booker helped with that. He is such a big part of my world now."

"I used to be a big part of your world."

Juliette could see the pain on her sister's face. "Eve. You have been my entire world since we were born. You will always be my twin sister. Nothing will ever change that. Did Jesse change that? Did Willow change that? No. My marrying Booker and moving will not change that. We will still be the Nicholas twins. We will still be Evie and Jules. I love you more than life itself, and I would give anything in the world for you."

By this point, tears were flowing freely down Juliette's cheeks, and she could see tears on Eve's face also. Both girls hugged and clung to each other until Willow made her discomfort known. They separated and laughed, Juliette taking the baby and holding her nose to nose.

"You, little Miss Willow, are such a blessing. Your arrival was unplanned by us, but completely planned by God. I love you so much, little angel." Juliette kissed the baby and smelled her skin.

"Juliette, how is it that you started out the God skeptic and are now totally religious, and now I have no faith at all?"

Looking at Eve, Juliette could see the pain in her face. Her sister truly had lost all her faith in the Lord. "I don't know, Eve. I don't think it's being religious; it's being faithful. The past year has been terrible for us both, and yet a blessing for us both as well. It was Booker who first got me to see what I was missing out on. And he got me to see that God had not been punishing me by what happened; he was allowing it to do two things. One was to get my attention because nothing else had worked. And secondly, it was to build my testimony and character so I could help others."

"So, what about me, Jules? Why was I allowed to fall in love with a man who left me pregnant and then died? And now I have a mixed-race baby with no father, and I'm still living with Mom and Dad."

Juliette's heart went out to Eve. She remembered what it was like to live day to day wondering why God had permitted what had happened. It was a lonely place. She had not realized just how far down into that hole Eve really was. She went to church with the family and smiled and recited everything she should. But Juliette realized that her heart had not been into it for some time.

After a quick and silent prayer, Juliette said, "Eve, I don't know why God let Jesse leave you. I don't know why he died. But I do know that this child is a blessing to you, me, and the entire family. I can only guess that God is using this situation to help you in some way. This is a part of your journey." Juliette hoped and prayed her response was accurate.

"It's not that I wish Willow wasn't here," Eve said. "You know that. I love my baby. But I hate how she came to be. I hate that her father lied to me."

"Willow's father might have lied to you and left you, but our Heavenly Father will never lie to or leave either of you. That I can promise." Juliette handed Willow back to her mother and leaned forward. "He was with me when I was raped. I know now that Buzz had worse intentions for me than what happened. And He was with you, too. Did He not allow you to get financial help from Mrs. Washington? And how about Mom and Dad letting you stay and keep Willow when they had discussed sending you away and giving her away?"

More tears slipped down her sister's cheek. Juliette took Eve's hands in her own and held tight, with Willow between them.

"I hadn't thought of it that way," Eve said. "I've just felt so alone and distant from everything, especially at church. The people whisper about me."

"They whisper about a young woman who overcame being lied to, who is managing to raise her child without a man, and who is strong enough to still go to church each week. If you ask me, they could learn a lesson from you," Juliette said with a smile. She was proud of her sister.

"That makes me sound like a saint, which I am not," Eve said with a laugh.

"And you don't have to be, Evie. God loves and accepts you as you are. All you have to do is accept Him back." Juliette searched her sister's eyes and prayed for God to guide her in the right words. "What is holding you back?"

Eve looked at Juliette. "Myself." Her lip quivered, and her shoulders shook. Juliette prayed that her sister would receive Christ as her Savior, but wasn't sure how to proceed. Thankfully, she didn't have to do it alone; she knew God was with her.

"Juliette, I'm so tired of being tired. I'm so tired of fighting for my life alone. How is God always with me?"

"No matter what we do, God is there, Eve. Even if we don't feel His presence. But I promise you, you will feel Him more if you accept the gift of salvation and let Him lead you from here on out." Juliette wished and prayed with all her might that Eve would agree.

And she did. "I want to, Jules."

Elation filled Juliette. She smiled and saw a huge smile grow on Eve's face as well. "Oh, Evie, I have been waiting for you to say that. It's so much freer when you let God take the reins of your life and follow where He leads as long as you're willing to listen." She sat next to her sister and hugged her close.

"What do I have to do?" Eve sniffed. She stood and put Willow in her bed. "Don't I have to sign something or do something?"

"Just pray, Eve," Juliette replied. "Just pray. Do you want me to help you? Booker had to help me."

When Eve nodded and sat back down, Juliette took her hand and closed her eyes. She asked God to fill them both in that moment, and she prayed, "Lord, I am certainly not an expert when it comes to faith. It's so new to me, too. But I do know that we need to pray to You, Lord. I know we need to ask Your forgiveness for the sin in our lives—past and present. Lord, guide Eve and me in the path You have chosen for us. She wants to follow You for the rest of her life and bask in Your glory. I want the same as well. Be with us, Lord, in this coming time of change and adjustment. Allow us to blossom and grow more into the women You would have us be. Amen."

Opening her eyes, Juliette glanced at Eve. Her eyes were still closed, her mouth moving silently. She was praying. Juliette could feel her heart swell in that moment. She prayed once more for Eve's heart to mend, for her to find and follow the path laid out before her. When Eve squeezed her hand, she opened her eyes.

"I feel so much . . . lighter," Eve said. "I feel better."

"I'm so glad, Eve. Accepting Christ is the best decision you will ever make for you or your daughter." Juliette stood and went to Willow's crib. The baby was already asleep. "Should I go and let you sleep?"

"I'm not tired," Eve replied. "But I am ready to get into some more comfortable clothes. I'm going to put on my nightgown." She stood and went to her dresser. Eve pulled out a nightgown and disappeared into her closet for a minute before coming out, crumpled green dress in hand.

This made Juliette realize she had not asked about her date with Patrick. "Eve, how was your date?"

Shaking her head, Eve said, "It was not a date, Jules." She took a deep breath. "Okay. I think it was a date. He said he really likes me and that he has to see where the relationship will go. He said he feels drawn to me, that God has put me in his life." Juliette watched as her sister blushed like a young girl.

"Oh, Evie, that is wonderful. Patrick is a great Christian man. What else?"

"And he said he loves Willow and didn't care that she was mixed race. And he's so nice and gentlemanly," Eve said as she put an elastic in her hair to make a ponytail.

Excited for Eve, Juliette asked, "Were there sparks?"

Thoughtful, Eve furrowed her brow. "No, not so much as sparks. It's not the giddy feeling I had with Jesse. It's more like comfort and ease. And it's like there's a low-burning fire in the pit of my stomach that grows each time I'm with him. It's growing from warming to getting a little too warm."

Juliette frowned. "Is too warm a bad thing?"

With a laugh, Eve quickly responded, "No! It's a good thing. I like him a lot, but I've been burned by fire before. Or burned by sparks, rather. This is warmth that might grow into heat. It's good, but I'm cautious. Both for my heart and for Willow's." With that comment, she quickly peered in at her sleeping child.

"I'm so glad, Eve. He's a great guy and seems to adore you and Willow. And you know, sparks don't last. It's the burning embers that keep you warm for a long time. Sparks fizzle out too quickly," Juliette said. She loved seeing her sister so happy. "We all like Patrick."

"Do you like him better than Jesse?"

The smile fell from both their faces. Juliette wasn't sure how to respond. She had liked Jesse as well. He had been a great guy up until he left Eve. Both Jesse and Patrick had been by her own side without question last summer. Did she like him better? With a slow nod, she affirmed that yes, she did like Patrick more than she had liked Jesse. Besides, Jesse was gone, and Patrick was here and willing to love a girl with a baby in tow. That made him more of a man than Jesse had been.

"Yes. Jesse was nice; but when things got complicated, he ran. That's not a man or a father. That's a coward," Juliette said. "And now, here's Patrick, who knows you have not only a child, but also a mixed-race child; and he still isn't backing down from you, and he cherishes Willow and spends time with her. He's the real deal, Evie."

"The real deal," Eve repeated. "He's a doctor. He goes to church and talks about God. He is great with my daughter, and he wants to be with me." She looked Juliette in the eye. "What do I do with that? How do I act?"

"You catch him and don't let go!" Both of them erupted in quiet laughter.

"I'd better go to sleep. I have a busy day tomorrow," Juliette said after they had calmed down. "And you have some sweet dreams to have. I love you, Eve."

"I love you, too, Juliette."

Without another word, Juliette slipped from Eve's room to her own and readied for bed. She fell asleep smiling, thanking God for the night she and her sister had shared.

Salty Shells

JUNE HAD ARRIVED TOO QUICKLY for Juliette's taste. Tomorrow, she, along with her father, would be going to Tennessee to prepare for Buzz's trial. Booker had wanted to come with her, but she had insisted on him staying behind. She needed to do this alone, she had told him. And he would make her only more nervous.

She would meet with the lawyer in the morning to go over her testimony for the trial opening the next day. As she put the final things in her suitcase, she took a deep breath and sat on her bed.

"Knock, knock," her mother said as she entered the room. "Are you ready?" She sat next to Juliette and looked at her expectantly.

"Yes, I just packed the last items."

"Good," her mother cooed, smoothing her hair. "Now. Are you ready?" The different tone in her voice told Juliette she had shifted the topic from baggage to trial.

After a deep breath, Juliette smiled at her mother. "I'm ready. As ready as I can ever be. I won't allow Buzz to do this to anyone else, and I want to send the message that rape is never okay. I want other women to know they can come forward if they have been abused, and I want to put this behind me. I'm ready."

"You are so brave, sweetheart. I have been praying for you since all this came out. That you would have the right words and that God will see justice served. And I pray for the Herbert family. I know Mrs.

Herbert is beside herself. And I hope that Buzz can get the help he needs from both professionals and from the ultimate Healer."

Juliette turned to her mother. "It never occurred to me to pray for Buzz. But that's the right thing to do, isn't it?"

Abby, with her hair clipped back and her face freshly washed, looked like an angel to her daughter. "That's the first step in forgiveness, Juliette," she said. "To pray for the person who offended you. That's how healing truly begins."

"I love you, Mom."

"I love you, too. Now, be safe. Mind your father, even if you are about to be married," Abby warned her. "And above all else, let God guide you. He will see that justice is served, even if the courts here on Earth don't do as much as you would like."

"Thanks, Mom."

Her mother left her alone, her long, blue skirt swishing out the door behind her. With a deep breath, Juliette picked up her suitcase and made her way to the living room. She said goodbye to Joey and Alisa, who both hugged her awkwardly. She looked at Eve, who for once did not have tears.

Eve wore a stern expression on her face. "Juliette, I will be in constant prayer for you until you return home. I thought I would be crying, but I realized I am so proud of you for doing this that tears would be unnecessary. And I know that things will turn out in your favor and the favor of the other women involved."

"Thank you, Evie. That means a lot to me," Juliette said with a nod. "And thank you for the prayers."

"You just go and let Buzz Herbert see that while he hurt you temporarily, he has not damaged you forever. Let him see that you are happy now. Let him know that he will not continue to hurt you for the rest of your life. And let those other girls know that the best thing they can do is enjoy their life and live it to the fullest."

Juliette smiled. "That's precisely what I plan to do, dear sister. And I'm glad to see that you are also following your own advice."

The girls embraced. Harvey picked up Juliette's bag and waited for her at the door. They made their way to the car and then down the road. The trip to Tennessee would be long, but Juliette knew that showing Buzz that she had moved past the pain would be worth it.

The next morning, she awoke bright and early to meet the prosecuting attorney in the hotel's conference room. Her father joined her for a quick breakfast, but said she should meet the lawyer on her own.

"I can't sit with you on the stand, so it's best if you do this on your own as well," he had told her. "But I will be right here, and you will never truly be alone as long as the Almighty is with you."

"Thanks, Daddy," she had whispered to him before going through the large wooden door to the man awaiting her.

The attorney was a tall man with wiry, graying hair and thick glasses. But he had kind eyes, Juliette noticed. She hoped he knew what he was doing as a prosecutor.

"Juliette Nicholas? Thank you for coming in this morning," the man said. "My name is Harold Conger, and I am the prosecuting attorney for this case. Please have a seat." He motioned to the chair opposite him.

Juliette sat silently, nervously, unsure of what to say. She tried to sit up as straight as possible, and she folded her hands on the table before her.

"It's perfectly fine to be nervous, Miss Nicholas," he said with a smile. "We just need to go over your testimony. Can you tell me what happened in your own words?"

Juliette took a deep breath, ashamed to tell the world of what had happened to her, but knowing she needed to. She closed her eyes and focused slowly on the in-and-out of her breathing. She carefully recalled the events of the night a year before. The party, the sound of the waves, the smell and taste of the drink. She told the attorney how she knew what was going on but couldn't move or scream for help. With a tear, she said that her sister had found her bloody and battered and that she had been too embarrassed to do or say anything at that time.

When she finished, she wiped the few stray tears off her cheek and looked at the lawyer. He nodded to her as he processed everything she had said.

"Thank you, Miss Nicholas. I know this is not easy for you," he commented. "Your story and that of the other girls is similar. We believe it was the same drug used on all of you, as they also were aware of what happened but seemed helpless to do anything. And they were also hidden away and left to be found. Though your case seems to be the only one with so much additional physical violence."

Juliette swallowed hard. "Oh, really? I—I guess that's good for the other girls. I mean, that they weren't hurt as badly."

"Now, the defense will try to make it sound like all of you were willing parties to the events that occurred. They will try to tell the judge that you simply regretted your choice to be intimate with Mr. Herbert and are now seeking revenge. Are you positive that is not the case?"

Shock came over Juliette, and she felt her cheeks redden. "Mr. Conger, I promise you I never had any intention of sleeping with

Buzz Herbert. He raped me and left me lying under a pier. I wish I could take that night back; but more than that, I wish I had reported it to the police that night, so other girls did not have to suffer the same fate."

"That's excellent, Miss Nicholas. Say that exactly," Mr. Conger said. "Alright. Please be in the courthouse lobby at two o'clock sharp. I will see you there. Do you have any questions?"

Juliette shook her head, and Mr. Conger stood. She followed suit, and he showed her to the door. Upon exiting, her father stood up from the chair where he had been sitting.

"Well?" Harvey looked as nervous as Juliette had felt. Juliette loved her father. Why hadn't she trusted him to tell him what had happened immediately after? She would never be able to go back and change things now.

"It was fine. I have to be at the courthouse at two."

Harvey rubbed her arms, despite the heat. "Do you want to rest a bit before we go?" When she nodded, her father guided her to the elevator. "Rest for a little while; then let's get a little bite to eat."

"I don't think I could eat, Daddy," she told him. "I'm too anxious."

"I understand, sweetheart. But you need something to keep up your energy, so you don't get sick. Maybe just some fruit?"

Juliette nodded and opened the door to her hotel room. She entered inside and sat upon the meager, little bed. She missed her mother and Eve, and she really wished they had been able to come with her for moral support. She also missed Booker and prayed with everything she had that he knew just how much she loved him. Mostly, she was looking forward to their wedding just over a week away.

Juliette laid on her bed and closed her eyes. She did not sleep, but she prayed for God to give her wisdom in her words and peace in her heart. She prayed for the other girls who would be coming forward and for their families. And she prayed for Mrs. Herbert—that she would be able to go on with her life after hearing what her son had done. Finally, Juliette lifted up the smallest of prayers for Buzz Herbert. For him to realize just how heinous his actions truly were and to find forgiveness in the Lord.

When Juliette saw the girls testifying against Buzz, she was astonished. They all looked similar to her with hair dark and texture ranging from wavy to tight curls like her own. They were all roughly her height with her milky complexion. There were five girls in all who would go on the witness stand.

Mr. Conger gathered them into a small conference room. One girl brought her father in with her, but none of the others did. They were invited to sit, but all chose to remain standing.

"Thank you, ladies, for being here. This is a trial to convict a man who is the most monstrous kind of criminal," Mr. Conger began. "A rapist. A man who forces himself upon young women. He needs to be put away, and we cannot do that without you. Each of you in here."

He walked along a narrow wall of the room, his voice getting louder as he spoke. It made Juliette mad. It made her blood boil to see justice done for herself and for the other ladies in the room.

"Now," Mr. Conger continued, "each of you will give your testimony of what happened. Nancy Saint Cloud, since you are still a minor, you will be the first on the stand; then your father is free to take you home. Remember, Mr. Saint Cloud, that your daughter might be recalled at another time. After Nancy will be Juliette Nicholas, who was the first victim. After her will be Jill Adams, Mary Sue Smith, and Theresa Farmer."

"I have to wait till last? I don't know if I can wait till last," one girl said excitedly. Juliette guessed she was Theresa Farmer.

"Miss Farmer, I know waiting to go on the witness stand is hard, but it is vital you are the last witness called," Mr. Conger assured her.

Juliette spoke up. "Can you not change the order?"

Peering over his glasses, Mr. Conger addressed Juliette swiftly. "No, sadly, we cannot. Miss Farmer was the final victim in all this and, apparently, the only one to conceive. Her being presented last will hopefully be the final nail in Mr. Herbert's coffin."

Juliette's eyes widened as Theresa Farmer quickly turned her back on the group, but not before Juliette had noticed the roundness of the girl's stomach. Comparing her to Eve, Juliette guessed the girl to be about six months along.

"Miss Saint Cloud, if you will, please," Mr. Conger said, pointing to the door. "Everybody else, stay either in this room or the lobby area. We will get to you as quickly as possible."

The Saint Clouds and Mr. Conger exited the room. Juliette made her way over to Theresa Farmer. "I'm sorry," she said quietly. "I did not mean to call attention to your condition."

The girl sniffled a bit. "Yeah, well. It seems I'm the only one that jerk managed to get pregnant," she said. "So, you're who, again?"

Juliette studied the girl. Her hair fell in loose curls to her shoulders, and her pale skin bore a few acne scars. She had circles around her eyes, and she twisted her hands in nervous energy.

"My name is Juliette Nicholas. I'm from South Carolina," she offered.

Theresa eyed her cautiously. "Oh. The one from the beach," she said. "How long has it been for you?"

Juliette was surprised by the bluntness with which Theresa spoke of the rape. "Um, just over a year ago now."

"Six months for me," she said. "Were you engaged before it happened?" She motioned to the ring Juliette wore on her left hand.

With a smile, Juliette played with her ring. "No. I wasn't. But I am getting married in less than two weeks."

"Lucky you," was the only thing Theresa said back to her. She then left the room, pushing past the other ladies, who now sat quietly.

With Theresa gone, one of the remaining girls spoke to Juliette. "You're getting married in two weeks?"

"Ten days, actually," Juliette said.

The girl narrowed her gaze. "Aren't you scared? Of what will happen? Of what the man will . . . expect?"

Juliette had thought a little about what would be expected on her wedding night. She had been praying about it—for all memories of the past to leave her and for her to be filled only with love and desire for Booker.

"I hope and pray to not recall anything of what happened with Buzz," she said quietly. "But my fiancé knows what happened, and I think he will be patient with me if necessary."

A second girl then added, "I'm surprised you began dating again. It's been since last August for me, and I can't stand to be in a room alone with a man."

"What's your name?" Juliette asked. This girl looked the most like her, and Juliette guessed she might be of mixed blood like Willow.

"I'm Jill," she said. She pointed to the girl who had spoken first and said, "This is Mary Sue."

"I'm Juliette. I'm pleased to meet you, though not so much under the circumstances."

"We know who you are. Jill and I are college friends," Mary Sue said. "We just happened to have met Buzz Herbert around the same time, and he attacked us within days of each other. We were the ones who came forward first, but he wasn't arrested until after he raped that poor, little girl in the fall and Theresa back in December."

"I wish we had reported it sooner," Jill added, shaking her head.

Juliette rushed to their sides. "No! I wish I had reported it sooner. It was last May for me. I was so scared and ashamed, I made my sister promise not to tell anybody, and I never did either. It wasn't until Mrs. Herbert came to our house to tell us what had happened recently that I spoke up."

"Regardless, we are all victims of the same man," Jill said.

"How old is the girl?" Juliette asked.

"Nancy is fifteen. She went with her cousin to a fraternity party over at UT, where she met him. He did the same thing he did to all of us. Put something in her drink, led her away, and had sex with her while she was unable to move or fight back." Jill spoke with a sheen of tears over her eyes. "Jerk. She's just a little girl."

"How old are you?"

"Me? I'm twenty-one, and Mary Sue is twenty-two."

Juliette nodded. "I was only eighteen when it happened."

Mary Sue looked surprised. "I didn't realize you were so young."

Just then, the door opened, and a dour-looking woman came in. "Miss Nicholas, Mr. Conger is ready for you." She held the door open and waited for Juliette to exit before her. Both Jill and Mary Sue nodded to her as she walked past them.

As she followed the woman, Juliette prayed for God to give her wisdom and courage.

Entering the courtroom, Juliette found the benches filled; not a space was left. She quickly scanned the crowd for her father; and when she spotted him, she let out a sigh of relief. She was instructed to wait against the wall for a moment until Mr. Conger called her; then she was to come forward.

It was then that she saw him. Buzz Herbert in the flesh. More than a year after the last time she saw him hovering over her unmoving body. Juliette felt sweat come to her brow and bile rise in her throat. She gripped the wall behind her, feeling for anything she could take hold of to keep herself upright. She had not expected such a reaction from seeing him again. She wanted to run away and lash out at him at the same time.

"Miss Juliette Nicholas, if you will step forward," the judge called.

"Yes, sir," she said meekly and approached where Mr. Conger was standing. He escorted her through a small swinging door onto the courtroom floor, the sound of her heels on the tile the only sound. He motioned to the witness stand, where Juliette took an uncomfortable seat.

Juliette blinked several times. There was a sea of faces before her, and she felt dizzy. The judge must have noticed her being ill at ease because he asked if she wanted some water, which she nodded to accept.

After a sip of cold water and a few deep breaths, she was ready when the bailiff held out the Bible and asked if she would tell the whole truth and nothing but the truth. Juliette agreed.

Mr. Conger stepped out from behind his desk and quickly asked, "Miss Nicholas, are you feeling well?"

After clearing her voice, Juliette said, "I guess I'm a little nervous, but yes, I'm well."

"You looked peaked and ill when you came in; are you sure?"

"Yes, sir. I just was not expecting such a reaction to being here. Thank you," she said, now embarrassed that everyone had noticed her flush.

"Why did you have such a reaction, Miss Nicholas, if you are not ill?" Mr. Conger stopped in front of the box she sat in and looked at her closely.

Juliette suddenly realized where the attorney was going with his questions. "I have not seen Buzz Herbert since the night he attacked me. Seeing him again brought up some very hard memories for me, and that is why I became flushed."

"But you are feeling better now?"

Juliette nodded. "Yes, sir. I am now that I can see my father in the room." She smiled weakly at her father, who sat in the third row behind Mr. Conger's desk.

"Very well," he said with a smile. "Can you please tell the court what happened to you on the night of May twenty-eighth, nineteen-sixty-eight?"

"I was invited to a party, where my drink was drugged. Then I was led away from the group and raped under a pier in Myrtle Beach and left there until my sister discovered me."

"Is the man who raped you in this room now, Miss Nicholas?" Mr. Conger moved backward, so he was not obstructing her view of anybody in the room.

A knot formed in her throat, but Juliette managed to say, "Yes, he is. Buzz Herbert, sitting at the desk, is the man who raped me." She nodded in his direction as tears tracked down her cheeks.

"Thank you. Can you now tell me exactly what happened to you?"

Juliette took several deep breaths. Before she spoke, she glanced at Buzz, who sat at the desk opposite Mr. Conger's. He sat back, appearing relaxed. Almost as if he was enjoying hearing his victims rehash what he had done to them. Juliette looked away in disgust.

"Yes, sir, I can," she said boldly. "I met Buzz Herbert when he and his mother came to my parents' home as dinner guests. They were new to our church, where my father is the preacher, and it is our custom to invite new parishioners over. Buzz invited me to a party the next weekend. I was permitted to accept by my father, so long as my sister accompanied us, which she did. When Buzz got me a drink, I thought it tasted strange; but I didn't want to seem ungrateful for the beverage, so I drank it anyway."

Juliette recounted the rest of the story—from Buzz leading her away from the party to Jesse taking her to his house and calling his doctor friend to come look her over. She wiped tears away every few minutes, but Juliette knew that her blouse was tear-stained. When she finished, she took a deep breath and squeezed her eyes shut for a moment before opening them.

"Thank you," Mr. Conger said when she opened her eyes. "Miss Nicholas, I hate being so personal, but it is vital to this case. Have you ever been with another man aside from the defendant?"

"No. That's not something I would do brashly without loving someone dearly and being married," she said. She took a deep breath and fought the urge to massage her aching temples.

"Okay. Did you tell the defendant that you were unwilling? Did you fight back?"

"I tried to yell for help, but no sounds would come from my throat. I also did my best to fight; but not only were my arms and legs heavy like lead, but he also had my arms wrapped up and pinned down. I was completely unable to move, but I was very aware of what was happening," Juliette told him. "When my sister found me, I was still unable to move and had to be carried to a car."

"And your sister and her boyfriend at the time tended to you?"

"Yes, and they called a friend, who is a doctor."

"Your Honor," Mr. Conger said, addressing the judge, "we have that affidavit in the file." The judge nodded.

"One more question for you, Miss Nicholas. How old were you when this happened?"

Juliette had never thought age was a factor; but in the courtroom, it added to the charges against Buzz. "I was eighteen at the time, sir."

"Thank you, Miss Nicholas," Mr. Conger said before turning her over to the defense.

"Miss Nicholas, you are wearing a nice diamond ring," the other attorney said. Juliette recalled that his name was Mr. Harper. "Where did you get it?"

"Objection!" Mr. Conger called.

"Overruled," the judge said. "Please answer."

"It's from my fiancé."

"Fiancé? Isn't that nice. How long have you been engaged?" Mr. Harper stood from his chair and came into the center of the room.

"About three months," Juliette answered.

"So, you have had no trouble moving on from your relationship with my client?"

Juliette sighed. "Buzz and I did not have a relationship. We didn't know each other long enough for a relationship to form."

"But you went on a date with him. Surely, that implies a relationship," Mr. Harper suggested. He threw his hands up in the air for a dramatic effect.

"One date is not a relationship. The one date we had wasn't much of a date in the first place, since all he did was put something in my drink and rape me," Juliette said, getting frustrated. "But yes, it did take time for me to move past the pain Buzz Herbert caused me."

"So, you were dating your now-fiancé at the time you went on this date with my client?"

"No. I had not even met my fiancé yet," Juliette said. Every word she spoke sounded silly, and she felt embarrassed to have her life open for scrutiny.

"So, you went from dating my client, Mr. Herbert, to dating another man and are now engaged to him—all within a year's time?"

Juliette blinked. "Yes. That's right."

"So, you did date my client," he said softly. Then suddenly, he loudly called out, "Miss Nicholas! How do you know he put something in your drink?"

"It tasted funny, chalky almost." Juliette fiddled with her ring, but then remembered to hold her hands still.

"Did you see him put something—a pill perhaps—into it?" Mr. Harper came closer to the witness stand and leaned in toward her.

"No, sir. But I—" But before Juliette could speak again, she was interrupted.

"Might I suggest, Miss Nicholas, that instead of being a victim like you claim to be, you instead regret having made the decision to be intimate with my client and decided to cry rape? Or perhaps your family found out about your loose ways, and you wanted a way to cover your sins?"

Mr. Harper raised his arm up with his voice. Juliette felt very small and scared on the witness stand.

"No," she said with a shaky voice. "No. I did not make any decision to be intimate with that man. Any choice I had was taken from me as I tried to get away from him and found my limbs tied up and unable to move. And my family had no idea about what had happened until Mrs. Herbert came to our house saying her son had been arrested. It was then that I told them what happened."

Tears came freely down Juliette's face, and she felt her curls springing free from the bun she had carefully twisted them in to that morning. Were all lawyers trained to scare the life out of people?

"So, why did you wait so long? Why did you not report it when it happened?"

"I was scared," Juliette admitted. "I was scared what other people would think of me. And I thought I had done something wrong. But I know now that the only thing I did wrong was to wait so long before coming forward. If I had told the police what had happened to me last summer, perhaps the other four girls testifying here would not have been raped as well."

Mr. Harper was silent for a moment as he thought. "So, you were scared of what people would think?"

"Yes."

"You were scared people would think you were nothing but a loose woman? Or that you allowed men you had just met to have their way with you?"

"No, not at all," Juliette said defensively. "I was scared people wouldn't believe me."

"Because the rape is a lie. You willingly had intercourse with Mr. Herbert, didn't you?"

"No!"

Mr. Conger stood. "Objection! He is badgering the witness."

"Overruled, Mr. Conger. Mr. Harper, please get to the point."

Mr. Harper got closer to the judge's bench. "My point, Your Honor, is that we believe Miss Nicholas to be a woman who made a mistake. She was intimate with my client and later regretted the action because of her impending nuptials."

"But that's not true."

"Let's talk about when you claim your sister found you. You said you had to be carried to a car?"

"Yes."

"Who carried you? Surely, not your sister?"

Juliette shook her head. "No, her boyfriend at the time carried me to his car, and we went to his home, where they called a friend who is a doctor."

"Do we have anything from this boyfriend on record?"

"I'm afraid he passed away earlier this year," Juliette said, taking a drink of the water in front of her and wishing the man would finish.

For another twenty minutes, the attorney kept trying to find a way to make her say she had willingly slept with Buzz, but Juliette held her resolve. She never consented; she never wanted it; and she was completely unable to defend herself from his advances.

"That will be all, Miss Nicholas," Mr. Harper said. "You can step down."

The judge repeated, "You can step down, Miss Nicholas."

The bailiff came forward and escorted Juliette down from the stand and to the swinging door that led through the audience. She quickly exited the room, her father on her heels.

In the lobby, Juliette collapsed in her father's arms with a fit of tears. "He twisted my words! I would never have been with him in that way, never!"

Harvey rubbed her back and led her to a bench. "I know, sweetheart. I know. But that's his job—to try to make you look as bad as his client already does. But you know what? It won't work. You were sincere. And he tried the same tactic on the young lady who testified before you."

"He did? How did she do?" Juliette lifted her head and looked at her father.

"She was scared, too. She is only fifteen, you know," he said. Juliette nodded. "But she was strong, just like you. I'm sure the others will be strong, also. There is no way all five of you are lying. And it's my understanding that his methods were very similar in each case."

Juliette nodded. "Yes, and did you know we all look alike? We all have dark, curly hair and pale skin. We're all even about the same height."

"I'll be sure Mr. Conger is aware of that in case he didn't notice. You know, we men don't always notice the little details," Harvey said with a slight smile.

The doors to the courtroom opened, and people began filing out. "Where are they going? Are we done?" Juliette was hopeful that things would be done quickly.

"Probably just recessed for the day. It is approaching five o'clock," her father said as he checked his watch.

Juliette frowned that they were not done, but she knew these could be lengthy ordeals. She was ready to go back to her hotel room and go to sleep. She felt like she could sleep for three days, given the afternoon she had just gone through.

"Miss Nicholas, a word?" A young man with a tie and notepad approached her.

Then another person came over with a video camera. And more followed. News reporters. Camera flashes started going off around Juliette, and she held her hands up in front of her face, trying to block their advances.

"Miss Nicholas! Did Buzz Herbert really rape you?"

"Were you conscious when it happened?"

"Was Mr. Herbert your boyfriend? How many times did you sleep with him?"

Tears streamed down Juliette's face. She was horrified that people would ask such imposing and rude questions. Her father tried to keep the reporters away from her as best he could, but still flashbulbs went off in her face.

"I heard your fiancé is a black man. Is that true?"

That question made Juliette's head snap up. How had they heard that? Would they go after Booker or her family back home?

Suddenly, the reporters began shuffling away, and Juliette could hear shouting coming from behind them. Several uniformed police officers were herding the news correspondents away from her like stray cattle.

"Come on, Juliette," her father whispered, taking her arm. "Let's get out of here."

Waves on the Horizon

WITH HER SISTER AND FATHER now home and Buzz Herbert behind bars, Eve felt like she could let out a sigh of relief. She had cried tears and shouted praises when her father had called and said that Buzz would be spending the better part of thirty years in prison.

Juliette's wedding was now only two days away, and everyone was frantically scurrying around trying to get the final things done. But not Eve. On this morning, Eve was going on her second date with Patrick McKenzie.

When he had stopped by the night before asking for time with her and Willow, Eve had suggested a breakfast date, so she could spend the rest of the day helping her mother and sister at the church. She was thrilled at the idea of another date with Patrick. They hadn't been alone together since weeks before when he had taken her to dinner, but he had come to the house for dinner at least twice a week since then. He and Booker now had their own places at the dinner table.

Eve was still unsure of how to proceed with Patrick. On one hand, he was everything a girl could want in a boyfriend—or more, if it came to that. But then again, she had been burned before by what she thought was love and had the child to prove it. Eve was also concerned that perhaps Patrick was more in love with Willow than the idea of a girlfriend. But her feelings for him were growing, and she thought of him more than she cared to admit.

She dressed Willow for their date and went downstairs while it was still quiet. Her mother and Alisa were already at the bakery making Juliette's wedding cake; her father and Joey were probably still asleep. Juliette was probably getting her beauty rest as well.

Glancing in the mirror, Eve turned sideways and studied her figure. In the almost four months since Willow had been born, she had slimmed down considerably. Of course, the diet she had put herself on had helped. She had been quite slim before, but now bore a mother's body. Her chest was rounder and firmer, her belly softer, and her hips wider. She was thankful she had not gotten many stretch marks.

Eve took a step back and assessed her outfit. She was nervous, but wanted to appear as casual as she could. She wore a purple sundress that ended above her freckled knees. The straps were thick and the neckline high to cover her now-ample bosom. She wore cork wedge heels that made her two inches taller than she really was.

"Stunning," a voice said behind her.

She turned quickly and saw Patrick standing before her in the doorway. "Oh, Patrick! You scared me." When Willow began to cry in her arms, she brought her close. "And I scared you. I am sorry."

"You're a great mother," he said as he took several steps toward her.

"I am amazed at how naturally things come to me," she admitted. "I thought I would be fighting to figure it out. But I love being a mother. I would love to have more one day." She smiled at him and nuzzled her daughter's neck so she giggled.

"I can't wait to have children," Patrick said, "as soon as I find the right woman." He raised an eyebrow at her.

A blush came over Eve, and she managed to hide her face behind her daughter for a moment while she recovered. She couldn't believe she had said she wanted more children. And then for Patrick to say he needed to find the right woman like that! Eve wondered if he thought she was the right woman, and she wondered it herself.

"Shall we go? There's that new pancake house up the beach a ways that I thought we could try out," Patrick said with a smirk on his face. "It's called Denny's. Have you been there?"

"I haven't been out for breakfast in almost a year, actually. So no, I haven't," she said as he held the door open for her. "And in the last few months, coffee is about all I manage while trying to sort through laundry and diapers and feeding this little one. Soon enough, she'll be moving around the house, and then I don't know what I'll do."

"Being a single mother is hard, I'll wager," Patrick said, opening the car door for Eve. She slid in and positioned Willow on her lap for the short drive.

When he got into the car, Eve replied, "It's not easy, but then I think even if I were married, or Willow had a father, it would still be difficult. But my parents and siblings have been wonderful. They have been so accepting of Willow and have really defended us against the gossip and stares."

"Because you're a single mom?"

"Because my daughter is black," Eve said matter-of-factly. When Patrick's eyes widened, Eve realized he didn't see the color of her daughter's skin, and that endeared him to her all the more. "You don't see it, do you?"

Patrick started the car but did not put it into reverse. He took the infant's hand in his and smiled at Eve. "No. I don't. I just see her. I see the daughter of an amazing woman. Now, she doesn't really look like you, but she looks like Juliette; and she does have the hint of red in those baby-soft curls."

"So, you're not bothered by her skin color?" Eve shifted uncomfortably; everyone seemed to care about Willow's skin color.

"No. I think her skin is beautiful. I think her dark color is just as beautiful as your porcelain skin and dotting of freckles." Patrick smiled at her quickly, and Eve could see him redden a little as he threw the car into reverse and backed out of the driveway.

After the short drive, they walked into the restaurant and were showed to a table by an older black woman. She eyed the trio as they sat. "You need a high chair for your . . . ?"

Eve met the woman's gaze. "My daughter? No, thank you. I will hold her."

Again, the woman just stared, her eyes going from Willow to Eve, then back to Willow. Eve could tell she was debating saying something further, but instead, she asked for their drink orders.

When she had walked away shaking her head, Patrick quietly asked, "Do you get that a lot?"

"Everywhere," Eve said with a heavy sigh. "Everyone cares about her skin color. Everyone cares how her coloring and my coloring compare. And I can tell that being out with you, with your blond hair, makes her stand out even more. I hate it for her. I can handle it, but she's just a baby. I don't want people judging her because her parents are different races."

"I'm sorry, Eve. I had no idea it was so difficult. I was raised to treat all people as part of God's family. I was never keenly aware of race," Patrick said with sympathy in his eyes.

"Same here. I never thought much about it until I was with Jesse, and we got stares and some unbelievably rude comments." Patrick did not respond, and Eve quickly spoke again. "I'm sorry. Should I not mention Jesse?"

"He's your past, not mine. And no matter what mistakes he made, he did make Willow, so he will always be a part of your life."

"And that's why I am so hesitant with you. I don't know if you can or would want to accept all the baggage I bring with me," Eve said honestly. "Jesse may have left me, and he may be dead; but he will always be Willow's father."

Patrick shook his head as drinks were set in front of them. The waitress left again, and Patrick said, "No. One day you will get married, and that man will become Willow's father. A father is someone who loves and raises a child, not the man who created the child."

Eve nodded in agreement. "You are very right. I had not thought of it that way. Jesse did give her life, but he gave up on her as soon as he knew she existed. He wanted to kill this precious child," Eve said as she gulped air, unable to imagine what she would have missed out on if she had given in to Jesse's request for an abortion.

"He wanted to kill her? What do you mean?"

Eve blinked as she looked at Patrick. "Have I not told you about what he said when I told him I was pregnant?"

Before Patrick could respond, the waitress came back with her pencil and pad of paper. She did not speak, just stood before them, waiting, and eyeing Willow. Eve was fed up with the woman's obvious scrutiny.

"My daughter is adorable, isn't she?"

The woman startled. "Yeah, she is. But you two is awful white to have a black baby."

Eve fumed and felt heat rise on the back of her neck. "I don't see where it's any of your business," she said, trying to keep her voice under control. "I birthed her; she is my child. The rest doesn't matter, does it?"

"I ain't askin', sugar. I just want to take your order," the woman said as she puckered her lips.

Patrick quickly spoke up, rattling off what he wanted. Eve's anger caused her appetite to leave her, but she still ordered coffee and biscuits with gravy. The woman left them, appearing to have as little interest in them as possible.

"Oh, that makes me so angry! Who cares if you are Willow's father? Who cares if she's black? I don't care," Eve huffed. "And really, she's only half-black. I'm white. But white people don't accept her because she's too dark; and black people don't accept her because she's too light, and she's with me."

"I'm so sorry, Eve," Patrick said, laying his hand over hers on the table. "People are nosy and rude. But I think you shocked her well enough. We can complain to the manager."

With a shake of her head, Eve rejected the idea. "No. It will just cause a scene. It's not worth the hassle."

Patrick left his hand on top of hers, and Eve noticed. As she cooled down, she felt the soft movement of Patrick's thumb sweeping over the top of her hand. Eve closed her eyes a moment, hoping Patrick would think that she was still trying to calm down; but really, she was trying to memorize the feeling of Patrick's hand on hers. She paid attention to how her pulse slowly quickened, and she could feel the heat rise from her midsection. She smiled.

"Is something amusing?" Patrick asked, his hand still staying in place.

Straightening her face, Eve replied, "Nothing. I just—well, despite all this, I'm having a good time. It's nice to have someone to talk to, someone who feels the way I do."

Flashing his perfectly white teeth, Patrick smiled. "Yes, it is. I think you were going to tell me something about Jesse; but if this is not a good time, I won't press the matter."

"Oh. That. No, I might as well tell you now before Willow is old enough to understand it. If, by chance, you are still around in any capacity when she is older, Patrick, I am swearing you to secrecy, just as I have Juliette and my parents. Do you understand this?"

"I believe I do, yes."

"Even if you are just her doctor or someone we pass on the street, you are never to tell her this." When Patrick nodded, she continued. "Jesse told me he was getting married at the same time I told him I was pregnant. When he said he couldn't have a mixed-race baby out in the world, he offered to pay for an abortion. I refused and told him my child was precious, even if he did not think so."

Shock came over Patrick's face. His cheeks blanched, and his brow furrowed. He shook his head as if the information wasn't registering with him. "He what?"

"Jesse offered to pay for me to kill the child I am holding in my lap. Right after he told me he was going to seminary to become a preacher." Eve laughed then.

"I cannot believe that. The Jesse I worked beside last summer would have never suggested such a thing. He must have been a masterful liar."

"What a hypocrite he was. How did I not see it?" Eve tried to blink back tears, but knew she would be unsuccessful.

The hand that had been resting on her own moved, leaving a cold shadow behind. Eve looked up at Patrick, knowing tears swam in her eyes. What would he say to that, she wondered.

"You were in love," he said quietly, his hand retreating under the table.

"I thought I was in love. But I wasn't," Eve said plainly. "We had sparks, but nothing lasting. As my wise sister told me, sparks fizzle out. It's the burning embers that keep you warm."

She smiled at him then, a genuine smile that made her wonder if Patrick McKenzie would be the one to fan those embers into a long-lasting flame. She prayed in her heart that he would be, and the thought both startled and excited her. Perhaps her heart was moving along faster than her head.

Their conversation shifted as their breakfast was served. Willow fell asleep in the crook of Eve's arm, and she struggled to eat and hold her daughter at the same time. Patrick—who seemed to have wolfed down his omelet, grits, and orange juice—offered to hold the baby.

"No, I'm fine; you don't have to bother," Eve said as she tried to scoop up a piece of biscuit and failed miserably.

"Come on, Evie," he said, using her family's pet name for her. "It's not a bother. Ever." He held out his arms. "I promise," he added.

Gently, Eve moved to place Willow in Patrick's waiting arms. She didn't want Willow to wake, especially since she was not in a place where she could take her to nurse. She stood and moved closer to Patrick, then lowered her body to his while extending the arm that held her daughter. Effortlessly, Patrick cradled Willow with both arms and held her close to his body. The child only sighed in response.

"You're an expert," Eve said as she stretched out her stiff arm.

"I hold a lot of babies." Patrick laughed.

"Oh, that's right. I guess you do," Eve said, suddenly feeling jealous that he paid attention to children other than her own. "I forget about that sometimes. What made you decide to be a doctor?"

As she ate, Patrick happily began to tell her about his childhood dreams. He had loved to bandage up his friends when they had scrapes and cuts and was even known to mend his sister's baby dolls from time to time. Doctoring had always been a part of him, he told her. And as he grew, his passion for helping children grew as well. When it came time for college, there had been no question as to what he would pursue.

"I wish I had known what I wanted to be last summer. Maybe I would have some direction now," Eve said. "I know I will need a job—and soon. I'm helping at the bakery when I can, but it's certainly not my calling like it is for Mom and Juliette. I just don't know what I would pick as a career."

Patrick glanced from Willow to Eve and smiled. "I think your career picked you."

Leaning back in her chair, Eve frowned. "As much as I love Willow, she doesn't pay me. I can't live with Mom and Dad forever and mooch off of them until Willow is grown. I need a job."

"What interests you?"

"I don't know," Eve said, shrugging her shoulders. "I don't have a passion like you do for medicine or like Juliette and Booker do for food. I like to read. I like to laugh. And I love being a mother."

As she thought, Eve realized she really did not have a passion. When she wasn't busy being a mother or keeping the house in order while the rest of her family worked, Eve was found with her nose in a book. She read to Willow every day. She loved escaping to the lands of mystery novels and romantic stories. But she didn't tell Patrick that for fear he would think it odd.

"Being a mother suits you," Patrick said as the nosy waitress brought their bill over. He rose from the table and added, "If God has anything else planned for you, you will know when the time is right."

Eve nodded as she followed Patrick toward the counter to pay.

As she walked, a woman she passed grabbed her arm. "Excuse me, darlin'," she said. Eve looked at the woman, afraid she would make a comment about Willow. "I just have to tell you that the sight of your husband holding your baby is just precious. Cherish these moments with your family."

She quickly looked up and saw what the woman saw. A handsome, young man, strong and in his prime, cradling a tiny bundle in pink close to his body. He was protecting her, both of his arms wrapped around Willow with only her socked feet and a sprout of curly hair peeking out for spectators to see. Eve felt like the picture before her suddenly knocked the wind out of her. It was beautiful. A father and his child—the picture of happiness. The embers that stayed warm when Patrick was around grew a little hotter in that moment.

Her eyes misted over, both out of affection for the two people she looked at and for the pain she felt in knowing that they were not father and daughter as the woman had assumed.

As she fought back tears, Eve looked again to the older woman who must have taken her misty eyes for love. "I know it's a sweet sight. I miss those days. Enjoy it, young lady; they'll be gone in a flash."

She released Eve's arm, and Eve whispered, "Thank you," to her before slowly moving past to where Patrick was waiting for her.

"What did the woman say? Did she say something rude?" Patrick looked ready to jump to her defense.

"No, no," Eve said, seemingly in a daze. "She told me to cherish the memory of my husband holding my child."

"Oh," Patrick said as he blinked several times. "I am sorry, Eve. I—I don't know what to say." He paused where he was and looked at Willow, still fast asleep in his arms.

"I do," Eve said softly. "Thank you. Thank you for giving me and my daughter something that should be normal. One day, you will be an excellent father," she told him. She stood on her toes and brushed a light kiss on Patrick's cheek before taking Willow from him and pushing through the door.

The grin on Patrick's face did not escape her notice one bit.

The wedding ceremony had been gorgeous, Eve thought. Juliette had been a vision in her lace overlay gown, her dark curls peeping out from under her veil. And Booker had shed tears as he watched his bride make her way down the aisle of Respite Baptist Church.

Both of their fathers had officiated, since both were pastors, and jointly pronounced them as husband and wife. The mothers had appropriately cried; the congregation had uttered a collective sigh at their first kiss; and Eve herself had applauded wildly as they made their way back up the aisle as a married couple.

During the ceremony, Eve, of course, had one eye on her sister and one out in the crowd, making sure Willow did not act up. But, she realized, she didn't need to worry because Willow sat quietly, patiently—not in the lap of her grandmother, but in the lap of Patrick McKenzie. He had given her a pair of sunglasses to hold, and she pleasantly shook them and chewed on them, never once making a peep during the entire ceremony. And when she observed Patrick adjust Willow in his lap and plant a kiss on her chubby cheek, Eve felt her knees go weak and let out a sigh so loud, she was sure everyone had heard her.

She was falling, hard, for the man holding her child.

At the reception held, of course, at the Blue Rooster, Eve was announced with the rest of the bridal party and made her way over to her mother, who was now holding a drowsy Willow in her arms.

"She needs to lie down. Do you have that seat in the car?" Eve whispered to her mother.

"Yes, I'll send your father out to get it after the father's dance," Abby told her. "Do you think Willow will sleep?"

"Maybe we can find a quiet corner for her," Eve said, shrugging. "She was so well-behaved during the ceremony."

Her mother looked her in the eye. "The minute she saw Patrick, she lunged forward for him," Abby said. "She loves him. And he seems to love her."

Eve smiled. "I know." The memory of watching Patrick kiss her daughter came back to her.

Abby's face turned serious, and she asked, "And you?"

Feeling a blush rise on her cheeks, Eve nodded her head to her mother. "And I think I love him, too."

Abby nodded and gave her eldest daughter a knowing smile. "I know."

Eve settled in next to her mother and watched as Juliette and Booker entered to a rousing round of applause and took the floor for their first dance. As the band began a steady, slow tune, Eve closed her eyes and swayed to the music. After a moment, the crowd began to chuckle; and Eve opened her eyes to see her father butting into the dance, whisking Juliette away from her groom. Booker laughed and graciously gave up his bride for her father.

The band's lead singer announced, "The bride invites all fathers and daughters to the dance floor to join them."

Slowly, men and their daughters filled the dance floor. Some girls were little, others teenagers. Abby passed Willow to Eve when her own father, Nathan Walker, held out his hand for her to dance. Eve's grandfather winked at her as he swept his daughter into the group.

"I know I'm not her father," a deep voice said behind her, "but I would like to ask Willow and her mother to dance."

Turning to see Patrick, Eve immediately embraced him, feeling tears threaten to come forward. Eve suddenly realized at that moment that she did think of Patrick as Willow's father. He had been a father figure to her since she had been born. He gently wrapped his arms around her and Willow, and they began to sway to the music.

As she rested her head on his chest, Willow's head on her own, she whispered to him, "Patrick?"

"Yes?" His baritone voice reverberated in his chest against her ear.

"You—you are like a father to Willow. And I'm ready to move to the next level, Patrick," Eve said, sighing against him.

"Eve, do you mean that?" He stopped moving and cupped her face in his hands.

Gazing up into his piercing blue eyes, Eve nodded. "I think God brought us together. I realized it watching you during the wedding. I want what Juliette and Booker have. I want that with you."

A smile broke out onto Patrick's face as he bent down over Eve and Willow. "That is the best news I have ever heard," he said as he lowered his face to hers.

Patrick's lips brushed against Eve's softly, tentatively at first. And with one hand on her and one hand on Willow, Eve felt Patrick deepen the kiss. Her heart racing and her mind reeling, Eve could feel the heat of the burning embers in the pit of her stomach burst into flames as her heart broke open with love for the man kissing her.

Pulling away, Eve quickly scanned the crowd around her. Spotting Alisa, she darted to her and passed off an almost-asleep baby, promising to take her back in a few minutes.

She returned to Patrick and pulled him into a back corner of the restaurant, where nobody else was standing, and smiled. "Now, tell me that one more time," she said as she laced her fingers behind Patrick's neck.

"I think I love you, Eve," Patrick whispered in her ear as he nibbled on the lobe. "No, I know I love you."

Feeling a slight urgency, Eve pulled him closer. "Do you, Patrick? Oh, do you?" She kissed his neck and his cheek before he found her mouth again. "I love you, too," she said between kisses.

With a hard moan, Patrick broke away from Eve and looked her in the eye. "What about taking it slow?"

"It's hard to take it slow when you know what you want. When you know what God wants for you," she said. And she did feel like God had told her exactly what He had planned for her. And a life with Patrick and Willow was it.

"I know how you feel. That's exactly how I felt when I saw you this spring at the bakery. It was like God had opened my eyes and shown me you. And when I met Willow, I instantly felt like she was my daughter."

"Did you really?" Eve could hardly believe her ears. She had feared that she was destined to never find a man accepting of her previous relationship and the daughter it produced. And here was a man who not only knew about it, but who also loved her child wholly.

"Eve, when we get married . . . " He licked his lips and paused. "One day, when we get married, I want to adopt Willow as my own."

Eve jumped into his arms once again, not caring that tears freely flowed down her cheeks, ruining her make-up. "Patrick, I didn't think I could love you more, but I do now!"

He laughed and said, "Mind you, that was not a proposal. I'm just saying that one day, I will adopt Willow and be the father she deserves to have and the husband you deserve to have."

With a sly smile, Eve wiped the tears from her face. "I know, and I thank God. I hope one day I can be the wife you deserve." And she kissed him again.

An Ever-Changing Sea

JULIETTE HAD LOVED EVERY MOMENT of her wedding ceremony. It was exactly what she wanted—fun, full of family and friends, and centered on the Lord, Who had blessed them. With the main dances over and everyone seated to feast on the fare before them, she scanned the crowd for her twin sister.

As Juliette's gaze focused in on the trio her eyes found, she instantly knew. Her sister was in love. She watched as Eve snuggled into Patrick, his arm draped protectively over her shoulder. They were looking deep into each other's eyes, without a care for anything else in the world at that moment. And Willow lay in the crook of her mother's arm between them, sleeping soundly. Juliette could feel her heartbeat quicken as she saw them; joy for her sister overflowed.

Almost as if by instinct, Eve tore her eyes from the man at her side and met Juliette's. Their gazes locked; the twins were instantly able to read each other's mind. Juliette could feel her sister tell her that this was it—she had found the same love in Patrick that Juliette had found in Booker. Juliette nodded to her sister and smiled as her sister nodded in return.

"What was that?" Booker asked at her side. "Who are you nodding to?"

She motioned to where Eve and Patrick sat. "That," she said. "My sister has found the same happiness I have with you. That makes this day twice as perfect."

Booker kissed her on the cheek. "I know you've been praying for them, Juliette. I'm happy they're happy. And I'm happy they have made you happy."

Turning to her husband, Juliette whispered, "Oh, but you have made me happiest of all. This truly is the perfect day. I can't wait for the fireworks later."

With a soft kiss, Booker replied with a smile, "I can't wait for the even better fireworks after that."

Juliette ducked her head down so nobody would see her blush, and she grinned at Booker.

She was nervous about their first night as husband and wife. And thankfully, Booker understood that. She had been praying for a month that she would be able to overcome any fears she had about them joining as one. Juliette wanted any and all lingering thoughts of what Buzz had done to her gone; and thankfully, seeing him being led in shackles to the jailhouse had eased much of the heaviness on her heart. But still, she prayed again that nothing would hinder her desire for her husband on this night or any after.

When the meal had been cleared away and the guests began to roam around, talk, and dance, Juliette sought out her love-struck sister.

"Oh, Evie, I am so happy for you!" She embraced her sister, not caring if her dress wrinkled.

"For me? Jules, it's your wedding day! I am so happy for you," Eve said as she smiled at her sister. Juliette felt her heart swell with love for her sister. They truly had an unbreakable bond.

"God has blessed us both, hasn't He?" Juliette asked. When Eve nodded, she added, "It's been a long year. It's been a tough year. But

Evie, look at the blessings that have come from sadness. Last year, I never would have thought we'd be where we are now."

Putting her arm around her sister, Juliette saw a tear slip down Eve's cheeks. "Oh, Juliette. It's hard to think that without the bad we went through, we wouldn't have the good we have now."

"So, you love him?" Juliette asked her sister.

Eve nodded. "And he loves me. And he wants to adopt Willow officially."

This time, tears swam in her eyes as Juliette clung to her sister.

A voice came through the microphone and called to the duo. "Why don't we have a special dance for the bride, Juliette, and her sister, Eve?"

The pair laughed as Aretha Franklin's "Natural Woman" began to play. Juliette led her sister out to the dance floor, and they began to dance around each other, laughing all the way.

With the reception over and the guests waving them on, Juliette and Booker sped away in a borrowed Ford Mustang convertible, Juliette's veil blowing behind her. They headed to Hilton Head Island, where they would honeymoon for a few days before going to Washington, D.C., to look at apartments for their upcoming move.

The three-hour trip was pleasant, and the pair spent the entire time talking about who had come to the wedding, what the dances were, and recalling other wedding details.

"I hope the photographer got a picture of me and Evie dancing tonight," Juliette said with a smile. "That was the best part of the reception."

"More fun than dancing with me?" Booker asked with a teasing laugh.

"That's different," she said. "This is my sister."

"I know," he said with a grin. "I think he did get a picture. I'm glad I suggested a dance for you two to the wedding singer."

"Was that you?" Juliette said with surprise. "Thank you! It really meant a lot to us both."

"You're welcome," Booker said as he turned into the hotel parking lot. "I know how special Eve is to you."

"She is my twin sister, and the only one I'll ever have."

Epilogue

CHRISTMAS, 1978, FINALLY SAW THE entire Nicholas family together for the first time in almost a decade. Abby and Harvey had cleaned every nook and cranny to fit their ever-expanding family into their house. What had once been a spacious and roomy home had turned into cramped quarters when their children, children-in-law, and grandchildren trooped into town for the holidays.

Juliette and Booker still resided in Washington, D.C., where they had opened a successful chain of restaurants called Equal Bites. Booker had hand-created each and every recipe served in their five District-area restaurants. Juliette, for her part, had become a pastry chef and had created the amazing dessert menu. In addition to the five restaurants, Juliette was also a successful wedding cake baker who was highly sought after by the political elite.

After moving to Washington, they had wasted no time in setting up connections all throughout the city. Both appreciated the fact that nobody seemed to mind their being a mixed-race couple—at least, not enough to mention it. Booker had begun to work as a chef in an elite restaurant, and Juliette had gone to pastry school. Two years later, they had opened their first restaurant in downtown D.C.

A year after that, their first child, Eric, was born. With a mop of curly black hair and light skin, the only nod to his father's ancestry was his decidedly Asian eyes. Juliette thought her son was the most beautiful child God had ever created until three years later when their daughter, Jewel, came along. With skin coloring more like her father and her aunt Eve's auburn hair color, Jewel was an exotic beauty if ever there was one.

Now at seven and four years old, they ran through their grand-parents' house, squealing in delight over candy canes and the idea of Santa soon arriving to bestow gifts to all the children.

Eve's family had also grown exponentially in ten years' time. Patrick McKenzie had made good on his promise to adopt Willow after marrying Eve at Christmastime, 1969. His formal adoption of Willow happened right before her first birthday, and it was no surprise that the child's first words on her birthday had been "Dada."

Eve and Patrick had wasted no time in adding to their family when Starla and Isla were born, one after another. Both with whitish-blonde hair and blue eyes, they were the spitting image of their father, with the exception of their curly hair that matched their older sister's. Eve had surprised them all with the birth of their first son, Nathaniel, earlier this year.

With four children, Eve kept busy as a full-time mother, and Patrick worked hard as a pediatrician. Eve had recently decided that she wanted to write and had set to working on a novel in the recent months between diaper changes and homework.

Willow had taken charge of the grandchildren as the oldest of the lot. She toted her baby brother on her hip through the house with ease —the same way her mother did.

Abby marveled at how far her eldest children had come since that fateful summer over ten years before. For a time, Abby had worried they would never recover from the hurts they had received—both individually and jointly. The girls had grown apart and back together several times as they sought their paths on their own without the other by their side.

As for her other children, with the birth of their first child, Pete and Linda had asked if they could call her and Harvey grandmother and grandfather. Abby had been only too happy to oblige. She thought of Pete to be just as much her own child as he was her brother's. Abby knew Peter and Emmeline watched over their son and three grandchildren from Heaven.

Joey had married earlier in the year, and Abby was thrilled to have a nice girl named Anita as a daughter-in-law. Both Joey and Anita were photographers and had fallen in love while competing for clients. They now worked side by side in their own joint business.

As for the youngest, Alisa had blossomed in the midst of her sisters' drama, and Abby had nearly missed it. Now at twenty-four years old, Alisa had gotten her undergraduate degree and was now in the midst of law school. She had high aspirations, and Abby knew her youngest child would go far. She had been talking with many young men over the years, but Alisa had been too focused on her career to worry much about settling down.

It was Christmas Eve, and Abby sat on her weathered couch and smiled. She and Harvey had been married thirty-five years and raised five beautiful children. She was still as in love with her husband now as she had been at the start of World War Two. And she still had a hard time not mothering her brood. She had nine grandchildren to her name this year, and she knew more would come.

Sweet Treats had been sold, so Abby could enjoy both retirement and the grandbabies. She watched Pete and Linda's trio every afternoon until they got off work. She spent as much time as possible with the other four, who lived close, and even spent weeks at a time visiting Juliette and her children in Washington.

As she thought back on the blessings of her life, Abby remembered the times when she doubted God, the times when she had been angry with Him. The death of her brother and sister-in-law, leaving her with an infant to raise. The infertility that stole joy from her year after year. The loss of innocence for her twin daughters in the span of one summer.

But then, she realized how God had used those things for joy in the end. She was able to raise a piece of the brother she cherished. She appreciated the four children she later gave birth to more because of the years she yearned to fill her arms. And even though the summer of 1968 had been almost impossible for her family, Abby gained a beautiful and smart granddaughter and two amazing sons-in-law from it.

God had surely blessed her and had been faithful to her family. And she marveled that each and every member of her large family placed their faith solely in their Father above. And for that, she was eternally grateful.

WAR-TORN HEART

Read Abby and Harvey's Story . . .

Abigail Walker, a young woman from rural South Carolina, is on the cusp of womanhood, aching to be able to run wild as the younger children do, yet yearning for things she has yet to understand. Awkward and unsure of herself, Abby is flustered when she meets Harvey Nicholas, the nephew of a family at her church and a cadet from Clemson College. As summer begins, Abby finds herself constantly in the company of Harvey and falling quickly in love with him.

As rumors of war begin to reach the States, Abby begins to fear what may come for her older brother and Harvey. Once Pearl Harbor is bombed, the boys are eager to protect their home and the women they love. But will Abby and Harvey's love be able to withstand distance, rumors, loss, and hurt? Or will the war be what tears apart Abby's heart?

War-Torn Heart is a Kleenex-box book with a story of hope, of love, and of perseverance through World War II, which will make the reader cry, scream, and long for more.

More from Ambassador International

In 1817, a young man faces life with an alcoholic father and imminent financial and social ruin. In 2018, a gifted artist can't paint anything but the same theme over and over, until she unearths this young man's history and his noble rise from rags to riches in Antebellum America. Based on a 200-year-old letter collection, Once Upon an Irish Summer brings to life and weaves together a true story of romance, mystery, and hope.

Once upon an Irish Summer
by Weny Wilson Spooner

Emma has high hopes when her family moves to the North Carolina mountains. Here Emma meets Edgar Moretz, an intelligent, passionate, and godly young man. Things are looking up for Emma, but when she is captured by a Cherokee raiding party, her problems have just begun.

Cleared for Planting

by Janice Cole Hopkins

Elderly Sarah returns to her hometown of Adare, Ireland with her daughter-in-law, Anna. The suffering that World War II brought them was unimaginable, but they still have each other. With all their loved ones killed in the war, the two women have nothing but a hope that one distant relative will help them. Will this new beginning bring the healing that both of them have prayed for?

A Little Irish Love Story

by Amy Fleming

For more information about
Allison Wells
&
When Waves Break
please visit:

www.allisonwellswrites.com
www.facebook.com/allisonwellswrites
@OrangeAlli
AllisonWellsWrites@gmail.com

For more information about
AMBASSADOR INTERNATIONAL
please visit:

www.ambassador-international.com
@AmbassadorIntl
www.facebook.com/AmbassadorIntl

*If you enjoyed this book, please consider leaving us a review on
Amazon, Goodreads, or our website.*

www.ingramcontent.com/pod-product-compliance
Lightning Source LLC
Chambersburg PA
CBHW060529260626
47161CB00003B/821